KU-591-813

Chris Brookmyre was a journalist before becoming a full-time novelist with the publication of his award-winning debut *Quite Ugly One Morning*, which established him as one of Britain's leading crime writers. His 2006 novel *All Fun And Games Until Somebody Loses An Eye* won the Everyman Bollinger Wodehouse Prize, and his 2016 novel *Black Widow* won both the McIlvanney Prize and the Theakston Old Peculier Crime Novel of the Year award. Brookmyre's novels have sold more than two million copies in the UK alone. His work has been adapted for stage, television, radio and, in the case of *Bedlam*, a video game.

Also by Chris Brookmyre

Quite Ugly One Morning
Country of the Blind
Not the End of the World
One Fine Day in the Middle of the Night
Boiling a Frog
A Big Boy Did It and Ran Away
The Sacred Art of Stealing
Be My Enemy
All Fun and Games Until Somebody Loses an Eye
A Tale Etched in Blood and Hard Black Pencil
Attack of the Unsinkable Rubber Ducks
A Snowball in Hell
Pandaemonium
Where the Bodies are Buried
When the Devil Drives
Bedlam
Flesh Wounds
Dead Girl Walking
Black Widow
Want You Gone
Places in the Darkness
Fallen Angel
The Cut

Ebook only

The Last Day of Christmas
Siege Mentality

The Cliff House

CHRIS BROOKMYRE

Little, Brown

LITTLE, BROWN

First published in Great Britain in 2022 by Little, Brown
This paperback edition published in 2023 by Little, Brown

1 3 5 7 9 10 8 6 4 2

Copyright © Chris Brookmyre 2022

The moral right of the author has been asserted.

Quote from *Bull Durham* © Orion Pictures/MGM 1988
Quote from *Alien* © 20th Century Fox 1979
Lyrics from 'She Knows' by Balaam and the Angel reproduced with
kind permission from Balaam and the Angel/Illegal Music
Lyrics from 'Feet to the Flames' by the Wonder Stuff reproduced with
kind permission from Miles Hunt/Downtown Music.

All characters and events in this publication, other than those
clearly in the public domain, are fictitious and any resemblance
to real persons, living or dead, is purely coincidental.

All rights reserved. No part of this publication may be reproduced, stored
in a retrieval system, or transmitted, in any form or by any means, without the
prior permission in writing of the publisher, nor be otherwise circulated in any form
of binding or cover other than that in which it is published and without a similar
condition including this condition being imposed on the subsequent purchaser.

A CIP catalogue record for this book is available from the British Library.

ISBN 978-0-3491-4385-9

Typeset in Caslon by Palimpsest Book Production Limited, Falkirk, Stirlingshire
Printed and bound in Great Britain by Clays Ltd, Elcograf S.p.A.

Papers used by Little, Brown are from well-managed forests
and other responsible sources.

Little, Brown
An imprint of
Little, Brown Book Group
Carmelite House
50 Victoria Embankment
London
EC4Y 0DZ

An Hachette UK Company
www.hachette.co.uk

www.littlebrown.co.uk

For Fiona Brownlee

Jen

They had been on the island less than five hours and already the whole thing was falling apart.

There was a bite to the breeze as Jen stood outside the house, a reminder that though the calendar said late June, it was still night-time on a remote Scottish island on the edge of the Atlantic.

She saw no sign of Samira. She had said she was going to grab some air, but from the state of her there was a greater chance she was actually off to be sick. It turned out Jen's future sister-in-law was a mouthy rage-monster who couldn't handle her drink, and she was the least of Jen's problems.

She glanced back at the house, where she could see the others through the drawing room's huge windows. None of them was speaking. This whole shebang had been a stupid idea, and she was an eejit to have let herself get talked into it.

It hadn't helped that Zaki, her fiancé, had been thoroughly encouraging of the notion. She'd wondered if that was because he had big plans for a stag weekend. If so, they hadn't materialised.

She pictured him back at home, popping open a can and getting comfy in front of the TV. She wished she was there instead. Suddenly she just wanted to be with Zaki, and Zaki alone. That was a good sign, right?

Then she remembered how they had left things.

She had as good as told him she didn't trust him. It hadn't come out of nowhere; it had been a background hum to their relationship from the off. But that she had put it out there in the open on the morning she departed for her hen weekend was a hell of a red flag.

He had been acting secretive of late, shifty and evasive. A couple of weeks ago, she had suspected that he had gone through her bedside drawer. Nothing was missing, but she got this instinctive feeling that the things in it weren't quite how they had been before. Then last week, in the documents folder of his laptop, she found a scan of her passport. Zaki didn't have a private log-in for the laptop, something he had presented as a sign of openness, but it struck her that it also ensured she *believed* she was seeing everything.

Then last night he had shut the lid just as she walked into the kitchen, trying to be nonchalant about it but merely having the opposite effect. She had caught a glimpse of what was on-screen. He was replying to an email from an account identified only as grimpox02@vapourmail.com. Jen had looked up the domain and found that it specialised in disposable email addresses. But more troublingly, she had accessed the laptop while he was in the shower this morning, and couldn't find the incoming email or the reply he was composing. She checked the inbox, archive and sent folders. There was nothing. He had deleted all trace.

That was why, when he emerged from the bathroom, she had asked him directly. 'Who were you emailing last night?' she asked. 'Who is grimpox02?'

'It's nothing you need to concern yourself with.' He tried to sound casual, though he surely knew it was pointless.

'If it's nothing, why did you delete it? Yes, I looked. You emptied the trash too. That's a lot of steps for nothing.'

He had seemed angry at this, though he tried to disguise it by appearing hurt. 'For God's sake, Jen, you need to chill. Not everybody's playing an angle all the time.'

'So why don't you just tell me?'

'Because maybe I'd rather you took me at my word. I could prove it's nothing you need to worry about, but then we'd be no further forward, would we?'

'I'd know the truth. That's a step forward.'

He looked exasperated. 'You'd know the truth, but you still wouldn't trust me. That's the issue, not whether I'm deleting emails or who grimpox02 is.'

It was the moment she should have said she did trust him, even if they both knew it was just lip service. But it hit her that they were past the point of pretending, and Zaki had nailed why.

He stared at the ceiling, like he was asking for strength, and when he looked at her again there was frustration in his eyes. 'I'd like to say I can't marry someone who doesn't trust me, but the sad fact is I'd marry you anyway. But *you* shouldn't marry someone you don't trust. And you've never trusted me.'

It hurt to hear this because it was the truth, and it hurt more to contemplate the consequences.

She finally said something conciliatory. 'We should take the weekend to talk this through. I'll cancel the trip.'

'No,' Zaki replied. 'You should take the weekend to have some distance, have a good time. Maybe it will let you get some perspective.'

'I don't need perspective on us. I think we're great. It's just—'

'Not perspective about us, Jen. Perspective about you.'

He had been right. It was her problem. She had never fully

trusted him, and at the root of it was this inescapable fear that he was too good to be true.

Not everybody's playing an angle, Zaki had told her. But that was what a man who was playing an angle would say, and she had been fooled by such a man once before.

Zaki *was* different, though. She had to accept that. He was insisting on paying for the honeymoon, which she knew was his way of demonstrating that he wasn't expecting to leech off her. Unfortunately that meant they were only having a few days in Skye rather than the luxury trip she would have happily sprung for, but it was important to let him have this.

She *wanted* to trust him. Right now, standing outside the house on Clachan Geal, she wanted to be able to tell him how she was feeling, to confide her thoughts and opinions on everyone and everything. Wasn't that what marriage, what companionship was about: having someone you could tell anything and know they'd keep it safe?

But that was all moot for now, because it was Friday night and the helicopter wasn't due back until Monday. Before that, the only other way off the island was their host Lauren's boat. Jen would have to make the best of it. The booze and the outpouring of aggro might have vented some of the underlying tensions, so maybe there was hope for this weekend yet.

As for the wedding to which it was supposedly an overture, that was another matter.

Jen took another lungful of the cool air, gulping it in like it could magically sober her, then ascended the front steps. She was reaching for the door handle when she heard the scream.

Ten hours earlier

Jen

'So, what's the trip? Business or pleasure?'

The taxi driver sounded chirpy. Jen took that as a good omen. She wasn't superstitious, but there was this one indefatigably miserable bugger you sometimes got whose conversation was entirely dominated by previous passengers' cancer diagnoses. He had picked up her and the kids for a flight to Majorca this one time, and it rained the whole holiday. She was convinced he had jinxed it.

'Would you believe a hen weekend?' Jen couldn't keep a chuckle from her voice. She was finding it difficult to believe it herself. How had she been talked into this? The idea seemed to have evolved from a vague notion into an imminent reality all by itself.

'Ooft. Fasten your seatbelts. Who's getting married?'

It took her a moment longer than it should to answer that question. She'd need to watch that if she didn't want to be answering harder ones.

'Me.'

'Oh, nice. Congratulations.'

'Thanks,' she replied, though in her head she was saying: Don't speak too soon, we're not over the line yet.

'Where are yous away to? Prague? Barcelona? Budapest?'

'Clachan Geal. It's south of Barra.'

'Oh, right. I'm finding it hard to picture male strippers and nightclubs.'

'No. We're all a bit old for that. Just a get-together with some pals.'

She caught his reflection in the rear-view, their eyes meeting briefly. He was checking her out, estimating her age and a whole lot more, she suspected.

'First time, or you been around before?'

She knew he wasn't talking about Clachan Geal. 'Second time.'

'Aye, me as well. First time lasted less than two years. Second time nearing thirty. You know nothing when you're young.'

Ain't that the truth, she thought.

'How long you been divorced?' he asked.

'I'm not.'

It seemed to take him a moment to process the implication. 'Oh. Sorry to hear that.'

'Don't be. I wasn't.'

She watched his brows jump in response. She had actually surprised herself with her vehemence, and her candour.

'How long you been a widow, then?'

'Technically three years.'

'*Technically?*'

'That's when he was legally declared dead. He was missing for seven before that. Though I can't say I looked that hard.'

The driver smiled. Either he approved of the sentiment or he was pretending he did in pursuit of his tip. 'Does that mean you got the life insurance?'

She scoffed. 'He'd have needed to be paying the premiums before he disappeared.'

'Oh, like that, was it?'

No, she thought. That was the merest fraction of what it was like.

'Do you ever worry what would happen if he turned up? A bit awkward if it was at the wedding. "Any person here present who has a reason why these two should not be wed, speak now or forever hold your peace" – "Aye, I'm no deid!"'

She couldn't help but laugh. There were many worries that kept Jen awake at night, but her husband ever coming back was not one of them.

Jen

The fare had been forty quid. The airport run was normally thirty-six or -seven. When she queried it, he insisted it was the standard rate, which was when she remembered that the cab was from a different firm. Jen paid up and tipped him, but it was too late. The moment had left a bad taste, and it was her fault. Again. Was it really worth souring the mood over three quid? Especially now, when she had so much in the bank?

Not everybody's playing an angle.

She endeavoured to shake it off as she made her way into the terminal and up the escalator towards security. Even though she was only taking a puddle-jumper to the Hebrides, something about this place tapped into a sense of adventure that went right back to childhood.

As she placed her toiletries into a tray, her eye was drawn to the open case of the woman at the adjacent bay, in which sat an unmistakable pink and blue box. The label stated 'Muffin in Particular': the variety four-pack of Jen's own product.

Muffin Finer had started as a single shop on Bothwell Main Street, expanding a few years later to two more premises in Glasgow and Edinburgh. The locations were strategically chosen for building brand awareness, but the real marketing success was driven by the names. Every variety of muffin Jen sold was labelled with a daft pun. Muffin Serious, Better than Muffin, Muffin But Trouble. She seldom missed a tie-in opportunity either: You Know Muffin, Jon Snow for *Game of Thrones*, and Muffin Really Matters when the *Bohemian Rhapsody* movie came out.

Once the brand was established, Jen had concentrated on expanding manufacturing, getting the product into supermarkets rather than just her chain of coffee shops. That was when the big boys had come calling. She had done a deal last year to sell the company, though she would still be in charge.

Something in her swelled. If she was reading a chirpy cab driver as a good omen, then this was a sign from the heavens. And God knows she needed reassurance. She was gathering six women from completely different periods of her life, some out of sentiment and nostalgia, some out of wishful thinking, and some out of obligation. It was a Venn diagram in which she was the only mutual overlap. Many of them didn't know each other, one of them didn't know anybody, including Jen, one of them quite possibly hated her, and two of them definitely hated each other. What could possibly go wrong?

Jen assumed she would be the first one here, as she was meant to meet Samira, her prospective sister-in-law, off a flight from London. But as she emerged from the duty-free labyrinth into the departure area, she spotted Helena up ahead. She was hovering just outside the Jo Malone shop like she was afraid if she crossed the threshold she wouldn't be able to control herself.

Jen had suggested her taxi could pick Helena up en route, but she had insisted she would make her own way. Jen hadn't pressed the offer. Helena had been acting cagey of late, untypically so. She was normally candid to the point of oversharing, the way

11

you get after years of motherhood have utterly eroded all sense of personal privacy, dignity and discretion.

They had both become mothers around the same time, and now they were both dealing with the empty-nest thing. The difference was that while Jen had embraced it as a chance for a new beginning, Helena seemed to be focused on what was coming to an end. Though to be fair, Helena's husband leaving her hadn't helped.

Helena seemed lost in her thoughts, oblivious of Jen's approach. Jen cupped her hands around her mouth. 'Bing-bong. Passenger Eckhart, the next flight to PARTY ISLAND will soon be boarding at gate number . . .'

Helena took a step towards Jen and pulled her into a hug. 'Are you Dunne?' Helena asked.

'No, I'm just at the tickly bit.'

It was an in-joke dating back to schooldays, when they met in first year at secondary. They were seated together for registration class because their surnames were adjacent alphabetically: Michelle Cassidy, Jennifer Dunne, Helena Eckhart. But despite knowing each other for so long, Jen and Helena had never felt like best friends. That was largely because Helena had known Michelle since Primary One, so when Jen met them they already came as a package. You were never getting as close to either of Hel and Shell as they were to each other, even when they fell out for a few days. Or even when they fell out for seventeen years.

'So how is the beautiful bride-to-be? Counting the days until you're Mrs Hussain?'

It took Jen a moment too long to respond, and Helena noticed. 'What?' she asked. 'Something up?'

'Oh, nothing. Just nerves. Worried it's all too good to be true.'

12

'That's a *good* sign,' Helena assured her. 'Better than worrying you could maybe have done better.'

Jen wasn't sure whether Helena was talking about how she now viewed her estranged husband or how she thought Neil had viewed her.

'You ready for this?' Jen asked, eager to get away from the subject of husbands past and (possible) future.

'I can't wait.'

It sounded like Helena's words were genuine; or at least that she was making a genuine effort to sound so. It's easier to tell if someone's putting on a face when you've known them all your life. Or maybe it's just that they don't feel the need to hide the truth quite so much.

They locked eyes for a moment, a beat to acknowledge that it was reasonable to *not* be ready for this.

'Fun, goddammit,' Jen said.

'Fun, goddammit,' Helena replied.

'What time is Salena's flight due in?'

'Samira. About half an hour.'

'And what time are Nicolette and . . .'

As Helena said this, Jen's phone chimed. She smiled and held it up, showing a message from Kennedy, their tennis coach. *This is Sergeant Goodtime of the Party Platoon. Recruits are to report for duty at table thirteen in the Caledonia Bar.*

'She made it, then,' Helena said.

Jen felt a surge of relief. They had got a WhatsApp from Kennedy yesterday with a selfie posted from A&E. She had gone over on her ankle during a game. She assured them she would still make the trip, but Jen couldn't help but worry. She knew Kennedy was the glue needed to hold this thing together.

Jen and Helena walked briskly through the departure lounge

to where they could see Kennedy and Nicolette waving to them. Kennedy's left foot was lodged inside a support brace, a burdensome plastic affair that looked like a ski boot. They were seated at a table bearing a bottle of Prosecco and five glasses. They had remembered that Samira was also joining them, which was thoughtful, but the sight prompted a nagging memory of something else Zaki said last night. 'Don't let Samira drink too much. She can't handle it at the best of times, and this is her first time let loose in forever.'

They exchanged excited greetings: four people who played tennis together twice a week now acting like none of them had seen each other in months. It was like everyone was getting into character, but there was something fun about the mutual complicity.

'How's the ankle?' Jen asked.

'It's not broken. This is just so I don't aggravate it. I'm allowed to take it off, like if they ask me to for the plane, but I'm not supposed to put weight on it without the brace.'

There were no hugs, for which Jen was kind of grateful. If your relationship hasn't reached that stage over a decade, as was the case with Nicolette, it would feel weird to suddenly start. And as for Kennedy, well, she didn't hug anyone. Even on nights out she was bubbly but not tactile. The only time Jen had seen her in direct physical contact with anyone was adjusting their posture as she taught them to serve. Maybe it seemed more noticeable because Kennedy was much younger than the rest, late twenties at most, and Jen's impression of that generation was that they were more physically affectionate with each other.

Kennedy was wearing jogging pants and a plain T-shirt, but managed to look dressed up at the same time. Some people just had that about them, a natural grace that made them look well-presented in whatever they wore. Michelle had always been like that.

Nicolette was looking super-glam, of course, but in contrast to Kennedy her appearance indicated that much planning and effort had gone into achieving the result. Nicolette's husband Paul had grassed to Jen that she had once cancelled a match because she had run out of foundation.

What was more surprising was how well Helena had scrubbed up for this. She looked smarter, younger even. Helena often looked mumsy and bedraggled, but she had splashed the cash on a new wardrobe. If it had happened six months ago Jen would have assumed it a response to her husband leaving, but she suspected such a recent transformation had been driven by a different motivation. Helena had a point to prove, and Jen knew who to.

'Now that Jen's here, the weekend is officially underway,' Kennedy announced, lifting her bag from the floor. 'So it's time for these.'

She pulled out a stash of bright red T-shirts wrapped in cellophane. Jen's eyes immediately went to Nicolette to take in her horror at this honking article that was about to banjax her carefully chosen ensemble. She was wearing a purple silk blouse with the top three buttons undone to display a precisely calculated expanse of cleavage.

Kennedy held one up, showing the back first, which read: 'Jen's final fling'. Then she turned it around to display the front: 'Fun, goddammit!'

It was a catchphrase at tennis, something Jen said when someone was taking things too seriously. Jen's first crush had been Kevin Costner, back in the early nineties. It was one of his lines from *Bull Durham*: 'This game's fun, OK? Fun, goddammit!'

'Get these on you,' Kennedy commanded, handing them around the table.

'Do we have to?' Nicolette protested. 'It's all a bit clichéd, and this really isn't my colour.'

'No exemptions,' Kennedy replied.

'Geeza break, Nicolette,' Jen said. 'We know you don't want to cover up your best assets, but let's be honest, we've all seen enough of your tits to draw them from memory.'

'I just want my money's worth,' she replied, thrusting out the features in question. 'These tits cost me more than my first car, they turn more heads than it ever did, and I'm hoping to get better mileage out of them.'

Nonetheless, Nicolette accepted the proffered garment and everyone donned their matching horrible T-shirts.

They all clinked their glasses and Jen took a gulp, feeling the bubbles, the burn and the buzz, all of which seemed more intense for it only being eleven in the morning. The chat soon started to flow along with the fizz, though she kept an occasional eye on the departure board.

Her gaze was briefly drawn to a TV monitor showing a building she recognised from a visit to Barcelona, her last trip abroad before the pandemic. From the subtitles she gleaned it was something about a corruption scandal involving 'the Catalan Kardashians', at which point her interest waned.

That was when she noticed a young woman hovering at the end of their table, as though waiting for a pause in the conversation to ask something. She was smiling shyly, eager but apprehensive. It took Jen a moment to realise this was Samira. Jen had only seen a couple of photos of her, the main focus of which had been the twin babies also in shot.

Jen had the impression of her being petite because Zaki always talked of her in protective tones. She was six years younger than him, not long turned thirty. However, Jen wasn't ready for just how slight she appeared in the flesh. She looked five feet tall and seven stone soaking wet. She was the in-house lawyer for a TV production company, and a bit of a Rottweiler by reputation, so Jen knew not to make any assumptions regarding her apparent meekness. However, she also looked knackered, and Jen knew she was safe to make assumptions on that score. Samira wasn't working at the moment, being five months into maternity leave after having the twins, and she was not having an easy time of it.

It had been Zaki's request, bordering on insistence, that Jen invite Samira along to the hen weekend. It was ostensibly so that they might get to know each other, but mostly to give the girl a break. Jen had been happy enough to oblige. She was more worried about how Samira would feel knowing absolutely nobody, not to mention being thrown in with (Kennedy aside) a bunch of women in their forties. However, Samira had all but bitten Jen's hand off, sounding almost tearily grateful on the phone.

'Everyone, this is Samira,' Jen announced.

'How did you find us?' Nicolette asked, a joke reference to the T-shirts.

Kennedy handed one to Samira, who gamely pulled it over her head. It drowned her. Helena slid a glass of fizz along the table towards her as Samira took a seat next to Jen.

'Oh, no thanks, but someone else ought to have that,' Samira said, holding the glass delicately by the stem and nudging it away. 'I've hardly touched the stuff in months and I need to pace myself. I'm a total lightweight at the best of times.'

Jen was pleased to see Zaki's request rendered redundant. She had considered it a wee bit unfair, as the last thing she wanted on her hen weekend was to be responsible for anyone else.

Jen did the introductions, Samira shaking hands or waving in response, depending on who was in reach. 'And is that everybody?' she asked.

'For now,' Jen said. 'We're meeting Beattie on Barra. She's got a boat and she's sailing there herself from her holiday home on Islay.'

'Why not all the way to Clachan Geal?' Helena asked.

'I don't know. Maybe she didn't want to miss out on arriving in style.'

'And what about the celebrity special guest?' Samira asked, with a curiosity that made Jen wonder whether Michelle's attendance had been part of the draw.

'She's doing some kind of spiritual retreat on Rum. She said she would charter a boat to get her across from there.'

'But she's definitely coming?' Kennedy asked. She sounded anxious rather than excited. In her case it was not so much that she was keen to meet Michelle as that she had become so invested in the outcome of Jen reaching out to her.

Jen had known Kennedy less than a year, but there were ways in which she had become as much life coach as tennis coach. After everything that had happened to her, Jen had issues with self-esteem, which was why she had been reluctant to bother Michelle about the hen weekend. Kennedy had been the one who helped her see that just because Michelle was famous and they hadn't seen each other in a long time, it didn't mean her old friend wouldn't make the effort for something special like this. Kennedy was probably worried that if Michelle didn't show up, it would set Jen's esteem back further and prove all her counselling and positivity wrong.

'I don't know for sure,' Jen told her. 'Nothing's ever one hundred per cent certain with Michelle.'

'Oh, she'll be there,' said Helena. 'She just didn't confirm because she knows it makes everyone all the more grateful when she does turn up. Classic showmanship.'

'I'm just not making any assumptions after what Michelle's been through in recent months,' Jen replied. 'She might not want to be around a bunch of people.'

'Why, what happened to her?' asked Samira. 'I've never been very up on celeb gossip.'

'But Jen said you work in television,' Nicolette said.

'I do, which is why I've become adept at filtering out showbiz bullshit. That, and being lost in baby-land for five months.'

'She was in rehab or therapy or something,' Nicolette told her. 'It all stemmed from her sex tape.'

'Someone hacked Michelle's cloud storage and posted explicit pictures and videos all over the internet,' Jen explained.

'Fuck. I'd need *all* the drugs and therapy after that,' Samira replied.

'In my case I'd just be shocked there was footage on something more recent than Super 8,' said Nicolette.

'What's she like?' Samira asked. 'Is there anything we should know in advance?'

'Depends who you ask,' replied Helena archly.

'Oh, that's right,' said Kennedy with a gossipy giggle. 'She did the dirty on her bandmates, didn't she? Took a big-money solo deal but told them they could stay on as her backing musicians. That must have been awks.'

Jen gave Helena a kick under the table by way of prompting her to come clean before anybody said too much.

'Can't say it's my favourite showbiz memory,' Helena said.

Kennedy and Samira looked puzzled, Nicolette astonished. In the latter's case she had at least put two and two together, but was having trouble accepting the answer.

'Helena was in Cassidy,' Jen clarified. 'She was the guitarist.'

'Oh my God,' Kennedy said, sounding embarrassed. 'I'm so sorry, I didn't know.'

'It's fine. I generally don't like to talk about it, but it's kind of unavoidable this weekend.'

Jen guessed this explanation was more for Nicolette's benefit than anyone else's. They had known each other all these years and Helena had never mentioned this fairly juicy aspect of her past.

'I must look you up,' said Samira. 'Are you in the videos?'

'Please don't. It was a long time ago. You would barely recognise me. And as Kennedy indicated, it didn't end well.'

'Does this mean we're going to be Team Helena or Team Michelle by the end of the trip?' Samira asked, a hint of relish in her eyes. Jen recognised an appetite for mischief that Zaki had not prepared her for.

'No. Absolutely not,' said Helena. 'This weekend is all about my oldest mate Jen, so I'm going to be on my best behaviour. Remember—' she ran her hand under the slogan on her T-shirt '—Fun, goddammit!'

'Fun, goddammit!' they all replied, some raising glasses like it was a toast.

'Let's get a picture,' said Nicolette.

'I'll take it,' Kennedy offered.

'No, I'll do a selfie. We want everyone in it.'

They all crammed around the table in an ungainly pose. Nicolette took an age about it. She made out she was ensuring she got everyone in shot, but Jen knew she was holding off pressing the button until she had the best angle on herself.

Sure enough, when she showed it around, Nicolette was looking elegantly composed while everyone else just happened to be there. Kennedy's face was partly obscured by the glass she was holding, but nobody could be arsed with taking another. 'That one would be shit as well,' said Kennedy. 'I'm cursed when it comes to photos. My eyes are always closed or I'm looking the wrong way, or somebody's finger is over the lens.'

Jen glanced at the departure board and saw that their flight was being called. A voice in her head asked whether missing the plane would be so bad, but she ignored it.

The group responded with surprising obedience, immediately getting up and grabbing their bags. The only straggler was Nicolette, who noticed that there was still a near-full glass on the table.

'Kennedy, you barely touched your fizz.'

'Too busy gabbing, as usual,' she replied, grinning.

'Never mind. I've got the flight covered anyway,' Nicolette said with a wink.

They made their way towards their gate, Kennedy fairly spry despite the ski boot. Jen reckoned she would still beat any of them in a singles game, even with the brace on.

There were jetways and aircraft visible through the windows to their left. Jen saw an Emirates jumbo next to a BA 737. The further they progressed along the walkway, the smaller the planes seemed to get.

Nicolette started handing out an assortment of miniatures she must have picked up in the duty-free shop. 'I didn't imagine there would be much of an in-flight service on this thing,' she explained.

Jen accepted a bottle of Stirling gin. Again, Samira refused. 'I'm not always the best flyer. Don't want to risk feeling sick.'

Her fellow millennial Kennedy said no thanks also. Just the old soaks, then.

As they neared the end of the corridor, Jen noticed Samira looking out the window then checking her boarding pass. She suspected the words 'operated by Loganair' were taking on a deep significance as she noted the name printed on the tiny aircraft.

'You are joking me.'

'Ach, don't worry,' Nicolette said. 'We'll be down on the beach before you know it.'

'You reckon it's going to be warm enough for the beach?' Samira asked sceptically.

'No,' Jen told her, 'the plane *lands* on the beach.'

Samira's eyes bulged, then she turned to Nicolette. 'I'll take that miniature after all. And Kennedy's as well.'

Helena

As the helicopter ascended above Barra, Helena was more conscious of its motion than on even the tiny plane they just got off. The pitch and yaw felt more immediate, prefaced by the vertical nature of the take-off, which seemed weird without the attendant acceleration. She was grateful for the lack of wind. It had felt pleasantly warm outside, not something ever guaranteed so far north.

She looked around the cabin. Everyone was smiling at each other whenever it banked and they all felt it in their guts. She was pretty sure everyone was equally terrified but pretending to enjoy it, which felt like an appropriate leitmotif for the weekend ahead.

Helena glanced at Beattie, who she had known since she was in primary school, and who had worn the same expression of sour disapproval for three decades. It wasn't so much that Beattie was in her fifties as that she was one of those women who was *born* in her fifties.

They say keep your friends close and your enemies closer, but Jen inviting her former sister-in-law on her hen weekend had sounded like a step too far. As it was clearly an implicit way of asking for Beattie's blessing on her new marriage, Jen was gifting her the opportunity to demonstrably withhold it. Maybe enough time had passed for her bitterness to have faded, but Helena was not convinced. She of all people was qualified to recognise someone reluctant to let go of a grudge. Jen would do well to watch herself around that one.

Samira was nearest the window, looking down at the waves with a queasy expression. Helena was seated opposite, Beattie to her left. The noise level meant it was difficult to talk to anyone further away. Jen was seated closest to Samira but Nicolette was already in her ear.

'We're probably not as low to the water as it looks,' Helena assured Samira.

'It just looks so cold and unforgiving,' she said. 'It's weird, but I'd actually feel safer floating on the water than flying above it like this.'

'I know what you mean,' said Beattie. 'A boat's *meant* to be on the water. Whereas if this thing hits it . . .' She gave a shudder.

'Why didn't you sail to Clachan Geal, then?' Helena asked.

Beattie's reaction was briefly defensive, then her expression softened. 'Nowhere to moor. There's a jetty near the house, I think, but it's small, just for dropping off and picking up. I couldn't tie up there as it would be an obstruction. I'd certainly *rather* have taken my boat.'

'I used to be pretty fearless,' said Samira. 'But now all I can think about is how I can't let anything happen to me because of the twins. I'm hoping it's just a phase.'

Helena and Beattie shared a look, a moment of connection.

'I'm afraid not, dear,' Beattie said. 'Something they don't tell you about becoming a mother, or indeed a grandmother, is that you just see potential danger everywhere, and your state of vigilance never ends.'

24

Samira glanced at Helena as though appealing for a second opinion, but she was coming to the wrong place.

'I was looking forward to a time when I no longer needed plastic covers on the plug sockets and safety catches on all the cupboards in case they drank the bleach,' Helena told her. 'Suddenly they're crossing the road themselves, getting buses into the city, then before you know it they're learning to drive. But here's the kicker. You change into a completely different person until you can't remember who you were before they came along – and then they fuck off.'

Samira laughed, though Helena hadn't entirely meant it as a joke.

Helena was facing forward, so she was the first to see that they were approaching Clachan Geal. She had read on the website that it was Gaelic for 'white stones', and there had been photos of a sandy beach, turquoise waters lapping it beneath a clear blue sky. She couldn't see anything matching that description on the southern shoreline, which was mostly grey and rocky. The beach must be to the north, at the bay where the house was situated.

Beneath them she could see a boat speeding towards an inlet. It was a RIB with an outboard motor, a single figure aboard dressed all in black. It was probably a wetsuit or waterproofs, but from up in the chopper it looked like the SAS or something.

'I thought we were going to be the only people here,' said Nicolette in the tone she might use to complain that there were kids in the adults-only pool of her hotel.

'People love to explore all these wee islands,' said Beattie. 'It's not like you can stop them. At least this one looks like he knows what he's about. You'd be amazed at how many people end up needing rescued because they go for a nosey without checking the charts first.'

'Looks like some extreme outdoorsy type,' said Samira. 'One of those blokes who are always boring on about the isolated and inaccessible places they've slept in a flimsy tent. He's probably looking forward to bragging about Bear-Gryllsing it on a remote and uninhabited Scottish island. He'll be gutted when he discovers there's a mansion house with its own spa and a six-hole golf course.'

The mansion was also named Clachan Geal, built as some Victorian aristo's retreat. It was Nicolette who had first shared an article about it on WhatsApp: a magazine feature about Lauren Combe, the property developer who owned it. She specialised in renovating houses and flipping them, but in this case she had held on to the place. In the Airbnb era, she had realised she had a unique quantity on her hands: stately-home grandeur blended with high-end luxury on what was effectively a private island.

The accompanying photos showed a heated infinity pool, alongside a hot tub sunken into a slate-tiled terrace overlooking that unspoiled beach. All the rooms were individually decorated in a measured blend of the traditional and ultra-modern. Four-posters and sleigh beds, claw-foot baths and hydromassage shower cabins, 4K TVs and fibre-optic broadband. The only caveat was that there was no mobile reception, but that was marketed as a plus. If you couldn't leave the outside world behind for a couple of days in a place like this, you were doomed.

Given the remote location, it was harder to imagine a finer image of exclusivity. And for that reason it was booked out until forever, proving an irresistible draw for corporate retreats, fashion shoots and the odd celebrity wedding. It was the kind of place Helena had never imagined visiting in a million years. But then Kennedy somehow got wind of a cancellation: some tennis connection who knew somebody who knew somebody. And though it was costing Jen more than if she had flown everyone to New York for the weekend, she had jumped at the chance, still feeling super-flush after selling her business.

They had all been posting about it non-stop, counting down with far more anticipation than over the wedding itself. No point going somewhere so upscale and indulgent if you couldn't boast about it on Facebook in advance and then spam out Instagram stories while you were there.

There was a fitness trail and a gym as well as the swimming pool, spa and golf course. You had to let Lauren know in advance if you wanted the groundskeeper to visit, or an instructor for sports. Similarly, there could be staff on-site if requested, otherwise they would prepare everything in advance and leave you to it. You could take the house purely on a self-catering basis, but Jen had chosen to have a private chef at their disposal.

Plus, of course, there was the helicopter transfer, intended to make you feel like an A-lister before you even set foot on the place.

Helena remembered being in a helicopter once before, when they were playing a music festival in Germany. They weren't exactly top of the bill – they were on at four in the afternoon – but it was still one of the main stages. The helicopter had been laid on by the record label to fly them from the nearby town where they were staying and thus avoid the traffic around the festival site. This was despite their second album failing to set the heather alight. At the time she remembered thinking this was a sign of the label's long-term confidence in the band. She later understood it was all about them buttering up Michelle ahead of her going solo.

She felt the chopper descend, which meant the flight was

mercifully nearing its end. Down below she spotted a row of derelict cottages and wondered when they had been inhabited; wondered what kind of miserable existence anyone had eked out here in those days.

The helicopter banked again, heading back out to sea. It's never over till it's over, Helena thought. The pilot was doing a circuit of the mansion so that they could all get a long look at the place from the air, with its towers and crenellations, the glass dome of its winter-garden conservatory, its walkways and terraces, its gardens and its landing pad.

As they began their final approach, two women emerged from the grand entrance. By process of elimination, Helena was able to identify the brunette as Lauren, their host. This was because even from this height and distance she recognised the blonde beside her as the diva known to millions as Mica, but known to Helena and Jen once upon a time as Michelle Cassidy.

Helena felt something lurch in her gut, and it wasn't caused by the helicopter's vertical descent. When she had so confidently asserted that Michelle would be here, it had been much the same as when Neil predicted a defeat for his beloved Rangers. It was like an insurance bet. She had been hoping to be proven wrong.

Helena often worried how it would feel to be in Michelle's presence again after everything that had passed between them. Now that the time was at hand, she remembered that seeing her face to face was never the danger. It was when your back was turned that you had to worry.

Nicolette began hauling off her red T-shirt. She had agreed to wear it throughout the journey, but now that the chopper was touching down she had evidently decided she was free once again to show off her designer blouse and her designer cleavage.

Helena used to feel intimidated by Nicolette's confidence in her physical appearance. Helena had been busty from around the age of fourteen, which proved the source of unwanted attention and painful self-consciousness growing up. She remembered an A&R guy talking about Mica's success and telling her that if she had undone a few buttons in the videos, she and Michelle would be a pop duo now. She had done well not to deck him.

It used to bother her how conceited Nicolette could be, but that was before. Although Helena couldn't pretend to anyone that she was happy to be back in Michelle's company, she wasn't lying when she told Jen she was looking forward to this weekend. Sometimes when you have a secret it makes you feel vulnerable. You are afraid of what you could lose, afraid of what everyone might discover. But what Helena had come to learn of late was that being the one who knew a secret gave you power over everyone who didn't.

Lauren

Watching the helicopter coming into sight was normally when Lauren could start to relax, confident that her part was done. By the time the guests were planting their feet on the ground, all appropriate preparations had usually been made, meaning she could simply welcome them to Clachan Geal and leave them to it. That was often what they wanted: they sense that the place was entirely theirs, nobody watching, nobody judging.

Sometimes she would be off the island within an hour of the guests reaching it, particularly on weekend bookings. She wasn't kidding herself that her daughter Darcy still needed her to cook the tea or make sure she was tucked up in bed at a sensible hour, but Lauren was always impatient to get back to her anyway.

Not today, though. This weekend she would be observing at a discreet distance, staying in her private apartment within the house.

Darcy was with her dad this weekend, though that wasn't the main reason Lauren had decided to stay on-site. Sometimes she just got a feeling, a sixth-sense tingle. It was never a genuine fear that they were going to trash the place, but there were occasions when she felt uneasy, and this being a hen weekend must have put up some subconscious red flags. She knew they weren't all twenty-one and about to get pissed on cheap vodka, so she didn't need to worry about anyone puking in her planters or ending up drowned in the hot tub. Nonetheless, a bunch of women over forty on the randan unsupervised could be a danger to themselves in less predictable ways. She wanted to be on the spot in case some firefighting was required, though hopefully not literally.

As she stood before the main entrance alongside a woman whose every album she owned, Lauren had to admit that, just maybe, another reason for staying was simply that she wanted to spend some time around Mica. She was not above deriving a thrill from being introduced to certain celebs who had visited, seeing them enjoy the environment she had so lovingly created and hearing them compliment her taste. For a lassie who had grown up in care homes and council schemes, there was no shame in wanting to rub shoulders with the stars.

Michelle had arrived on a Quicksilver motor launch a couple of hours ago, her hair protected from the wind by a headscarf, eyes shielded from the spray by a pair of sunglasses. She looked like a sixties Italian movie star arriving in Sorrento, and Lauren suspected she knew it too. Lauren had expected an entourage or at least a PA; if not for the whole weekend, then at minimum to drop off her charge along with a list of instructions, including details of when Ms Cassidy would be picked up again. Instead it had just been her and the gnarled-looking bloke who was piloting the boat.

Lauren was fairly certain she had come from Rum, specifically the Askival Spiritual Retreat Centre, which was the discreet name of a rehab and counselling facility increasingly favoured by high-profile clients due to its remoteness from prying eyes and zoom lenses.

She was taller than Lauren had imagined. From what she had seen on video, Lauren had pictured her as petite, but she could see now that it was all in the proportions. Instead, she was tall and stringy, athletic even. If she didn't know otherwise, Lauren might have thought she was some kind of sports star.

Lauren's Sealine was tied up at the jetty, bobbing in the wake as the Quicksilver accelerated away. She remembered the moment when it had dawned on her that boats would be her primary means of getting to and from her new investment. It was the one thing that made her think she might have made a mistake, as it struck her that she would either have to remain reliant on other people or learn to pilot her own vessel. Neither had seemed an attractive option.

She had been tremulously anxious the first time she sailed here unaccompanied. Now she felt much the same way about getting behind the helm of her F42 as she did getting behind the wheel of her Tesla.

Lauren had greeted the goddess at the foot of the gravel path that led up to the house. 'Ms Cassidy, welcome to Clachan Geal.'

She had a confidence to her poise. A woman with a good conceit of herself, as an acquaintance used to say.

'Ms *Michelle* Cassidy,' Lauren had stated, making a show of reading the details from her iPad. 'You're Mica, right?'

Again the thin smile. 'That's right.'

'I find it's best to acknowledge these things up-front,' Lauren explained. 'We have a lot of high-profile visitors here, and I have learned that coyness can have its pitfalls. I've no poker face and I'm easily star-struck, but it's all allied to a healthy respect for boundaries.'

'It can be a balancing act for both sides,' Michelle had replied. She sounded at ease, which made Lauren feel that bit more

32

relaxed too. It was a gift, one she recognised. That confidence and poise, she wondered: did it come with success, or did naturally having it help success come along?

'How is it you know Ms Dunne?' Lauren asked now as the chopper overshot the house, the pilot giving them the full bird's-eye experience.

'Oh, Jen and I were at school together,' she replied, this time with a warmer smile. 'We don't see enough of each other, you know how it is. Life gets in the way. But you've got to make an effort for something like this, especially as I doubt I'll be free for the wedding itself. Tour rehearsals start next week.'

She added this last as though an explanation was due, then frowned as if reflecting that it wasn't a very good one. Maybe attendance at a hen weekend as one of seven was easier than turning up at some massive hotel bash full of strangers, and the rehearsals were a convenient cover.

'So is this weekend going to be like a miniature school reunion?'

'God, no,' she replied, relief evident in her laughter. 'I only know a couple of the other guests. But I'm here as Jen's mate Michelle, so no showbiz bullshit.'

Lauren nodded, though she wasn't quite clear what she meant. 'Is it easier socialising with people who knew you before you were famous?'

'It can be. But that said, having a public persona is a shield sometimes. If I'm answering questions about being a pop star, it means nobody is prying into the side of me that's real. Do you know what I mean, or am I sounding like an arsehole?'

Lauren gazed out at the sea, at once a frightening threat and a protective barrier. 'Not so long ago I wouldn't have had a clue, but a while back there were a few magazine features about me and about this place, and that's given me a glimpse of what it must be like. I got a lot of business inquiries out of it, which has been great, but there was also . . . some unwelcome interest.'

Michelle nodded, a bitter, knowing smile at the corners of her mouth. Lauren felt like she had just described a minor rain squall to a sailor who had rounded the Cape of Good Hope.

'All I do is sing and dance,' she said. 'How can that be pissing people off? I used to wonder. Comes a point where you realise that existing while female is your primary offence. You have to remember it's not personal. Just the irrational hatred of sad, angry randos screaming into the void.'

These were the sage words of someone who had navigated the roughest seas, but they weren't as reassuring as Michelle intended. What troubled Lauren was that the hatred in the messages she'd received was not entirely random or irrational. And though Clachan Geal was not the most accessible place, if someone wanted to make good on an online death threat, they'd know exactly where to find her.

Worse still was that she couldn't tell anyone she had been targeted, because then she'd also have to tell them why.

She heard the door swing open behind them and saw that it was Joaquin, the chef Jennifer Dunne had booked, come out to confirm her arrival. Lauren noticed him steal a look up and down at Michelle, then observed Michelle steal a similar look at him before he headed back inside. She met Michelle's eyes, sharing a smile that she had been caught ogling. Lauren didn't know what his desserts were like, but the guests would certainly be well-served for eye candy.

She hadn't recognised him. Sometimes when people insisted on booking their own personal chef, it turned out to be one of the guys on her own list. Not this one, though, because it wasn't just his name that stuck out. Joaquin Hernandez was built like a boxer, chiselled features atop a ripped physique. When Lauren first saw him get off the boat she wondered if he had been booked as a stripper. That was until she saw him hefting a box of provisions.

Lauren had heard music from the hallway as Joaquin pulled open the front door, audible while the chopper was downwind, banking over the bay. She thought for a mortifying moment that it was Mica's last album, which she had been playing yesterday on Spotify. Fortunately it wasn't, but it prompted an important consideration.

'We've got this networked speaker system throughout the house,' she told Michelle. 'It means Ms Dunne or whoever can have her own playlists in the public rooms, but if not, it will default to random songs based on previous lists people have made. I'm mentioning this in case you want me to vet what's likely to come up; you know, make sure there isn't some of your material on there if that's awkward.'

Michelle gave a light shrug, though she smiled to acknowledge the offer. 'I don't mind. I'm not one of those artists who pretends I'm precious about hearing my own songs. Sometimes there's something fresh about encountering a song in a different context.'

'So we're good to leave it to chance?'

'Sure. I mean, I think it would be conspicuous if *nothing* by me showed up over three days. Though maybe Jen's playlist will blank me.'

Her smile suggested how unlikely she thought this.

The helicopter slowed to a hover, then came down to the landing pad in a gentle descent. They stayed where they were, watching as the pilot secured the blades then opened the door.

Lauren glanced at Michelle to take in her reaction, witness the moment when someone caught a first glimpse of old friends emerging onto the steps.

There was a smile of anticipation, but a flicker of something else too: an anxiety. A wariness, even.

She turned to Lauren, once again wearing that thin smile. 'Actually, regarding the music. Can you make sure there's no Cassidy? Especially not . . . you know.'

She knew. 'Are you sick of the sound of that one?'

'Something like that.'

Nicolette

Nicolette let the breeze play on her face for a moment, savouring the feeling of being back on the ground. In the weeks running up to the trip, everyone had been posting about what a legit perk it was, the notion of arriving by helicopter synonymous with glamour and luxury, but for Nicolette that was not the first association that came to mind. Sure, her first time on board one had been plenty glam and luxurious, a private transfer in the Maldives at the start of her honeymoon. Nobody needed to convince her of how special it could make you feel to be stepping out of a Sikorsky on the way to your hotel, as opposed to stepping out of a Tui chartered coach with the rep's fake-cheery voice still ringing in your ears. But her second time had created an altogether different association with this particular means of transport.

Alongside her, everyone seemed so intent on getting out of the small cabin and grabbing the right cases that it took a moment before anyone noticed who was standing waiting for them in front of the house.

'Oh my *God*,' Jen shrieked, excited. Relieved too, maybe. She had been acting like she wasn't fussed whether her famous bestie showed up, but Nicolette reckoned she just didn't want to set herself up for disappointment.

'I told you,' said Helena, in a way that did not entirely suggest she was delighted to have been proved right.

Nicolette was still processing the revelation that Helena had been in Mica's band. That Helena had been in *any* band. She knew Helena was a music teacher, but if someone had asked Nicolette to picture her as a musician in her youth, it would have been one of those orchestra-geek types whose mothers never had a television in the house.

By contrast, one look at Michelle Cassidy in the flesh and there was no question she was a pop star. She was standing at the end of the path in a white trouser suit, composed in her posture and framed in front of the house like she had stepped off an album cover. These record company execs knew what they were doing. With marketing and autotune they could make anybody a star these days, but some people were a better fit to hang it all on, and Michelle was one of those.

She was someone you instantly pictured in high definition, a wind machine blowing her hair as five ripped guys gyrated in sync behind her. Though of late it was hard not to also picture her on all fours with one particular ripped guy hanging out the back of her. Because of course Nicolette had watched the video. Price of fame. Michelle ought to consider it a *badge* of fame, in fact. Because these days you're nobody if you're not important enough to have your iCloud hacked and for the whole world to see you with a face full of dick.

Jen let go of her pull-along and covered the last few paces at speed, Michelle skipping towards her at the same time until they collided in a tight hug.

'Oh, God, Michelle, I'm so glad you came.'

'Barbara! I wouldn't have missed it.'

Barbara? Nicolette wondered.

'So good to see you. You look amazing.'

'That goes without saying,' Michelle replied, joking not-joking. Self-deprecatory and yet somehow quite the opposite.

Nicolette had often heard mention of Jen being friends with Mica down the years, but had always assumed it was some tenuous connection. Now that she had seen them together, it made a lot of sense. Jen always had a certain energy about her. That was how she had built up a business: something she was born with, something she exuded. If there was a name for the opposite of needy, that was what she had, this take-charge quality about her. Nicolette had first recognised it partnering her at tennis. If you were 1–5 down, most of the group – Nicolette included – would be happy enough just to lose the next game and move on to another set, or move on to coffee and a comfy seat, because what did any of it matter? Jen was the kind of person who still saw it as salvageable at set point, and if she got back that second game, you could feel the momentum shift.

They reluctantly broke off their hug, tears forming in Jen's eyes, then Michelle turned to greet the others, looking first at Helena.

There was no embrace there, Nicolette observed, and there was a lot going on behind the polite smiles they traded.

'Helena. Long time. How you doing?'

'I'm good. You?'

'Can't complain.'

Watching this uncomfortable little exchange, it struck her what a sacrifice Helena was making for Jen. It wouldn't be easy spending time with someone who had dumped her on the road to fame and riches. But if there was a part Helena was cut out for, it was that of loyal friend. She was one of life's supporting players. Maybe that had once been her role with Michelle, and now she was performing it for Jen. Nicolette guessed she needed to find a purpose now that her husband had bailed and her daughters were growing up.

'This is my friend Nicolette,' Jen said. 'Nicolette, this is my old friend Michelle.'

Michelle shook Nicolette's hand as she took her in. 'Oh wow, is that from Reiss?' she asked, accurately identifying Nicolette's purple blouse. 'The one in Princes Square?'

'It is indeed,' she confirmed, basking in Michelle's approval.

'Nicolette works for Reiss,' Jen added. 'In design.'

'Oh wow.'

'It's more the design side of marketing,' Nicolette clarified.

Nicolette had first been taken to Princes Square when she was about ten years old and it had not long opened. She remembered thinking it was the most glamorous and sophisticated place in the world and that working in it would be amazing because you'd get to be there every day. It was much the same as how she had once thought being an air hostess was glamorous too.

'I love it,' Michelle said, stroking the material. 'I just wish I had the curves to pull off the low cut. And I can see why you're not hiding it under one of those red T-shirts. It would be a crime.'

'That's what I've been trying to explain,' Nicolette said. 'The T-shirts were Kennedy's doing.'

'And this is Kennedy,' said Jen.

Kennedy stood back a moment even as Michelle offered a hand, rocking on her heels as though afraid to approach. It was unusual to see her looking in any way meek. For a tense moment Nicolette even feared she was going to cry.

'For God's sake, Kennedy, don't give us a showing up,' said

Jen. 'It's just my mate Michelle. It's not like she's Serena Williams. She's only a singer.'

Jen and Michelle shared a knowing look at this. Nicolette glanced at Helena to gauge her response, but she was looking along the path towards the woman Nicolette recognised as Lauren Combe, on her way to greet them.

Kennedy put a hand to her face and did indeed wipe a tear from her eye, though it looked now to be one of embarrassment. She gave a sniff then stepped forward and gripped Michelle's outstretched hand. 'Sorry. I'll get it together. I'm not normally like this.'

'What happened to your foot?'

'Stood on a ball while lining up a smash.'

'Did you at least win the point?'

Kennedy shook her head then stepped aside, looking like she wanted a hole to open up and swallow her. Samira was approaching at her back, Beattie bringing up the rear.

Samira was this dainty little thing in skinny jeans and a Karen Millen cami top. Jen had been giving out to Nicolette about showing off her cleavage, but she noticed that Samira was quick to ditch the hen weekend T-shirt too. They had been told she'd been invited because she was wrung out from being stuck at home with twins, but to Nicolette's eyes she didn't look like she had been pregnant any time in the last decade.

There was something sleekit about Samira, Nicolette decided. She had made a great show of grabbing those miniatures but Nicolette hadn't seen her actually drink either of them. Given that tiny frame and having said she was a lightweight, Nicolette would have expected to see some effects. Everybody was different, though.

'I'm a bit calmer than Kennedy,' Samira told Michelle, 'but that's because I'm altogether less impressed with you.'

41

She added a giggle at the end of this. It sounded like dry humour, a way of making light of Kennedy's reaction, but there was something unguarded about the way it had spilled out, which made Nicolette reappraise whether Samira had indeed knocked back the miniatures.

The look on Michelle's face was of someone with little choice but to make out she was on board with the joke. That was also the price of fame: pretending to be a good sport when someone is pushing their luck because there's just too much blowback if you tell them to go fuck themselves.

'This is Samira,' Jen said.

'Your future sister-in-law,' Michelle stated.

Did Nicolette detect a bit of a pause before Jen replied?

'She's Zaki's younger sister,' Jen said. As opposed to, for instance, simply 'yes'.

'Zaki's *much* younger sister,' Samira added.

'And you've got twins.'

'Where?' Samira looked around in a fake panic. 'Not this bloody weekend I don't. That's the whole point.'

Michelle scrutinised her a moment, curious. 'Have we met before?'

'I don't think so. It's probably just that all us brown people look the same.' She left it long enough for there to be the beginnings of mortification before clarifying that this was also a joke. 'I'm the lawyer on *Sunrise*. I was probably hovering in the background one time when you were on the sofa. We wouldn't have been introduced unless you said something actionable.'

'That must be it,' Michelle agreed. She remained smiling but her expression was wary.

Nicolette was right there with her on that. She had seen Samira's type before: acting flaky and disengaged, but all the while observing everything and filing away the fine details for later use. Nicolette had got that vibe off her brother too. It was hardly the thing she was about to confide in Jen, especially this weekend, but there was something about Zaki she didn't quite trust.

Michelle turned finally to Beattie. 'Beattie, it's been forever.'

'Michelle. Glad to see you're doing so well.'

There was a sympathetic note to Michelle's manner, like an acknowledgment of Beattie's sorrow. Nicolette hadn't realised they knew each other. If they had been in the same circles as teenagers, Michelle must have known Jen's late husband, Jason, and Beattie through him.

In that moment Nicolette realised that Michelle's tone wasn't merely about acknowledging that Beattie's brother was dead. It was about acknowledging what had come out about him in the years since he went missing.

'And everyone, this is Lauren, our host,' Michelle said, Lauren having waited quietly to one side while they all exchanged greetings.

Nicolette noted how Michelle had played that, introducing the woman as though Lauren was the proprietor, but *she* was the weekend's MC. She was reminded of Helena's words about Michelle having a talent for making herself the centre of things.

Lauren led them the short distance to the house along a slate path between two manicured lawns. She was sporting a Jacquemus linen blazer and trouser combo which Nicolette recognised from Lauren's Insta feed. It was the one she favoured when there was a celeb in the party. She had a slightly more sober Low Classic one if it was high-level corporate personnel, and a Nanushka faux leather affair if it was some funky tech firm.

Lauren stopped just in front of the main entrance and handed them each a white card. 'I've allocated your rooms just to avoid arguments, but you're free to swap or negotiate. I can give you a tour later if you want, or you can just explore at your leisure. I'm assuming you probably want to unpack and settle in first.'

Nicolette looked at the card. Her room was called Glenmorangie. A glance at the others showed they were all named after malts. The card also listed the wi-fi network, 'clachangeal1', but no password, though why would there be? Nobody was going to piggyback unauthorised in this place.

'Your chef, Joaquin, is all set up and getting things ready in the kitchen. He is also a trained mixologist, he tells me, and will be serving cocktails in the drawing room from six.

'If you need me, I will be in my private apartment in the north tower. I am here purely for your convenience, so don't hesitate to ask if you need anything. Otherwise I will endeavour to be invisible, as I want you to feel the one true essence of the Clachan Geal experience: splendid isolation.'

Beattie

Beattie was giving herself a leisurely tour of the place when she observed Helena and Samira at the far end of a hallway. They were heading for the stairs, both dressed in fluffy bathrobes and towelling slippers.

Jennifer had told her to bring a bathing suit, to which her private response had been 'Sod that'. She wasn't keen on the idea of gadding about in next to nothing in front of younger women, and wasn't it always those who were younger and in better shape who suggested such activities? But upon reflection she had changed her mind. She was used to donning a uniform to get a job done, and in that regard the garment would serve as a constant reminder of her purpose. She was not here to enjoy herself; she was here on a mission.

She had assumed they were heading outside to the pool, but when she got back to her room, from her window overlooking the terrace she could see only Kennedy down there, swimming lengths. Her stroke was elegant, her hands barely throwing up a splash each time they broke the water. The support boot was sitting at the side, next to her towel. Clearly she was the type who had to find any form of exercise open to her, which made Beattie wonder why this lively young thing would want to spend a whole weekend with all these older women. She had been told Kennedy was late twenties, but she seemed so much younger than Beattie had ever felt at that age. She'd had three kids, the oldest of which was already seven by the time she hit thirty. Beattie guessed it was a reflection of the fact that Kennedy had reached the same marker without knowing any real responsibility. Never mind having no kids, making your living doing something as frivolous as teaching a game meant she'd never really had to grow up.

There was an aromatic scent filling the corridor as she approached what she assumed to be the spa. In fact, the first facility she encountered turned out to be the gym, where upon first glance there appeared to be several identically dressed women working with weights, like there was a class in progress.

It took a moment for her to resolve the image into the single figure of Michelle reflected in the mirrors lining three walls. The fourth was entirely glass, including the door. Michelle was holding the weights at her side as she performed slow-motion lunges, perfectly balanced, her movement smooth.

Michelle gave her a smile, waving with the dumbbell in her right hand. Beattie assumed that would be the extent of their interaction, but then Michelle put the weights carefully down on the floor and popped her earphones into the palm of her hand as she made for the door. 'I meant to ask, how is Kathleen getting on? I heard she had a baby, feels like a month ago but I'm assuming—'

'Xander. He's nearly two,' Beattie told her, smiling at the mere thought of the wee man, her youngest grandchild.

'And how's Kathleen herself? What's she doing these days? Or is she at home?'

Kathleen was Beattie's eldest. Michelle had babysat for her once upon a time.

46

'She's a pharmacist, at Wishaw General. Back part-time.'

'Her husband's a doctor there, is that right?'

'Michael, yes.' Beattie took her in. Michelle was forty-two, but a young forty-two by anyone's standards. Not that biology cared about that, but there were options these days; even more so than when Michelle was born.

'And still no plans to settle down yourself?'

'Maybe when I've grown up,' she said. It sounded like a mind-your-own-business answer.

To Beattie's mind, it seemed kind of ungrateful that Michelle seemed to have no intention of giving her parents grandchildren after so much effort and struggle had gone into having her. She had surely made enough money that she didn't need to keep doing this. It was just pop songs, for God's sake. But then, God love her, Michelle had always been all about Michelle.

Beattie had known her since before she was born. In a way, she could say that she had known Michelle Cassidy since before she was even conceived.

Michelle had been what they used to call a test-tube baby. Among the first, in fact. Beattie's family knew her parents, Tom and Gwen. They lived in the same cul-de-sac, just across the turning circle with its grass banking and redundant NO BALL GAMES sign. She remembered hearing her mum talking sympathetically about them trying for a baby and not being able to have one. It was before Beattie was old enough to fully understand the mechanics of it. Then there was excited talk about them having a 'test-tube baby', something that seemed a fraught and precarious process, and one the mechanics of which Beattie understood even less. Consequently, the image of the test tube itself cemented a notion in her head of Michelle being particularly fragile among infants. Michelle wasn't fragile, though. What she was, was precious.

She was a born princess, brought up with the impression that the whole world loved her. This was not simply because of how her parents treated her, but because so much of a fuss was made on their behalf. People were so happy for them, and took more of an interest in Michelle growing up than they would any other child. Beattie certainly had. She'd prick up her ears any time there was discussion of how wee Michelle was doing, the whole family invested in her progress because they had previously been invested in Tom and Gwen's struggle to have her.

Beattie's brother Jason had been born around the same time, only a few weeks earlier, and in her eyes their fates always seemed intertwined. Jason was a special child too. Beattie's parents had three daughters, of which she was the eldest. Then five years after the third of those was born, along had come a son.

Down the years Beattie had often heard people say that Jason was spoiled, but from her perspective what these uninvited comments seemed to be objecting to was simply that Jason was happy being Jason. Not only did he have two parents who adored him, but three older sisters in competition for his attention. Consequently he had grown up with a high opinion of himself, and it seemed a lot of people didn't like that.

He was a popular, good-looking and confident kid, someone who would always be able to take his pick of the girls, but there was never going to be anybody who could compete with Michelle. They had known each other from the cradle upwards, so there was something both inevitable and, to Beattie, deeply satisfying about how they became an item once they were old enough to become interested in that kind of thing.

And then something happened that she had just never seen

coming. Michelle's family moved away the summer she and Jason turned fifteen. It all seemed quite sudden, and there seemed to be something in the background nobody was talking about. To do with Tom's job, she deduced, which had implications for their mortgage.

Beattie knew it was folly to be tormenting herself with might-have-beens, but she couldn't help thinking that Jason would still be alive if Michelle's family had never left. They were right for each other. They were meant to be together.

'Have you any photos?' Michelle asked. 'Of Xander?'

'Tons. But my phone's upstairs.'

'Of course. You're on your way to the spa. Though we've got all weekend.'

It was Michelle's way of politely dismissing her.

Beattie carried on along the corridor, appreciating the thickness of the carpet underfoot now that she was shod in something less substantial. She lost herself in the simple pleasure of it: the lush texture, the crispness of the colours, the sheer opulence of the space. However, in doing so she invited that internal voice of censure, the one that reminded her she did not deserve such personal indulgences.

Not after what she had done.

Nicolette

Nicolette's room was on the first floor, with a view looking out to the bay through a six-paned lattice window. Directly in front of this was a free-standing bath, supplementary to the one in the actual bathroom. It was in that echelon of luxury that was just skirting the edge of decadence, which was the echelon Nicolette always aspired to inhabit. There was a great temptation to fill the tub right away and just sit there looking out to sea, but she was restive after being cooped up in the turbo prop and then the helicopter. She felt like she wanted to drink this place in, not hide herself away in one – admittedly generous – corner of it.

She wandered down the return staircase, noting how the carpet was matched by the Farrow and Ball wallpaper that rose from the skirting boards to the cornicing, all of it further comple-mented by the filigree patterning etched black-on-gold into the Paladin cast-iron radiators.

When she was a wee girl, she used to wish she could step inside the pictures in a catalogue. Today it felt like she finally had.

There was music playing everywhere, the sound following her wherever she went, but not intrusively. She couldn't see where the speakers were, and she must have been listening for a good thirty or forty seconds before she realised it was *that* song by the Manic Street Preachers. The one everyone conspicuously tried to shield her from, people awkwardly scrambling to change it whenever it came on in her company, thereby just drawing more attention to the bloody thing. It was a relief to be in an environment where its coming on could be ignored as incidental.

She strode outside, continuing enough of a distance down the path to be able to fully appreciate the house and its situation. It was so much more striking in real life than any number of Instagram posts might convey, no matter how famous the people posting them. Not even professional photographs could do justice to an approach framing a triple-decker fountain between four roman columns, to say nothing of the smell of the sea, the feel of the breeze and the way the light hit the stone towers with that mackerel sky behind.

The other quality that had to be experienced first-hand was the quiet, something she hadn't appreciated on the way in, with people talking and the helicopter taking off again. Standing between the lawns, she could hear the lapping of the waves at the foot of the slope. There was a calm to it, a sense of distance from the everyday; a kind of quiet you seldom knew in the modern world. Standing here, she understood that there was a difference between calm and stillness.

In the early days of the pandemic, she had been unsettled by the absence of the constant white noise of the motorway, something she had never really noticed until it wasn't there. Every sound she made seemed to reverberate uncomfortably, rattling around in a way that made her feel her house was empty. That her life was empty.

She continued a leisurely circuit of the property, past the winter garden. She saw a quad bike parked haphazardly at the side, which only served to emphasise the absence of any other vehicles. A modern building without a car park: when had she ever been in such a place?

Rounding the base of one of the towers, Nicolette saw Jen standing with her phone in her hand, looking back at the building and taking photos.

'What do you think?' Jen asked. 'Will this do? Do you reckon we can thole it for a couple of nights?'

'It's amazing, isn't it?' Nicolette replied. Half the buzz about staying in a place like this was acknowledging your good fortune to each other.

'How's your room?' Jen asked.

'Spectacular. There's a bath in the window. How's yours?'

'Beautiful. But it's not just the room, it's the whole vibe,' Jen explained, gesturing to the sea and the island all around. 'I feel like I'm breathing for the first time in I don't know how long.'

This struck Nicolette as an odd thing to say for someone imminently expecting nuptial bliss. But then the run-up to a wedding was always stressful, and even the run-up to the hen weekend couldn't have been short on anxieties.

'Your mate Michelle turned up too,' Nicolette observed, suggesting one of the reasons she might be breathing more freely.

Jen nodded. 'I would have totally understood if she couldn't make it. I think she's been dealing with some difficult stuff, so I appreciate her making the effort, especially as being around us eejits is maybe not what she needs right now.'

'Maybe being around her oldest friend from the real world is exactly what she needs,' Nicolette suggested.

Jen gave her a grateful smile. 'Maybe,' she said.

'What about Helena? I honestly had no idea about all that. Will she be okay?'

'Ach, this might be what she needs too. It was all a long time ago, and you only get one life: you shouldn't waste it being in the huff. The way I see it, we've probably all done something to hurt somebody, even if we didn't mean to. If you feel you deserve to be forgiven for that, you should be prepared to forgive whoever hurt you.'

'That's very philosophical, Jen.'

'I told you, it's the surroundings.'

As she said this, a door opened at the side of the building and Nicolette gawped as a tattooed Adonis emerged, carrying a chopping board laden with assorted squeezed-out citrus fruit. He was in chequered chef's trousers and a tight T-shirt, the sleeves stretched around taut biceps.

'And speaking of the view,' Nicolette said.

She and Jen shared a look. They stifled a giggle until he had gone back inside, then it spilled out.

'Jesus. That's the chef?' Jen asked.

'Never mind what's on the menu,' Nicolette said. 'As far as I'm concerned, he *is* the menu. And I'm up for sampling every course.'

'Aye, very good,' Jen replied. She gave a look, seeking reassurance that Nicolette was joking.

A possibility floated before Nicolette to say something like 'What's sauce for the goose', but she let it pass. She couldn't lay something like that on Jen this weekend. It wasn't a time for anything real. She wasn't sure she and Jen had that kind of relationship anyway. They just played tennis. But she hadn't confided in anybody, and that was why it was eating her up from the inside. She couldn't imagine stating it directly, saying aloud that she was one hundred per cent certain her husband Paul was having an affair.

Apart from anything else, she wouldn't be able to handle the sympathy. Jen would be gratifyingly astonished, but that would only emphasise the humiliation. Jen would be thinking a guy like Paul must know he was punching above his weight and surely wouldn't do anything to blow it. But that was actually the problem. When you married somebody who worried you were out of his league, you imagined he'd be grateful, but in practice you were always dealing with his insecurity.

As Nicolette made her way back through the house, she felt altogether less comfortable in her surroundings, the matching patterns on the walls and floor now seeming oppressive in their uniformity. It was suddenly less like she had stepped into a catalogue and more like she was trapped there.

She was conscious of the hairs prickling on the back of her neck, and it seemed so much greater than any bog-standard irrational unease. This was what people meant when they said it felt like someone had walked over their grave.

We've probably all done something to hurt somebody, even if we didn't mean to, Jen had said, talking about Helena and Michelle. *If you feel you deserve to be forgiven for that, you should be prepared to forgive whoever hurt you.* The sentiment ought to have reassured her, but there was ground that it didn't cover. Darker ground.

What if you *did* mean to? And what if you didn't deserve to be forgiven?

There was something Nicolette had been trying to suppress in the run-up to this weekend. Having arrived and settled into her room without giving it any thought, she was confident she had neutralised it. It was all a long time ago, she had reassured herself, and if it was going to come back on her it would have done so by now. But as she walked inside the entrance hall, it struck her that whether anyone knew anything or not, for the next three nights she was trapped in this house, trapped on this *island*, with someone she had hurt.

Michelle

Michelle had just rounded the corner and stepped onto the terrace when she saw Jen approaching from the house, wrapped in a bathrobe and clutching a towel, intent upon the same thing. The sight drew her eye and delayed her noticing that there was someone already in the pool, face down, executing a perfect crawl. The plastic brace by the poolside told her it was Kennedy, the younger woman who had been weirded out when they were introduced.

The swimmer lifted her head as she reached the end, noticing Michelle's approach. She immediately climbed out and hurriedly towelled herself down before replacing her support brace and hobbling away without a word. Evidently, and despite her stated intentions, she had failed to get it together.

Michelle wasn't sorry. Some fans could be overcome in her presence, and that was preferable to the over-familiar types who imagined you were going to be best friends. When meeting the public there was pressure to come across as down to earth. People wanted to believe being a star was an act, a persona you adopted on stage. It was the same reason they loved talent shows: they wanted to believe that anybody could do this. Michelle knew that vanishingly few people could do this, and for them, it was being down to earth that was an act.

'Sorry about Kennedy,' Jen said. 'She's normally the most level-headed of any of us. I knew she was excited to meet you, but I didn't realise she was *that* excited. I'm now worried that she left because she actually peed in the pool. I hope she calms down soon, because she's my insurance against it all turning to awkwardness and huffs this weekend. She can get on with anybody: it's her superpower.'

'She reminds me of someone,' Michelle said. 'It's doing my head in trying to think who.'

'I know what you mean. Just the way she carries herself. I sometimes think Saoirse Ronan but that's not quite it.'

'What's her surname? Or is Kennedy her surname and . . .'

Jen looked faintly embarrassed. 'I don't actually know. That's terrible, isn't it? She's in my contacts as just Kennedy, tennis coach. I think I created the contact the day she arrived. The previous coach got fired for inappropriate use of the computer, and I do *not* want to know what that entailed. Anyway, there comes a point beyond which you can't ask because you've got to admit you've not known for all this time.'

'How about I find out for you? I don't know her so I can come right out and ask.'

'You *are* a brick.'

Michelle laughed. She hadn't heard that in forever. They used to love using vocabulary from stuff like *Malory Towers* and *The Twins at St Clare's*. It was the vibe she had aimed for by calling Jen 'Barbara'. That one went right back to first year in secondary school. There was an old Lloyd Cole song her dad liked called 'Jennifer She Said'. She and Helena used to sing the chorus, 'bah-bah-ra-ra-ra-ra', whenever Jen came into a room.

Christ. Helena.

'So are you for a swim,' Jen asked, 'or would you rather just sit in one of the hot tubs and have a blether?'

A week ago, Michelle's instinctive response would have been to hit the pool and clock up a hundred lengths, even despite the rarity of spending such quality time with an old friend. It had thoroughly altered her perspective to think she had put in all that effort just to be in perfect nick for a million wankers watching her naked without her consent.

'Hot tub sounds divine.'

Jen hung her bathrobe on a hook and climbed into the warm water, hitting a button to start the jets. She looked in great shape. Michelle had heard that Jen's fiancé was seven years younger than her. That tracked. It would take a younger guy to keep up.

Jen wasn't someone who seemed younger than her years; more like someone for whom it had taken all her years to make her this complete. That was what Michelle told herself anyway. It served her conscience to think that Jen wasn't carrying too many scars.

Michelle climbed in opposite and thrilled to the feeling of the jets pounding her. She could hardly call it a simple pleasure, but she was aware that she didn't slow down and smell the roses often enough.

'This is the life,' she said.

'I thought you lived the life every day,' Jen replied, winding her up.

'There won't be much time for this kind of thing once the tour starts, believe me. I'm looking at weeks of rehearsals then months of shows. And just to add to the fun, one of the backing musicians just broke three of his fingers playing bloody cricket. I mean, replacements aren't hard to find in terms of technical ability, but it's the chemistry, on stage and off. You've got to get that right.'

'I'm sure it'll be fine. Everything you touch turns to gold. Just how huge are you these days?'

'Well, I don't think Adele is looking over her shoulder yet, but I'm big enough to actually make money from Spotify, which is saying something. Alan my manager told me Ellie Goulding's people point to me for where she should be aiming, but maybe that's just his polite way of saying I'm getting old.'

'Didn't I just read that you made a fortune in Bitcoin or something?'

'No. I already have a fortune, remember? And when you have, you can gamble on things. My geeky financial adviser kept going on at me, so I put in half a mil a few years back. Now it's worth about five times that, apparently.'

She let out a wistful laugh. 'There was a time when that kind of money would have been life-changing. Now I'd give ten times that to go back a year and say: "Actually no, let's not film ourselves doing this."'

Jen reached out a hand and squeezed her shoulder. It was a small gesture but it was worth as much as half the therapy and counselling Michelle had been through.

'I wanted to say again, Michelle, thank you so much for taking the time this weekend. I appreciate it might not be easy for you and Helena being around each other. Greater love hath no woman than to tolerate some bitch you can't stand in order to please an old friend.'

'I didn't say I can't stand her.'

'I wasn't talking about you.'

Michelle sent a splash arcing towards her by way of friendly rebuke.

Jen's expression became sincere. 'Joking aside, I do think it's harder for Helena.'

'I am aware I'm painted as the villain in this tale.'

'It's not about blame, Michelle. More that if there was a

winner and a loser in this thing, it's kind of obvious which is which.'

Michelle nodded, coming to a decision. She didn't want to mess with the mellow vibe, but she knew Helena would have given Jen her version of events plenty of times, and she'd never get to air her side if she was waiting for the perfect time.

'Then I guess I'm the one who doesn't see it being about winners and losers. Because I know Helena probably regards this as something she lost or something I took away, but the fact is it wasn't something she wanted as much as she makes out. Everyone's heart is in it during the good times, on the way up. When you're out promoting a second album that nobody is buying, playing songs the audience doesn't want to hear, different story. That's when Helena started asking herself what she was doing in crappy motorway hotels in Belgium.'

'I think it was what happened after then that she's a bit sore about,' Jen said archly, letting Michelle know she wasn't getting to vent without pushback.

Good, she thought, because this was the part Jen needed to hear, the part nobody else seemed to understand.

'What I'm saying is that I took Helena on a journey she'd never have dared go on herself. But I could only carry her so far. She isn't bitter that I went solo. She's bitter because that was an option for me but not for her.'

Jen didn't look entirely convinced. 'Helena knows she was never cut out to be the star attraction,' she said. 'But I think some of her bitterness stems from the contribution she feels she made in getting you to that point.'

Michelle glanced out to sea and allowed herself a wry smile. 'Helena had been practising several hours a day since she was five, and thought that was the pathway to success. She couldn't handle that sometimes just one song can propel you so much further than every other factor combined. That for all her effort in honing her craft, we were playing to packed crowds because we covered an obscure number written in the eighties by three hairy blokes from Motherwell, a track which had failed to push them to the same level. There's no logic or reason to it.'

'"Clockwork motion and magic potion"?' Jen asked, quoting *that* song. The one she never played any more.

'Don't. But the main reason my sympathy for Helena is limited is that ultimately, she did get what she wanted. Deep down, Helena wanted to be a suburban mum, teaching music. If she wants to be pissed off at me all her life, that's on her. The bitterness is only going one way. And my conscience is clear.'

On that score at least, Michelle thought.

She decided to change the subject, asking Jen about the sale of her company. If there was anything that spoke to the qualities of Jen Dunne, it was that she had built up a successful business while raising two teenagers as a single mother. Michelle had been keen to hear all about it anyway, but now in particular it helped drown out what was creeping into the edges of her mind.

Despite the luxury of the surroundings, Michelle was feeling strangely vulnerable and exposed. The worst thing she had felt when the videos and images went online wasn't shame or embarrassment; it was the unmistakable hatred, people's delight in humiliating her. Soon enough she had gone from wondering why she was hated by random strangers to wondering if she might also be hated by the people she knew.

As the details had emerged about Jen's late husband's true nature, Michelle had worried that Jen would think she ought to have warned her somehow. She had known him first, after all. They were only kids of thirteen, fourteen, but still?

Beattie, forever overprotective and indulgent of her baby brother, had been vocally sceptical of all that came out after Jason went missing. To everyone else, the only thing that remained a mystery was whether it was one of his associates in the underworld or one of his bent colleagues in the police who disappeared him.

To be fair to Beattie, the wider perception of Jason had always been of a thoroughly happy individual, the kind of bloke whose presence unfailingly cheered everyone up, so it was hard for people to imagine him any other way. Being on his good side felt like such a special place that it had always made Michelle forget how scary being on his bad side was. No matter how afraid he made her feel, when the sun came out again, she felt the glorious sensation of having pleased him, or of being forgiven by him, which made her focus on what she must have done wrong. All of which was another way of saying she had always done what Jason wanted because she was afraid of the consequences if she didn't.

That was, until she discovered that doing what he wanted could have frightening consequences too.

Looking back, she often thought she should have told someone that he sometimes made her scared, but it was easy after the fact. When you're fourteen and your boyfriend is manipulative and controlling, you can't be expected to predict all that he would become. That didn't stop her feeling guilty, though, or afraid that Jen blamed her for keeping secrets.

It was at such times that she had to remind herself they *were* still secrets. But the source of her life-long fear was that nothing stays secret forever.

Beattie

Beattie passed through a heavy wooden door into a space that seemed to belong in another house, maybe another country. The walls were covered with tiny green tiles that sparkled in reflection of a thousand LED lights embedded in the ceiling, while all around her was an ambient sound, something that was not quite music and not quite anything else.

She could also hear conversation, polite laughter, and feel the warmth that was waiting to envelop her, from steam, from wood, from easy company. She was ambushed again, confronted with a contrast: the awareness that somewhere else, another woman was sitting in an empty house, broken in a way that could never be made whole.

She followed the voices and opened a frosted-glass door to enter what was neither sauna nor steam room, pleasantly warm rather than oppressively hot. There was water running down the walls, draining into lipped channels on the floor. It sounded like gentle rain, and the air was full of the scent she had smelled outside.

Helena and Samira were seated opposite one another, sipping from paper cups. Beattie had noticed a dispenser full of cucumber water next to the door, beneath a sign urging users to stay hydrated.

They both flashed friendly smiles as she stuck her head around the door. Beattie withdrew again and hung up her bathrobe before coming fully inside.

'This is lovely,' she ventured, taking a seat next to Samira.

'Isn't it?' Helena replied. 'I could fall asleep, except this almost feels better than sleep. It's as relaxed as you can feel while still awake.'

'Just not hearing any crying in the immediate vicinity is enough to relax me these days, so this is beyond bliss,' said Samira.

'You deserve it,' Beattie told her. 'We all do,' she added, leaning into the spirit of the occasion.

Helena offered a smile that had a solicitous quality to it. Beattie knew what was coming. That was the hardest thing about it. Everybody knew. Everybody cared. Everybody asked.

'And are you doing okay? I heard about the accident.'

'I'm fine. The only lasting impact is the occasional flashback to the fear, knowing Xander was in the front.'

'What's this?' Samira asked.

'Beattie was in a car accident a few weeks ago. A pedestrian walked right in front of her, off his face on drugs. Her grandson was in the car too.'

'Thankfully I doubt the wee fella knew much about it.'

'But the pedestrian was killed,' Helena added.

'God. How awful for you. So the police were involved? That can't have been easy, on top of everything else.'

'It wasn't a treasured experience, no, but the main thing is that Xander was okay. Everything else was just . . . inconvenience.'

Samira seemed to scrutinise her for a moment, as though trying to piece something together. 'Sorry,' she said, 'I'm kind of catching up all the time here, trying to remember who everybody is.'

'I'm Beattie,' she reminded her.

'And tell me again, how is it that you know Jen?'

Beattie must have waited a moment too long to answer, enough for Helena to fear an onset of awkwardness, because she stepped in and answered for her. 'Jen's late husband was Beattie's younger brother.'

That was Helena all over the back. Sensitive. A good girl. Beattie had known her since she was five years old. Helena's mum had been a music teacher, and in the end that's what Helena had ended up too. Beattie had always heard music whenever she walked past the Eckharts' house, somebody practising something or her mum giving lessons. Helena started on the piano but became very keen on the guitar. She was always a diligent and industrious wee thing, shy and quiet with it. Beattie had been amazed when she learned that Helena was in a pop group, playing concerts. It was no surprise that she hadn't lasted in that game though, and had done something more sensible instead, settling down and having a family.

'Jen's . . . Oh, I see,' said Samira. 'It's nice that you're still close,' she added.

It was a seemingly neutral statement until you contemplated the implicit question: Why wouldn't they be?

There was sympathy in Samira's face, which indicated she knew the answer. And in that pitying expression Beattie saw the reason she had come here. It was the same look Michelle had given her when she stepped off the helicopter. It didn't say *I'm sorry for your loss*. It said *I'm sorry for your shame*.

Beattie had to respond before a growing pause became conspicuous. 'It's family, isn't it,' she said. 'Jen and I are aunties to each other's kids.'

Beattie hid her true feelings behind a smile. It stuck in her craw to hear certain sentiments, and she was choking on the idea of being here ostensibly to celebrate Jen's future happiness. But this was an opportunity, an undercover mission.

Samira seemed a bright young thing. Beattie wondered if she was bright enough to see past the surface to the truth of who her brother was planning to marry. Because people had only ever heard Jennifer Dunne's version of events.

Jason was different after he married her. Beattie didn't doubt he had gone off the rails and done some things he shouldn't, but nobody ever asked about the extent to which Jen was the one who drew him into that.

You couldn't tell Beattie there wasn't a whole load of skeletons rattling around that family's closet. Jennifer's dad had started off running a tiny pub in Airdrie: the kind of place where the bouncer frisked you for weapons, and if he didn't find any, gave you one before he let you in. How did he go from that to owning a huge nightclub in Hamilton only a few years later?

Jen said Jason had been dealing drugs out of the place, like she and her dad never knew a thing about it. Beattie understood how these things worked. Having a policeman involved would have been an indispensable part of the operation.

Jen also told everyone he had stolen money from the nightclub. Funny how she never said a word about that to anybody until Jason wasn't around to speak for himself. Then suddenly he was a convenient scapegoat, not just for her, but for a whole host of people: gangsters and bent polis alike.

Jen had said that in the early days after Jason's disappearance, bad people from either side of the law had been actively looking for him, each thinking he was lying low to get away from them. It felt like such an insult to the brother she knew that it took Beattie a long time to realise that her anger over the lies being told about him had blinded her to a much darker truth.

Here, now, was her chance to bring it all into the light. Jen had gathered her closest friends together in this small and isolated place. Unfortunately, those she was most likely to have confided in were also those likely to be the most loyal. But with drink flowing and bonding easily mistaken for intimacy, people's guards could be lowered. All sorts of secrets could spill out over a weekend like this if you created the right circumstances.

If you gave people the right motivation.

Kennedy

Kennedy was almost swallowed by the sofa, her plastic-encased foot barely touching the carpet when her back was against the rear cushion. There was laughter around the room, an air of giddiness fuelled by the variety of cocktails the chef had left on the sideboard. He had walked them through the selection, explaining a little about each before apologising that he couldn't serve drinks on request as he had to prepare the meal. He was providing instead what he assured them in his accented English was 'a superabundance', prompting the predictable response of 'We'll be the judge of that.'

Kennedy had observed the lingering looks he received as he made his brief presentation. Most had been content to steal a glance when they thought his eyes were elsewhere. Nicolette had been less subtle, eyeing him much as an owl might a field mouse.

He had left at least an hour ago, and most of them were onto their second cocktail, some their third. Kennedy was still nursing her first, taking the occasional micro-sip but mostly keeping it out of sight on the side table next to the sofa. Being conspicuously dry on a hen weekend was to invite a question to which there could plausibly be only one answer. If it came to that, she would let it play out, but she'd prefer to avoid the issue and there seemed enough distraction.

She was seated to the right of the fireplace on one of three sofas forming a horseshoe around a low table made of driftwood, which emphasised the proximity of the sea. A glance through any of the three large windows afforded a view of the coastline, where it was easy to imagine wood washing up. The vista also took in the terrace and the infinity pool, the jetty beyond out of sight due to the slope.

There was music playing over a speaker system that was so sympathetically integrated as to be invisible. Kennedy literally couldn't see where the sound was coming from, though she could see what was playing, as there was a hub sitting on a table by the window. The titles were scrolling across a tiny LCD panel: 'Crash' by the Primitives had just given way to 'Celebrity Skin' by Hole.

'Kennedy, is this the playlist you made?' Nicolette asked, her tone indicating disapproval.

They had all given Kennedy their Spotify usernames so that she could find out what they normally listened to, and she had also asked them for suggestions that might have special significance for Jen.

'No,' she replied. 'Lauren said we should have access but I can't seem to get the system to recognise my device. Or it does but it overrides me and sticks with what it's already playing. I can give Lauren a ring and ask what's up.'

'It really doesn't matter,' said Jen. 'Let's not disturb her for anything like that. Though if it becomes non-stop jungle . . .'

'Or experimental jazz,' said Michelle, striding back from the sideboard with another mojito. She sat herself down next to Kennedy, in the space vacated by Beattie, who had just left the room, presumably to visit the loo.

Kennedy felt this weird heightening of the senses, an acute perception of Michelle's presence that was not replicated around anyone else. She tried to remind herself that she was twenty-seven years old, not some pubescent tween, but that backfired because it only underlined that Michelle's music had been a presence throughout much of her life. Her songs seemed to have matured in parallel with Kennedy's own development, from the cheerful pop tones of Cassidy that lightened the gloom of her teenage years, to the minor-key meditations that formed the more sophisticated soundtrack of adulthood.

She could still recall where she was and how she felt when she first heard 'She Knows'. It wasn't just the hit single; the whole of Cassidy's eponymous debut album had been balm to a lonely soul in her pitiless dorm at Logiealmond Academy in Perthshire. She had been sent to boarding school by two parents who didn't actually want *her*; they just wanted the idea of themselves as a mother and a father.

'So, Kennedy,' said Michelle, 'is that a first name, a surname, a nickname?'

Kennedy took a sip of her cocktail. Just one wasn't going to do much harm, and she needed to take a little of the edge off.

'It's actually a middle name, but I prefer it. Nobody calls me by my real name. If I hear it called out at something official, it takes a sec for me to realise they mean me.'

What she didn't say was that she only started going by her middle name because it sounded a bit like Cassidy.

'And what is your real name?' asked Michelle. She sent a brief glance towards Jen, sharing something that was lost on Kennedy.

'It's Kathleen Boniface,' answered Nicolette, making this unprompted intervention with a mischief bordering on malice. 'I found a photo of you on a website from the early 2000s.'

As she heard this name uttered for the first time in years, Kennedy felt an involuntary ripple of shock, quickly turning to anger that Nicolette had been rooting around in her past. She hid it behind a fake laugh. 'It's not, actually. It's Fiona Gilmour. Fiona Kennedy Gilmour.'

Nicolette's expression was a mixture of confusion and scepticism, like she thought Kennedy was messing with her. Nicolette held up her phone and displayed the picture she was talking about. It showed Kennedy at fourteen. The image was grainy and low-res, a scan of a headshot, but it would be hard to convince anyone it wasn't her.

'Where did you find that monstrosity?' she asked, making it sound like she was merely bashful. She thought she had managed to delete everything.

'Just trawling old tennis sites. I was planning a kind of guess-who quiz this weekend, but I couldn't find old-enough pictures of everybody. You're saying this isn't you?'

'No, it's my photograph all right, but it's wrongly captioned. Kat Boniface and me were a doubles partnership back then, and our names got mixed up in admin stuff all the time.'

'Yes, people are always screwing up registration forms,' said Helena. The remark appeared to be aimed at Michelle, but she blanked it.

Nicolette appeared to buy the explanation, though.

'So you were on the junior tour?' Michelle said, sounding genuinely interested.

Kennedy had to remind herself that Michelle being interested was no different to anyone else being interested.

'What was that like?'

Like boarding school, except that it moved around. It served the same purpose: to have someone other than her own parents

71

responsible for her. But she learned a lot in those years: how to blend in, how to get along, how to present an affable face to people who didn't really care.

She said none of that, of course.

'Mostly it was fun, but the standard was so high, and I wasn't quite good enough. Actually, I was nowhere near good enough.'

'Did you know anyone from those days who went on to be huge?' asked Nicolette.

'Maybe she doesn't want to talk about something that didn't work out.'

It was Helena who had spoken. Kennedy guessed her words were intended for Michelle's ears as much as Nicolette's.

'I'm not asking her to probe a sore tooth if she doesn't want to,' said Nicolette. 'But if I'm two degrees of separation from Emma Raducanu, I want to know about it.'

'Actually,' said Michelle, 'what I want to hear more about is Jen's intended.'

Kennedy wondered if Michelle changing the subject was out of consideration towards her, or that she genuinely hadn't already heard lots about Zaki. She certainly seemed to have picked up that Kennedy wasn't comfortable talking about her failed ambitions in a way that Nicolette would have been happy to ignore.

'He's gorgeous,' said Helena. 'I mean, seriously. He's young, he's stylish, charming. It's as if God sent him to Jen as compensation for—' She cut herself off, suddenly aware of Beattie having come back into the room.

Helena sounded a bit tipsy, though she wasn't the only one. Nobody had eaten anything and the cocktails kept disappearing. Kennedy was mindful of the drink Samira was working on, sitting on a side table at the other end of the sofa opposite.

Samira's arm kept flailing in gesticulation whenever she spoke, and she could see the drink getting knocked over.

'How did you meet?' Michelle asked.

'It was at a catering trade fair,' Jen answered. 'I saw him at this stall, this extractor system demo thing, talking to the sales rep. I didn't need a new ventilation system, so I won't pretend I hadn't gone over because I saw this very attractive bloke standing there. An inauspicious beginning, no question, but here we are.'

'And what are your honeymoon plans?' asked Michelle.

Jen wore an odd expression, like she was regretful, or concerned everyone would get the wrong idea.

'Nothing fancy. Zaki's business is a bit hectic just now, so we're just going to Skye for a couple of nights. We'll take a proper holiday in the autumn.'

Kennedy looked at Jen standing there against this beautiful backdrop, framed between the sideboard and the fireplace like she was posing for a portrait. It was hard to comprehend how someone she had never met seven months earlier could become such a big part of her life. She really ought to be used to that by now.

She used to be jealous of other people's friendships, imagining them to be something she would never have. It just took her a while to realise she had merely misunderstood their nature, seeing them from the outside and assuming them to be more substantial. Being around Jen had taught her that there was an important difference between an open person and a trusting one. You didn't need to trust someone, or for them to trust you, in order to be their friend. Jen trusted nobody.

According to the LCD display, the invisible speakers were pumping out the intro to 'Goodbye Earl' by the Chicks, OMD's 'Messages' having just finished.

'Didn't we just hear this one?' Samira asked. 'And the one before it?' She gestured again with her hand and this time did knock her glass over. Fortunately there was only ice left in it.

Kennedy took the opportunity to get to her feet and offer to fetch her a refill.

'Maybe a fizzy water?' she suggested.

'Fuck, no,' Samira replied, giggling.

Kennedy noticed Jen checking her watch, no doubt wondering when they were getting the call for dinner.

Nicolette returned from the toilet and plonked herself between Jen and Michelle, though not before grabbing one of the last few cocktails.

Having placed Samira's new drink on the side table, Kennedy perched on the far end of the sofa opposite, next to Beattie and Helena, who each seemed to have positioned themselves the furthest from the people they wished to avoid: respectively Jen and Michelle.

'So tell me, Michelle,' said Nicolette, 'which movie about the music business would you say is the most accurate?'

'I can tell you which ones I like,' she replied, 'but from my own experience I can't say any of them is particularly accurate. My favourite is still *The Bodyguard*, probably because of the age I was when I first saw it, which was on VHS. That's how ancient we're talking. Jen and Helena and I must have watched it a hundred times back then. We all loved Kevin Costner.'

'My favourite is *Almost Famous*,' said Samira. 'All that tension between the singer and the guitarist over which one is the star. Except they reversed it because it was the seventies: the genius guitarist was the real talent and the singer knew it deep down. In reality it's usually the singer who is the star.'

Kennedy could feel the temperature drop a notch as Samira

spoke. She wondered if she was oblivious to the parallel or squiffy enough to think it was funny.

'I haven't seen it,' said Michelle diplomatically.

'Oh, you've got to,' Samira insisted. 'The best bit is this scene on a private plane in a storm, where all their secrets and confessions spill out because they think they're going to die.'

'I think Michelle's had enough secrets spill out,' said Nicolette, which felt like the record-scratch moment of the evening so far. Kennedy couldn't tell if it was a pissed pitch at making light of the issue, but it didn't land well. In fact, there was no good way for it to land at all, which was why it should never have taken off.

There was a moment of silence, enough to hear the words '*I will never forgive you*' being sung over the speakers, then Michelle got to her feet. Kennedy assumed she was going for the door but she stopped at the sideboard and grabbed another drink, the last one on the tray. Jen had stood up, ready to follow her out, but Michelle gestured to sit as she took a large gulp of whisky sour. 'It's okay. It is kind of the elephant in the room. In fact, that's the whole thing about my sex tape: it's always there. Everybody knows.'

She stayed by the sideboard, leaning against it as she addressed the room. It looked like she needed the distance. 'It's so pervasive. Every man you speak to, you're asking yourself the whole time, did you download it? Have you seen me doing those things, seen my body? Women too. Even as they smile politely, you wonder if they have secretly watched you, if that's what they're picturing. And that's forever now.'

Jen got up again, walking across to clasp Michelle's hand. Kennedy heard the closing bars of 'Feet to the Flames' by some band called the Wonder Stuff playing for the third time by her count. The vocalist was insisting again that '*I will never forget that. I will never forgive you.*' It was followed by a track called 'Hater'.

Jen had evidently decided it would help Michelle to talk about something happier, and so asked her about her new album. They stayed over by the sideboard, as though Michelle wasn't ready to rejoin the body of the kirk.

Alongside Kennedy, Helena spoke in a quiet voice, almost but not quite under her breath. 'I told you. It didn't take long for it all to be about her.'

Kennedy could only just make out what Michelle was saying to Jen now, which reassured her that Helena's quieter words would not be intelligible across the room. They were intelligible to herself, Beattie and Samira though.

'It's not like she started the conversation,' Kennedy felt compelled to point out.

'No, but it's amazing where the conversation always ends up, don't you think?'

'I think she's been through something truly terrible, something horribly damaging,' Kennedy countered. It was weird seeing this side to Helena, who was normally so sympathetic.

'Yeah, she's been telling everybody about being on some counselling retreat, but I think the more salient detail is what she's talking about now. She's got a new album coming out and a tour in the offing. Always check the context. Drama means column inches, means clicks, likes, follows, ticket sales.'

'Are you saying you think she leaked the sex tape herself?' Kennedy asked, keeping her voice barely above a shocked whisper.

Helena looked a little cowed at having been called on this. 'I wouldn't be the first to suggest it if I was,' she said, not quite backing down. She was definitely a bit pissed, though not as much as Samira, it had to be said, who was starting to look woozy. Kennedy noted that the glass she had given her was almost empty. The one not containing fizzy water.

'Are you okay?' Kennedy asked her.

'I'm feeling no pain,' Samira replied, over-loud. 'I haven't felt this good in fucking ages.'

Kennedy detected a slight wince from Beattie at the swear word, while Samira's volume alone caused Jen to look up from her private chat with Michelle.

'Just maybe slow it down a wee bit so that you can make the most of your weekend of freedom?' Jen suggested. 'You don't want to waste tomorrow feeling rough.'

'That's a fair point,' Samira conceded. 'I've just been so enslaved by these two minuscule tyrants. Honestly, you spend your whole life, I dunno, educating yourself to the highest level of attainment, then suddenly you're required to become nothing more than a . . . a . . . an appendage to these two barely sentient creatures. Everybody lies about motherhood. And nobody tells you how fucking *boring* it's going to be!'

Beattie's expression of sour disapproval worsened. Kennedy inferred that she found the sentiment more profane than the language.

'All they do is cry,' Samira went on. 'And then you've got to play "Guess what's wrong with me". It drives me fucking insane. And sometimes nothing's wrong. They. Just. Fucking. Cry.'

'Is it colic?' Helena suggested, in a tone indicating she was familiar with it.

'Whatever that means. But yes. They cry from about half five in the evening, all the way through until they finally, begrudgingly fall asleep sometime after ten. The only evening since they were born that I've had any peace was after they had their MMR.

While their wee bodies were dealing with that, it seemed to chill them out for some reason. It was bliss.'

Nicolette's eyes widened at this. 'I wouldn't be so sanguine if having the MMR vaccine knocked them for six,' she said.

'Why?'

'Because it's dangerous. There's all kinds of side effects. It's all about the money for the pharma companies, so they lie about the dangers, and if anyone tries to expose them, the medical establishment sees that they get destroyed.'

'So you didn't have the Covid vaccine?' Samira asked.

'Well, yes, obviously, but that was my risk to take. And okay, I don't have kids of my own, but I'm just saying, if I did, I wouldn't take the risk on their behalf.'

'You'd suggest that instead I take the risk of them getting measles, mumps or rubella? Fucking polio, maybe? It's as well you don't have kids then, because they wouldn't stand a chance if they were being raised by a fucking stupid cow.'

Jen's intake of breath was audible as Samira got up onto unsteady feet. 'I'm sorry. I need to get some air,' she said, making for the door.

Kennedy spotted a tear in Nicolette's eye, which she quickly wiped away.

'There was no need for that,' Nicolette said, wounded.

'She said sorry,' Kennedy pointed out weakly.

'She wasn't apologising. She said, *Sorry, I need to get some air*. She was just excusing herself.'

'Maybe you should have kept your conspiracy theories to yourself on this occasion, Nicolette,' said Jen.

'I'm just saying, the authorities and the mainstream media don't tell you everything. There's two sides to every story.'

'Isn't that the truth,' rumbled Beattie darkly, which struck

Kennedy as an odd contribution from someone who didn't have a dog in this fight.

'She's a new mum under pressure,' said Jen.

'That's no excuse for firing off abuse,' Nicolette argued. 'She's utterly shit-faced, totally off her tits. Out of control.'

'I think we should leave this,' Jen told her. 'Especially as she's not here to speak for herself.'

Beattie gave a bitter chuckle. 'That never stopped you when it came to Jason, did it?' she said, eyeing Jen.

It turned out her dog was in a completely different fight.

'What's that supposed to mean?'

'I'm saying the world has only ever heard your version of events.'

'I'm not sure how Jason's version of how he murdered Ronnie Bryceland would make it sound any better than it did in court, but the floor is yours if you'd like to speak on his behalf.'

Jen stared at Beattie for an unpleasantly long few moments, daring her to respond, then she held her hands up, as if trying to dispel her own anger. 'I need a minute,' she said, then walked out of the room.

Michelle made to follow her but seemed to think better of it, perhaps deciding that giving Jen space would be more helpful.

'I think everybody needs to chill,' Michelle said. 'Let's all dial down the aggro factor a notch.'

'We could do with some food,' Kennedy suggested.

Michelle glanced at her watch. 'Damn good point,' she said. 'I'm going to find out what the hell's happening with the dinner. Maybe the hot Spanish chef found a mirror and couldn't pull himself away from it. Everybody try to play nice in the meantime.'

As Michelle exited, a raw kind of silence fell upon the

remaining four, while OMD's 'Secret' finished and 'Celebrity Skin' came on once again.

'Christ, if we've to listen to some rando's playlist, it could at least be more varied,' Nicolette muttered, an edge of more than mere irritation in her tone. 'I must've heard this song about four times.'

'Kennedy's right,' Helena said. 'Everybody's drinking on an empty stomach and getting hangry. So let's not take anything to heart. We need to remember why we're all here. We came to have a good time. We came for a celebration. Fun, goddammit!'

That was when they heard Michelle scream.

Jen

Jen had never heard anybody scream for real before, not in horror or fear. In her experience, when people were genuinely shocked, they reacted with stunned silence, or let out an involuntary gasp.

What she heard reverberating through the house told her not only what a real scream sounded like, but also drove home its purpose. It had an effect similar to hearing her own babies cry, but massively scaled up: something primal, a reflex that set her adrenaline flowing, ready to respond, to flee, to fight.

Jen strode back into the entrance hall as Kennedy hurried from the drawing room. There was no question she had heard it too, and even the brace had failed to impede her reactions.

'I think it came from the kitchen,' Kennedy said.

As they rushed along the corridor, they saw Michelle emerge from the kitchen, pale and dazed. There was blood dripping from her right hand. Jen wondered if she had injured herself and the scream had merely been a cry of pain.

'Oh my God, are you all right?' asked Kennedy.

Michelle looked at her uncomprehendingly for a moment, then seemed to notice her own hand.

'That's not mine,' she said in a numb voice. It sounded like she could be talking about the hand as much as the blood. 'He's in there,' she added.

It was only when she said this that Jen looked past Michelle. Her eyes briefly took in the blood that was smearing the door handle, a mere trailer for the true horror beyond.

The chef was lying on the floor behind the kitchen island. His face was turned away, but she could see that his throat had been cut. There was blood pooling on the tiles, pints of it.

Michelle hovered in the doorway, like she wanted to get away but somehow couldn't leave the scene. Whether she was concerned about abandoning the chef or abandoning Jen to deal with him was unclear.

'Oh, my God. Oh my God!'

Jen recognised Helena's voice, and turned to see her and Nicolette arriving. In her own panic she had momentarily forgotten they were even here. She had reacted too late to stop them seeing him.

They all remained frozen in place for a moment. It was like there was a force field across the threshold. Nobody wanted to cross it. Then Michelle spoke.

'I think I saw him move. While I was in there. I think he might still be breathing.'

They all looked at each other, then, God help her, at Kennedy, who knew they were all thinking the same thing. She was a trained First Aider.

Her expression conveyed how enticing a prospect this was and how much of a difference she thought she could make. This guy didn't need a sticking plaster or a support bandage. He had spilled two pints on the worktop alone, several more on the tiled floor.

Nonetheless she went, prompting a surge of both admiration

and concern in Jen, who was already feeling protective towards her for reasons she could not disclose.

Jen had noticed that Kennedy was nursing the same drink throughout the evening. She had barely touched her champagne at the airport either. The latter could have been about travel sickness or it simply being too early in the day, but that she was quietly dodging the cocktails was more significant. Jen had been on the cusp of asking why she wasn't drinking when it struck her that the answer might not be something Kennedy wanted to make public.

Jen had seen Kennedy in a coffee shop a couple of weeks ago, in the East Kilbride Shopping Centre, spotting her through the window as she walked the mall. Kennedy had been looking at her phone and appeared to be crying. Jen wasn't sure whether it was appropriate to intrude but she couldn't ignore a friend in distress. Kennedy had seemed pleased that Jen had stopped and taken an interest, but she wasn't prepared to open up about what was upsetting her. 'Just boy trouble,' she had said.

Now Kennedy walked carefully into the room, lifting her encumbered foot delicately over a puddle of blood to crouch down beside the chef. Her hand went tentatively towards his bloodied neck, but she seemed to think better of it and took his wrist instead. She held two fingers to it for an agonisingly long few seconds, then shook her head minutely.

The gesture was all the more devastating for its simplicity. The man who had been serving them cocktails an hour ago, who they had been joking about for his desirability and Nicolette vocally lusting after, was dead on the kitchen floor.

Then something shifted, and not just in Jen's mind. She could feel it pass through the hallway like a wave. With Kennedy confirming that nothing could be done, it was no longer about what had happened to Joaquin. It was about what happened next.

Nicolette was the one who said it. 'We've got to get out of here.'

Kennedy rose and limped back towards them, eyes glazed. Her hands were trembling. The girl was a natural organiser, the one they were used to deferring to at tennis, but she was not cut out to take charge of this. Somebody had to, though.

'Okay, keep the heid,' Jen said, as much addressing herself. 'First things first. We need to call the police.'

'First thing is we need to get off this island,' said Nicolette. 'It'll take the police hours to get here, and meanwhile whoever killed the chef can't be far away. He could be in the fucking house!'

These were Jen's thoughts too, but she had to background them while she fished her mobile from her clutch. It was as she did so that she remembered there was no reception. She checked the phone anyway, but it showed no bars.

'Where's the landline?' she asked, looking back along the hallway.

As she asked this, Jen heard the thump of footsteps from the ceiling, someone hurrying along the corridor on the floor above. They all shared worried looks, nobody knowing how to respond. Then a few moments later, Lauren appeared at the foot of the staircase. 'What's happened?' she called, her tone indicating she already suspected it was serious. She must have heard Michelle's scream too.

Jen suddenly found that she didn't quite know what to say or how to say it.

'Somebody's murdered the fucking chef, that's what's happened,' said Nicolette.

84

Jen watched Lauren glance at the blood on Michelle's hand as she approached.

'Michelle found him,' Jen explained, anticipating Lauren's line of thinking. Though as she spoke there was a purely logical part of her brain, some calculating instinct, that disregarded all she knew of Michelle as a person, wondering about the time that had elapsed between Michelle leaving the drawing room and Jen hearing her scream.

As Lauren neared the point from where she would be able to see for herself, Helena intervened. She pulled the kitchen door to, though not fully closed as she had grabbed it by the edge to avoid touching the bloodied handle.

'You don't need to see this,' she said.

Witnessing Helena's instinctive empathy in action, it struck Jen that Lauren might have known this guy a while. They would have had a professional relationship and who knew what else. That logical, calculating instinct started asking questions there too.

'We need to call the police and there's no mobile signal,' Jen told her.

Lauren eyed the kitchen door. 'The nearest landline is in there,' she said.

Kennedy looked like she was about to volunteer out of sheer duty, on the grounds that she had been in there once already, but there was an argument for cumulative effect too. She was already trembling.

'I'll go,' Jen said. 'You've done enough.' She opened the door, trying not to pull it too wide. It was wide enough, though, because she heard a gasp from Lauren, followed by a stifled sob. Morbid fascination had compelled her to look. She covered her mouth, instantly pallid.

Jen stepped inside. The phone was on a charging station on a worktop against the near wall, from where mercifully the kitchen island shielded her view of the chef's face. From her angle of vision, she could only see the bottom of his checked trousers. She did however get a closer look at all that blood on the worktop, poured over what was intended to be their starters.

Joaquin was tall, stocky and ripped, a guy who looked like he worked out. He would not have been an easy man to overpower, so he must have been taken by surprise while his concentration was elsewhere. It looked like he had been slashed while he was leaning over the island, perhaps delicately placing the quails that were on some of the starter plates.

Jen lifted the handset from the cradle. It was a wireless one, so at least she didn't have to stay in the room while she called. She dialled 999 as she headed for the hall, resisting the instinct to glance back at the other end of the kitchen island. She couldn't avoid seeing the blood, though, which was starting to congeal on the cold tiles.

Jen held the handset to her ear, waiting for the click of connection, the pulse of the ringing tone. She heard neither. 'Do I have to press something to get a dial tone?' she asked.

'No,' said Lauren. 'Just press the green button.'

Jen tried it again. 'I'm not getting anything. Is it possible it's lost its connection to the main hub?'

'That *is* the main hub.'

Lauren took the handset from Jen's grasp and tried for herself. From her expression there was still nothing.

'Is the battery low, maybe?' asked Kennedy.

'It's fully charged. I used it myself about two hours ago,' Lauren insisted. She swallowed, looking Jen in the eye. 'Somebody's cut the line.'

Helena

When Helena heard the scream and recognised it as Michelle's, she had assumed it would turn out to be some melodramatic act of attention-seeking.

Then she had seen the cause of it.

'Enormity' was a word that people misused and misunderstood. They thought it merely described vastness of scale, when it specifically described something overwhelmingly terrible. That was what she found herself coping with as Kennedy took the wrist of the man lying on the kitchen floor and gently shook her head. It was too much to process, a storm of frightening possibilities.

But what Lauren just said caused something much worse to pass through all of them.

'Have we still got wi-fi?' Nicolette asked.

Helena checked her phone. Everyone did, like a reflex.

'Looks like it.'

'Then we've still got WhatsApp.'

'Can you WhatsApp the police?' asked Kennedy.

'I can WhatsApp somebody, anybody, and get *them* to call the fucking police,' Nicolette replied, already dialling someone as she spoke. 'But the main thing is we need to get off this island.'

'Nicolette's right,' said Jen. 'Lauren, can your boat take all of us?'

'Comfortably.'

'Then we need to get everybody together right now.'

'Damn right,' said Kennedy. 'Take off and nuke the entire site from orbit.'

'Where are the other two?' Lauren asked.

'Beattie's in the front room,' Jen said. 'Samira, I don't know.'

'She went to get some air,' Helena reminded her. 'Didn't you see her when you went out too?'

Even as she asked, Helena knew the answer.

'I'll call her,' Jen said, opening WhatsApp.

Nicolette was prodding at her phone again, a look of confused frustration upon her face. 'It says it's dialling then it just drops the connection.'

Jen was getting the same problem. '"Error message. Your internet provider has blocked this application."'

'What's wrong with your internet, Lauren?' Nicolette demanded, her tone accusatory.

'Nothing!' Lauren protested.

Helena had used WhatsApp when they first got here, and it was working fine then. She had been checking in with Erin, as she did obsessively. She was surprised her elder daughter hadn't blocked her as a contact. She was staying the weekend at a friend's student flat in Edinburgh. Half an hour ago, it had been Erin's safety she was worried about.

Helena's phone was still showing a strong wi-fi signal. She opened her browser. 'I can access Google.'

'What about Facebook, Twitter, messaging apps?' Nicolette asked.

'"This website has been blocked by your service provider,"' Jen reported.

Helena tried searching the word 'police' but got the same error message. The Google homepage had only appeared because it was cached.

'Somebody is restricting our connections,' said Kennedy, looking at her own handset. 'I've seen this on uni campuses and other shared networks. They apply a content filter restricting what you can access.'

'But this is *my* network,' said Lauren. 'Who could be restricting it?'

Kennedy glanced back towards the kitchen door.

'I'm going to grab some more life jackets then prep the boat,' Lauren said, priorities firmly focused.

'Nicolette,' Jen said, 'could you go and break the news to Beattie? Then maybe the pair of you could check if Samira went back to her room. She was looking queasy. I think she might have gone off to be sick, or maybe even fallen asleep.'

'What about you?' Nicolette asked, like Jen was somehow trying to stiff her.

'I'm going to take a loop around the building, see if she's somewhere in the grounds.'

'I'll come with you,' Kennedy volunteered.

'Me too,' Helena said. 'Safety in numbers.'

'And I'll go with Lauren,' said Michelle. 'Nobody goes anywhere alone.'

The sun was still weirdly high when they stepped out through the front door. Helena's watch said it was after eight, but this far north the light could convince you it was still late afternoon.

'Goodbye Earl' was audible from the entrance hall, the looping playlist proving inescapable. Helena remembered the video: Jane Krakowski and Lauren Holly playing two good friends who conspire to kill the man who hurt one of them. It prompted her to wonder whether Joaquin the chef was as unknown to everybody as they had assumed. Was there some connection? The man in Michelle's sex tape had never been identified, his face never appearing. Could it have been Joaquin? Could Michelle have thought *he* was the one who leaked it?

She thought of Michelle's hand and wondered whether she got it bloody grabbing the door handle, or whether the door handle had got bloody because Michelle grabbed it. And what about the interval between Michelle saying she was going to the kitchen and the sound of her scream? It had been several minutes. She could have just gone to the loo first, but . . .

No. She was being crazy, her brain feverishly looking for connections to make sense of the situation.

'Ordinarily I'd suggest one of us go around clockwise and the other two anti,' said Jen. 'Make sure we don't miss her.'

She didn't have to affirm that this was not the plan tonight.

Helena was looking beyond the terrace towards the sea when something occurred to her. 'We should have a quick check down at the water in case she went there. Paddling in the sea is the kind of daft notion you might have when you're pissed.'

'Good thinking,' Jen said.

They walked to the end of the terrace, Kennedy's brace making a distinctive thump on the slate with every step. Helena noticed her wincing. It was hurting more than she was letting on. She was slowing too.

More and more of the shoreline came into view as they neared the top of the slope. Their focus was initially on the beach, but it was the gradually revealed sight of the jetty that stopped them in their tracks.

Every pace and every further degree of visibility had increased a feeling of panic as an irrational fear became a dreadful possibility and then a confirmed fact.

The jetty was empty. Lauren's boat was gone.

Nicolette

Nicolette felt this dread burden of responsibility, of being the one who had to puncture the protective bubble around Beattie and drag her into the same horrific world as everybody else. For a moment she thought that the words might not come, but sheer urgency lent her what she needed. She got it out there, simple, plain and unambiguous because she didn't want to have to say any of it twice.

'It's the chef, Joaquin. He's dead. Somebody cut his throat. We've got to get out of here. We're taking Lauren's boat, but we need to find Samira first. Jen asked us to check if she's in her room.'

To her credit, Beattie didn't ask any stupid questions or request she repeat herself. She did spend a moment staring back, like her brain was processing what she had just heard, then her expression became this weird combination of dazed and determined. She got up from the sofa and began moving as though motivated by some force beyond her control, perhaps surrendering to conditioned reflexes. Jen said Beattie worked in a hospital. Maybe she was used to witnessing the moments when people's worst fears came to pass, and understood that sometimes very bad things did happen. It was something Nicolette had known for seventeen years.

'Which room is hers?' Beattie asked as they reached the first floor.

'I'll get the list.'

Nicolette hurried into her own room to retrieve it, leaving the door open so that she and Beattie could still see each other. She couldn't say whether this was primarily for her own protection or Beattie's, but either way it was pointless. She didn't imagine Beattie could do much if there was an attacker waiting inside Nicolette's room, or that she might successfully intervene if someone fell upon Beattie in the corridor. Safety in numbers was meaningless when the number was two and the threat was some maniac with a knife.

'She's in Lagavulin,' Nicolette read.

Nicolette would ordinarily have been delighted to get a sanctioned snoop round someone else's room, someone else's stuff, but even aside from the circumstances, there was nothing to see. Not only was Samira not there, you would barely have known she had been in the place at all. Her case sat unopened at the foot of the bed, not so much as a tub of moisturiser on the dresser. The only item unpacked had been her phone cable, which was plugged into a USB port built into the bedside table.

'No joy,' she reported, but Beattie bustled in regardless.

'I'm not fucking blind,' Nicolette protested. 'I'd have noticed if she was here. Where are you going?'

'Checking the bathroom. She was blitzed. Wouldn't be the first time I found someone passed out on the linoleum.'

Nicolette hung back by the open door, keeping an eye on the corridor and opting not to share her thoughts on the likelihood of Lauren Combe letting linoleum anywhere near her property.

Beattie re-emerged after a second or two, holding a phone. 'This was next to the sink. She can't have gone far.'

As they stepped back into the corridor, Lauren was emerging from a door marked Private. Nicolette could see stairs behind it, presumably leading to her apartment. Michelle was at her back, each of them carrying a couple of life jackets.

Nicolette had noticed how the pair of them gravitated towards one another, mutually recognising, perhaps, another of those people for whom everything in life just seemed to click. Even running for their lives, they both looked like the black harness vests were for a photoshoot.

As well as the vests, Lauren had a canvas bag slung over her shoulder. It made Nicolette wonder if it would be bad form to grab her case. She didn't know how much room was on the boat, but she couldn't help calculating the cost of the clothes and toiletries she would be leaving behind. She'd get them back eventually, she counselled herself. It wasn't like the place was on fire. Yet.

'Not in her room, then?' Lauren asked redundantly.

'No.'

Nicolette and Beattie were following Lauren and Michelle down the staircase into the entrance hall when through the landing window they saw Jen, Helena and Kennedy making their way towards the front door. They looked even more shaken than they had five minutes ago, if that were possible. And they were unaccompanied. Samira was still missing.

'Looks like we're not going anywhere quite yet,' Lauren said. She sounded like she was trying to keep panic from her voice.

Nicolette's panic was closer to the surface. 'Can't we go in two groups?' she suggested, as Jen, Helena and Kennedy hurried into the hall below. 'That way somebody can at least get to the mainland and raise the alarm.'

'Are you volunteering to be in the group that waits behind, then?' Michelle asked.

'I'm just saying, there's no point in us all staying here.'

'Nobody is going anywhere,' said Jen. 'There's no fucking boat.'

'It's gone,' Kennedy underlined grimly. 'We were checking in case Samira had gone down to the water. Someone's taken it.'

Lauren let one of the life vests drop from her hand, then threw the other one to the floor. 'Fuck.'

There was a lull while everybody dealt with the news. Part of Nicolette wanted to cry. Another part told her she couldn't afford to lose control. She had faced the worst before and lived through it, though that didn't mean she had entirely survived it.

Michelle was the first to speak. 'I'm not being funny, but could it have been her? Samira, I mean? Might she have taken the boat in some drunken huffy act of recklessness?'

'At roughly the same time as we discover someone has murdered the chef?' asked Jen doubtfully. 'It would be a hell of a coincidence.'

'And what if it wasn't a coincidence?'

The words were out of Nicolette's mouth before she even realised. Something in her instinctively didn't trust Samira, and this didn't seem like a time for politely suppressing suspicions.

'She's spent the last six months up to her eyes in nappies and barely sleeping a wink,' Jen spluttered. 'You think all that time she was also planning to murder a chef she'd never met?'

'No, but she was drunk and het up,' Nicolette reminded her. 'What if she went to ask what was happening with dinner and there was some kind of bust-up, or the chef tried it on? She could have freaked out and slashed him, then panicked and taken the boat.'

'It makes as much sense as anything else,' said Beattie, support from an unexpected source. She eyed Jen directly as she spoke:

something going on there that felt far older than tonight. 'People do desperate things when they feel threatened, I'm told. And it's fairly suspicious that these two developments should happen at the same time.'

Jen met her gaze with a coldness Nicolette had never seen in her before. 'You know what else is suspicious, Beattie? Everybody else responded to the scream by coming to find out what was going on. And yet you stayed where you were, not bothering your arse.'

Beattie tutted. 'I thought it would turn out to be a fuss about nothing, and that if it was important someone would come and get me. Which they did.'

'Michelle's screaming shook the whole bloody house.'

'I'm a midwife. I hear screams all the time.'

'So are you saying you thought Michelle was maybe going into labour?'

'This is helping no one,' said Lauren. 'We have to keep it together. We have to *stick* together. And we need to start thinking straight, work out what we know for sure. Who was the last person to see Joaquin alive?'

'We all did, when he brought the cocktails,' Michelle replied.

'That was nearly two hours ago,' said Jen. 'There was plenty of movement after that. People nipping back to their rooms, going to the toilet. Beattie was away a wee while. Nicolette too.'

'What are you suggesting?' Nicolette demanded. She knew she had annoyed Jen by accusing Zaki's sister, so she was ready for the retaliation.

'I'm not suggesting anything. Just saying maybe one of you saw something earlier, something you thought nothing of at the time.'

'I went back to my room to use the loo,' Nicolette said. 'That's it. I saw nobody.'

Beattie said nothing. Nicolette presumed this was because she had seen nothing, but equally it felt like she was reluctant to cooperate simply because Jen was asking the question.

'Whoever did this took the chef by surprise,' said Jen. 'You all saw him: he wouldn't have been easy to overpower. He had his throat cut while he was busy leaning over the kitchen island. It must have been someone he expected to see there, someone he wasn't worried about.'

'That could have been any of us,' pointed out Helena.

'Someone might have snuck up on him,' said Michelle. 'He still had his earbuds in. Probably so he didn't have to listen to this endlessly repeating playlist.'

Helena glanced back towards the closed kitchen door. 'What if this isn't about us?' she said. 'What if it's about him?'

All eyes turned to Lauren.

'How well did you know this guy?' Jen asked.

'I only met him today.'

'He never worked here before?'

'No. Sometimes people independently book a chef who's also on my list, but he wasn't. How much communication did you have with him?'

'None,' Jen replied, as though confused by the question.

'So who booked him?'

'You did. You said you would provide a chef.'

'No, I didn't. You emailed to say you were providing your own.'

Even as Jen made her denial, Lauren was opening the mail app on her phone and scrolling until she found the appropriate message. She showed it to Jen, who was doing the same thing.

'I didn't send that,' they both said simultaneously.

They each took a moment to look at the evidence presented on the other's phone.

'Our emails have been hacked,' said Lauren. 'Or spoofed, maybe.'

'What's spoofed?'

'That's when you send an email that looks like it came from a different account.'

'No,' said Jen. 'Definitely hacked, because whoever did it would have had to intercept and remove the true emails.'

'Jesus,' said Lauren. 'This means someone has had control of both our email accounts for weeks. Whoever is doing this has been planning it for a while.'

'But why would they parachute this chef into our midst only to kill him?' Jen asked.

'Unless it really is about him but they're setting us up to take the fall,' Michelle suggested. 'Isolating us here so that there's a delay to bringing in the authorities while they get away. Then when the cops finally get here, there's a murdered guy on an island and we're the only people around. It's going to look like one of us did it and the rest are helping cover it up.'

'It sounds more plausible than Samira killing him and running away,' Jen said, largely for Nicolette's consumption, she was sure. 'But we still don't know where Samira is, so I'm not liking the fact that what Michelle just outlined is currently the best-case scenario.'

Nicolette could only listen to so much of this pointless speculation. It sounded like they were trying to work out which ingredient caused a pan to go on fire, when they should be concentrating on escaping the flames.

'Look, I know everybody is trying to make sense of this, but the only thing that matters is getting out of here. Samira or not,

98

someone needs to get help.' She looked to Lauren. 'Is there another way off this island? Another boat somewhere?'

'No. That's the whole attraction, normally.'

Lauren had replied without hesitation. Despair was palpable from all sides. Then Jen contradicted her.

'That's not strictly true,' she said, but in a tone that was ominously distant from hope. 'There *is* another boat: the RIB we saw from the helicopter.'

There was quiet as the implications began to sink in. Quiet but not silence. Music was still playing, some number from the eighties called 'Secret', sounding out for what felt like the tenth time. It wasn't loud but the presence of any music felt intrusively inappropriate, and Nicolette wasn't the only one feeling it.

'Lauren, can you turn off the tunes so we can think straight?' Michelle asked.

'Gladly.' Lauren tapped at her phone for a couple of seconds. 'It's not mine,' she added, frowning.

'We don't care whose playlist it is. We just want it to stop.'

'No, I mean it's not my account, and I can't get in. I'm locked out of my own system.'

Nicolette looked around the entrance hall, at the surroundings that had felt like a childhood fantasy only hours ago, the catalogue world she once dreamed of stepping into. Then she recalled the paranoid feeling that had come upon her in the same place, of being trapped in that world rather than merely a visitor.

'So that's it, we're stranded here?' she asked. 'No phone signal, no wi-fi.'

'There is wi-fi,' Helena clarified, always bending over backwards to state what was strictly accurate. 'We just can't use it to communicate.'

'What about email?' Beattie suggested.

'I've tried,' said Kennedy, holding up her mobile. 'It's blocked.'

'I don't get why they would only block certain services,' Nicolette said. 'Why not cut the internet altogether, like they've cut the landline?'

A few moments later she got her answer. Every phone in the hall chimed simultaneously. Every single one.

They all looked at their screens, and everything got so much worse.

Lauren

As she heard the familiar sound of the alert announcing a new email, for one blessed moment Lauren thought that whatever was blocking the internet had resolved itself; that it had just been some temporary glitch to which, in their paranoia, they were attributing undue significance.

Then she saw the email.

It was from someone calling themselves the Reaper, the subject line a single chilling word: 'Samira'.

Nicolette had asked why they hadn't cut the internet altogether. This was why.

When Lauren tapped to open it, her screen filled with a video, frozen on the first frame, the image blurred and undistinguishable. The instinct to discover more overcame the instinct to protect herself from what she might be about to see. It worked the same for everybody. They all pressed play.

There was no sound from anyone's phone, only gasps as they saw Samira. She appeared to be slumped in a chair, but when Lauren looked closer she could see that she was tied to it, lengths of cord securing her wrists to the armrests and her ankles to the legs. Behind her was a wall of stone marked with haphazard moss-lined cracks and tufts of lichen. The definition was poor, the low-res image sparsely lit, so it was hard to tell whether she was inside or out, whether the backdrop was live rock or an ancient, crumbling wall.

Samira's eyes were closed, and she appeared to be unconscious. The mercy was that she was not aware of her predicament. Not yet.

There was a noose around her neck, the rope behind her head extending upwards out of shot. It was straight but not quite taut, so it took Lauren a moment to understand that the real danger in the image was not from above, but below.

The chair was sitting on a slab of ice. It was a couple of inches thick, and it was the only thing keeping Samira from strangulation.

Lauren watched Jen put a hand to her mouth. She was able to stifle a sob, but not the tears that started to spill.

'She needs a seat,' said Michelle. 'Everyone needs a seat.'

They all filed numbly into the drawing room. Lauren looked at the sideboard. There had to be thirty empty glasses on there, others dotted about the place. Earlier in the day she had thought someone vomiting in a planter was the biggest thing she had to worry about, but nonetheless an instinct had told her to stay in case she was needed. An unworthy voice told her that if she had ignored it, she would have been oblivious to all this.

Helena held up her handset, indicating not the video but the only two words of text in the message, forming a hyperlink: Download me.

'Has anyone . . . ?' she asked.

Heads were shaken. Despite the need for information, this time instinctive caution had won out, initially at least. People were reluctant to download files from unknown sources at the best of times. What if this was a virus to control or destroy their phones?

'I don't think we have a choice,' Jen said. 'We need to know what they want.'

'What if just one of us does?' Helena suggested. 'Just to find out what it is.'

'Okay,' Kennedy volunteered. 'My phone is a piece of cheap shit anyway, so if this thing bricks it, it doesn't matter.'

They all gathered around her, craning to see her handset as it downloaded and installed a piece of software.

Kennedy briefly glanced around at everyone, like she needed a sense of solidarity, then pressed open.

It launched a crude text-based messaging app, evidently one that had certain permissions from whatever was filtering their internet.

Kennedy typed a single word and hit send.

Kennedy: Hello

Lauren noted that Kennedy's name had appeared as the sender without her entering it anywhere.

A few moments later, there came a response.

The Reaper: All for one and one for all. Six downloads short. 🎁

'We all need to download it,' Jen said. It sounded more like an order than an observation.

Everyone complied, all of them posting a simple Hello. Like Kennedy's, their names appeared, pre-programmed, without their having to key anything in.

A few moments later, three dots indicated that the Reaper was typing.

They waited breathlessly for a response, everyone's eyes on their screens, occasionally stealing glances at each other.

Lauren felt disconcertingly alone, an outsider. She had no friends here. Few friends anywhere, if she was being honest. It had been about her and Darcy for so long. About building a future for both of them, one that nobody could take away.

A shudder passed around the room in response to a popping sound from each of their phones, an inappropriately minute herald for news of such enormity:

The Reaper: One of you is not the person you believe her to be.

One of you committed a sin that has gone unpunished.

You have no idea what she is capable of. She is more ruthless than you could imagine. And she does not care who else gets hurt as long as it protects her secret.

But tonight one naughty girl will post her confession and make reparation, or I will be forced to punish the whole class.

I have one rule. If the number of people on this island changes, I will do your friend like I did your chef. And I will send you all the video as a souvenir.

Welcome to Clachan Geal, where you will find only what you brought with you, and where only the truth can set you free.

Staring at her screen, Lauren heard a familiar song coming over the speakers, not one that had played already tonight. It was unmistakably Cassidy, despite Lauren complying with Michelle's request to make sure there wasn't any cued up. Worse, it was the track she had specifically alluded to, the band's breakthrough hit from the early 2000s. Its cheerfully jangly and floaty intro sounded not merely incongruous, but inescapably sinister. It felt like a taunt.

It was called 'She Knows'.

However, as Lauren scanned the Reaper's message, that feeling of isolation from the others returned in the unlikely form of reassurance. Lauren did not know these people, but they knew each other. This was not about the chef and it was not about Lauren either. It was about her guests. Her emails had been hacked purely because it was her house they were coming to, the staging grounds for whatever this was.

Most importantly, she had not committed any crime.

She read the words again. That was when it hit home: the message didn't say *crime*, it said *sin*. The feeling of reassurance proved as ephemeral as her relief that the internet had been restored.

Lauren had done nothing illegal, she often reassured herself. But just because she had done nothing illegal did not mean she had done nothing wrong. Indeed, someone had been in touch to let her know just how wrong they considered it, just how angry it had made them. To tell her how one day they were going to avenge themselves by taking everything away from her.

That was the thing about death threats in the age of social media. You told yourself they were merely a form of hate mail. That they were the screams of people who had no other means of making an impact on your life. They were best ignored. They were meaningless.

Until they were not.

With a grinding dread, she saw that it might be in her power to save Samira. But equally, it might not. The stakes were high, but so was the buy-in. The app was designed so that no confession could be private. It was not about penitence; it was about placing the sinner in the stocks, admitting her sin to everybody.

And that was only the beginning. The Reaper had not specified what was *meant* by reparation, and he had already killed one person tonight. But while that remained unknown, what was starkly clear was the price Samira would pay if nobody stepped up.

Lauren was going to say something. She had no choice. She *had* to say something. Then she looked around at the others. From their shamed expressions, from their silence, from their inability to meet anyone else's eye, it was clear that every person in the room thought the sinner might be them.

Jen

Jen had read the message at least three times and now she found herself watching the video again. She didn't know why. She wasn't sure what she was hoping to see and every frame of it was painful, but she couldn't stop herself. Maybe it was just easier than looking at anybody else right then.

Samira had been sitting here in this room, what, an hour ago? Less? Back in another time, when the biggest thing Jen had to worry about was that they were all getting pissed and starting to rip each other's knitting.

Samira had looked tiny and fragile enough on the sofa. Seeing her tied up like that, rendered unconscious . . . Christ. At least Jen didn't have to see the fear in her eyes.

But maybe that was what was missing. Because truth was, Jen did know why she was looking at it again. It was to see whether, on second viewing, the sight would be enough to compel her to confess. Seeing Zaki's wee sister with a noose around her neck, a sheet of melting ice the only thing keeping her from strangulation, that should have been enough, shouldn't it? But it wasn't. Not while there was still time. Not while there remained the possibility that the sinner was somebody else.

Everybody liked to think that they were a moral person, but

usually this just meant that they had never been truly tested. Jen *had* been tested, and could still justify to herself the worst thing she had ever done. Until a few minutes ago she could have still told herself she was a moral person. That was before she was asked to weigh someone else's life against revealing the thing that would destroy her own.

She was ashamed to admit it, but she was staring at that ice and wondering how long she could hold out, how much of it could melt before she broke. Ashamed also because she had been looking around the room and hoping one of her friends had done something worse than her.

It *was* her, though. It had to be, because there was that song that kept playing, again and again, revealed now to be no glitch, no fluke and no coincidence. It was a message. A naming of her sin. And then just to drive it home, as she read the Reaper's words, another song had told her: 'She Knows'.

It was Michelle's voice singing the words, but who was *She*?

Jen swallowed, afraid that more tears would be interpreted as guilt. She wasn't tipping her hand. She wanted to do the right thing, but she didn't know enough to be sure, and the ante was way too high. She wasn't putting her cards on the table unless everyone else did.

'I'm guessing all of us has something in our past we'd rather nobody else knew about,' she said. 'And probably good reason for having done it. But one of us has done something to piss this bastard off, and we're all stuck with the consequences. So could we have some kind of amnesty? Where we each admit what we *think* it might be, but we all understand that what gets said on the island stays on the island?'

Jen glanced around the room, taking everybody in, forcing them to meet her eyes.

'Yeah, okay,' said Nicolette. 'You go first.'

And there was the rub.

Another silence ensued, or maybe now you could call it a seven-way stand-off. And all the while, somewhere on this island, a sheet of ice was melting.

Then Helena spoke. She gave Jen a supportive look, but not one that seemed an overture to going first with a confession.

'Look, we have to be rational about this. Nobody's going to bare their soul if they think they've got nothing to do with this. This guy isn't doing it because somebody keyed his car or put in an objection to his extension. This has been a long time in the planning. We know that from Jen and Lauren's emails. For somebody to have gone to this kind of trouble takes resources. So it's not merely a question of who might we each have pissed off. It's who among us might have pissed off somebody with sufficient money and clout.'

Michelle responded with a slow handclap. 'Well said, Helena. I was wondering just how long it would take for you to decide this was my fault. I think Samira would be grateful that you're going there so quickly and not wasting any time.'

'I'm just saying that maybe we should consider the possibility that mine wasn't the only back you stabbed on your way to the top.'

'I don't think this is helpful, Helena,' Jen warned, intervening before Michelle could react with another salvo in a relationship that had long gone from BFFs to FFS. 'We're not going to help anyone by firing accusations around.'

'Not that it's ever stopped you before,' muttered Beattie.

Jen felt something boil up inside her, an anger long in the burn but given added ferocity that Beattie should choose now to make a dig.

'Have you got something you'd like to say, Beattie? About

109

your blessed brother? Well, spit it out, and don't let its utter irrelevance hold you back. I'm sure Samira wouldn't mind.'

She had expected to shame Beattie into silence, thinking mutterings and innuendo were all she would be bold enough to offer. Instead, Beattie faced her down, sitting straighter in her chair and meeting Jen's eye with a look of cold loathing.

'I think Helena makes a good point. She just makes it about the wrong person. If we're talking about crossing people on a journey to success, you've always claimed my brother was mixed up with drug dealers and gangsters and all sorts, yet you're the one who has ended up rolling in cash.'

Beattie looked away now, but only to address everybody else. 'She's telling us Jason is irrelevant to all this, but if everything she's claimed about him is true, isn't it possible that Jen has got on the wrong side of dangerous people at some point?'

'I built up a business, on my own,' Jen replied. 'I bake muffins, Beattie.' She looked around the room, unsure quite whether she was challenging them to argue or looking for support. Either way, not many eyes were prepared to meet hers for long. Even Helena stared at the floor. Jen understood why, though. Everybody was searching for a reason to believe the sinner was somebody else. But Jen also understood that you wouldn't need a reason to believe it was somebody else if you were genuinely sure it wasn't you.

'We need to remember what the Reaper wrote,' Nicolette said. 'One of us is not who she claims to be. Well, I've known Jen for at least a decade. Her, Michelle and Helena grew up together, and Beattie, you've known Jen most of that time too.'

'Whereas you've only known me six or seven months so I must be the sinner, is that it?' demanded Kennedy. 'If you want to go down that path, we've only known Lauren a day.'

This drew a prickly response from the host. 'If this was about me, why would it be happening when I'm surrounded by strangers and nobody I actually know is here?'

'I'm just pointing out that someone here isn't telling the truth about themselves,' said Nicolette. 'I didn't point the finger at you specifically. And given Kennedy's reaction, I'm inclined to wonder if the lady doth protest too much. We've only found out her full name today. If that *is* her name, given there's photos of her online labelled Kathleen Boniface.'

'Fuck you,' Kennedy retorted. 'My real name is Fiona Gilmour, but maybe I've got reasons for not wanting to *be* Fiona Gilmour. Have you thought about that? Or about how I might not appreciate being stalked online? I've lived in a lot of places. I've never put down roots. That doesn't make me a criminal.'

Kennedy's words hung uncomfortably in the air, no response arriving to dissipate them. It was her tone as much as what she had said: hurt and anger, with a note of warning too.

Jen felt bad that she hadn't weighed in on Kennedy's behalf. She always felt an oddly maternal protectiveness towards her, even though the girl was nearly a decade older than her own kids. She was confident and buoyant on the outside, full of good advice and positivity, but Jen had always felt there was something fragile about her, something a little bit lost.

Nicolette had misquoted, though. The Reaper's message said: *One of you is not the person you believe her to be.* It didn't necessarily mean that this was about their identity. *Not everybody's playing an angle,* Zaki had chided her. But Jen knew different. Everybody was selling you a version of themselves that hid things they would rather no one knew. And that meant the way out of this didn't lie in someone feeling compelled to show their true face. It lay in how far everyone was prepared to go to avoid that.

'Whoever we're dealing with here,' Jen said, 'let's not give them what they want until we've exhausted all other options.'

Kennedy turned to look at her, a flash of energy in her expression, like she was daring to hope, eager to hear more.

'What they're doing is clearly sadistic,' Jen went on. 'They're out for revenge. They say they want payback for some perceived crime against them, but they're not saying who or what. That's because they want us turning on each other. And that slab of ice? Yes, it's a ticking clock, but they want to draw this out. They *want* to give us time. Let's make them regret it.'

Jen

Helena's expression was a portrait of conflict between her two strongest instincts: wanting to offer support to a friend and reluctance to break someone else's rules.

'They aren't playing a game with us, Jen. They've already killed one person and they've explicitly said they'll do the same to Samira if we don't comply.'

'But that's just it,' chimed Kennedy. 'They're telling us what they *don't* want us to do. They're telling us how they're vulnerable.'

'They're not vulnerable while they have Samira,' Helena replied.

'And that's the whole ball game,' Jen said. 'If we get her back, it changes everything. We can dig in, fortify this place. We can do whatever it takes to contact the authorities.'

'We don't know how long that slab of ice will take to melt,' Helena cautioned. 'We could have all night, we could have two hours.'

'It's Scotland,' Michelle stated drily. 'It could take a month.'

'My point is, how will we know before it's too late?'

'My bet is they'll give us updates to keep the pressure on,' said Kennedy.

'And are you prepared to stake Samira's life on that bet?' Helena demanded.

'The alternative is to trust the honour and intentions of a psychopath who just cut a guy's throat,' Jen said.

'So what do you suggest?'

'First priority is we need to find Samira, because nothing else matters if we can't do that. How far could they have taken her?'

'How long was it between her going outside and us getting the video?' asked Kennedy. 'Forty minutes, maybe? An hour?'

'It felt longer because of everything that happened, so I'm thinking more like half an hour,' Jen said. 'And they'd have had to carry her, either struggling or unconscious.' She winced at the thought.

'I think I heard an engine earlier,' Beattie went on. 'While we were all sitting here having drinks. But there was the music as well, and it sounded miles away, so I didn't think anything of it. I thought it might be a passing motor launch.'

Lauren hurried to the side window and peered out. 'My quad bike,' she said. 'Someone's taken it.'

'How big is this island?' Jen asked her.

'Roughly three kilometres north to south, two and a half east to west.'

'So, she could be anywhere,' Beattie stated. 'And that's a big area.'

It sounded like she was being deliberately disheartening, like it would please the old cow if Jen's hen weekend led to the death of her future sister-in-law. But Jen couldn't afford to think that way, to let Beattie get in her head.

'No, she can't be just anywhere,' Jen said. She pointed to her phone, playing the video again. 'She's here, and not moving, which is both the whole problem and its solution. Look at this stone. It could be the side of a hill, a rock outcrop, or it could be a wall.'

'What about this place?' Kennedy asked Lauren eagerly. 'Does it have a cellar or deep foundations?'

Lauren shook her head. 'A cellar, sure, but it's full of unused building supplies from the renovation. It looks nothing like that.'

'We flew over some ruined cottages,' Helena said. 'Could it be one of those?'

'Hold on a sec,' said Lauren. She went to the wall at the far end of the room, where a map hung in a wooden frame. Nobody had paid it much heed before but they were looking at it now like it was a sacred object. Lauren laid it out on the low table between the sofas. It wasn't some modern OS map, but an ancient, yellowed thing.

Helena pointed to a row of squares on the map. 'Yes. That's them there.'

'They're not the only ones.' Jen pointed to another square on the west coast.

'That's an abandoned croft,' said Lauren. 'It's old, but I doubt you'll find any bare stone there. Just flock wallpaper.'

'It's worth checking, though, isn't it?' Jen asked.

'I suppose,' Lauren replied, sounding slightly irritated at Jen's insistence.

'Why does it say Claiggean Geal and not Clachan Geal?' Nicolette asked.

'No idea,' Lauren snapped dismissively. 'It's an old map. It's Gaelic. What does it matter?'

'Sorry,' Nicolette muttered, clasping and unclasping her hands in a gesture of agitated embarrassment. Nobody knew what they were doing. Everything was a danger and everything was a clue.

Zaki's email to grimpox02@vapourmail.com flashed unhelpfully into Jen's mind.

Lauren pointed to the map. 'The ruined cottages are here,'

she said. 'To the south-east of us, about a kilometre. The croft is to the west, close to the far coast, on the other side of the hill.'

Jen held up her phone, the video paused on as clear a frame as she had been able to get. 'Does this kind of stone look like either of them in particular?'

Lauren looked closely, but it was clear it was something she had never felt the need to notice. 'I couldn't say. It might not even be man-made.' This seemed to spark a connection. 'In fact, this could be the cave, here.'

She pointed to an area near the northern coast. There was no cave marked on the map, only a waterfall. Jen thought about how they were supposed to be going on a walk to see it tomorrow, in that lost world where normal things were still ahead of them.

'It's not really a cave, just an outcrop with an overhang, near the waterfall. It's quite sheltered, surrounded by trees on the other side. You have to go over this hill to get there. I mean, you can get there using the coastal track too, but it's much longer.'

Jen was looking at the now three possible locations. She sensed everybody was making an identical calculation, involving time, distance and personnel.

Helena didn't name it, but her intervention was driven by the same fear. 'If we're lucky enough to find Samira, what do we do then? It's not like they'll have left her there alone. Someone took that video. Someone will be keeping guard.'

Jen's mind had been occupied by little else. 'I've been thinking about what Kennedy said,' she replied. 'That they're telling us what they don't want us to do. They don't want us to bring in help and they don't want us to leave the island. We should be finding ways to do both of those things.'

'They said they'd kill her if we did,' Helena reminded.

'They want something from one of us,' said Michelle. 'Let's

not forget that. As you said yourself, they've gone to a lot of trouble to set this up. They're not going to cash in their leverage just like that. They're going to give us time, so I agree with Jen that we should use it.'

'If you ask me,' said Kennedy, 'they're telling us not to bring in help or to try to leave because they know they can't monitor those things. Not with so much ground to cover. We need to contact the authorities and we need to find a way off this place. Because if by some miracle we can get Samira out of their hands, it becomes about us getting away from them, pure and simple.'

'There *is* a way off,' Jen pointed out. 'The RIB. If there's one thing that's likely to be unguarded, it's a boat they probably don't think we know about.'

'Where did you see it?' asked Lauren.

'Heading for an inlet south of here, flanked by cliffs,' said Beattie. 'A small horseshoe bay with a rocky beach.'

'I know where that is,' Lauren replied, pointing to the south-west corner of the map. 'It's all the way down here.'

'Is there anywhere you can get even a hint of a mobile signal?' Jen asked her.

'There is sometimes faint reception up here, at the northern peak on the way to the cave.'

Jen looked at the ancient map, those calculations becoming starker. 'So, we've got the ruined cottages and the boat to the south, the abandoned croft to the west, and the cave to the north.'

She looked up from the map and said what everyone already knew but nobody wanted to hear.

'We're going to have to split up.'

Kennedy

Kennedy had been starting to wonder if she would have to be the one to say it, but Jen got there first. It was a stark fact that nobody could hide from, so there were no arguments, just fleeting eye contact; people thinking about who they did and didn't want to be paired with or parted from. Then everyone looked at her, or more specifically at her plastic boot. Another stark fact that nobody could hide from.

'I'm okay,' she insisted. 'I mean, I'd prefer if there's a route that doesn't go over any hills, but—'

'You're not okay,' Helena interrupted. 'I saw you outside. You're in pain.'

'And you're worried I'll slow you down, is that it?'

'No, but it'll only get worse, and what if you go over on your other ankle out in the middle of nowhere?'

'Well, we can't leave her here on her own either,' Jen argued.

'It's okay. Helena's right. It's not ideal but it's this or limiting the search. I can make myself useful here. I've got a laptop and I know a few tricks from leeching off other folk's wi-fi down the years. Maybe I can find a way to get around whatever's jamming us.'

She tried to sound optimistic about the possibility, disguising how unlikely she knew it was.

Jen gave her a look, silently checking if she was really okay with this.

Kennedy had known this was coming, knew what her role would have to be, but that didn't mean anyone believed she really wanted to be stuck here alone with a killer on the loose. She responded with a weak smile and a tight nod. Then she spoke again, hoping to move things forward.

'Speaking of which, how are we going to communicate with each other? I mean, if one of you finds her or someone needs help?'

'We could use the app,' suggested Michelle.

'Which they can read too,' Helena pointed out.

'Could we devise a code?' Beattie asked.

'It won't work beyond the house's wi-fi,' said Kennedy, at which Lauren's eyes widened.

'Of course it won't: that's why I've got walkie-talkies. I just remembered. We used them all the time when we were doing the renovation.'

'How many?'

'Four handsets.'

'So we're sorted for comms,' said Michelle. 'What about defence? Should we be thinking about weapons?'

'There are plenty of knives in the kitchen,' Lauren replied. 'If you can face going back in there.'

The bloody scene in the kitchen came vividly to Kennedy's mind.

'No,' she said forcefully. 'Statistically, if you pull a knife on an intruder, you are far more likely to get stabbed than he is. So unless you reckon you're more adept with a blade than whoever stealthed and slashed the chef, I'd leave well alone.'

'How are the stats on golf clubs?' Lauren asked.

'Less suicidal.'

Nobody said much while Lauren and Michelle went off to retrieve the equipment, but Kennedy was aware that Nicolette in particular hadn't said a word for a long time. She was unusually colourless, sinking into the background. They couldn't afford to have anybody falling apart. It felt like nobody had the right to, either.

Jen had noticed too. 'Are you okay?' she asked, her tone indicating this was more a command to get her shit together than an offer of sympathy. It was at that moment that Lauren and Michelle returned, carrying radios and golf bags.

Nicolette took a look at the kit, then out the windows.

'I'm not sure I can do this,' she said. 'It's not that I don't care about Samira, it's just that there's a dead guy in the kitchen and I don't want to go out there and run into whoever killed him.'

'We're all scared,' Jen told her sternly. 'That's why you have to think of it as an extreme version of truth or dare. We all know what the truth part entails, so which would you prefer?'

Nicolette didn't need to think about it. She swallowed. 'I'll take a seven iron, please.'

'Good girl.'

Michelle

The path south became compacted earth not far from the house, rutted and dusty from the recent dry spell. Michelle gripped the golf club in her left hand, a canvas tote slung around her right shoulder. She had changed into a pair of jeans, a long-sleeved top and her workout trainers, grateful she had packed for long walks while she was at the retreat centre on Rum. Michelle had never wondered how she might dress for outdoor survival and a possible fight to the death on a Scottish hillside, but she was damn sure this wasn't it.

The tote was hardly a tactical backpack, but she didn't have much to carry. She had the walkie-talkie in there, a bottle of water and a flashlight. Lauren didn't have torches for everybody, just one for each team. It was late June, so it wouldn't be fully dark for a while yet, but night was coming nonetheless. They didn't know how long they would be out here, and nobody wanted to be relying on the charge on their phone to see in the dark.

She and her allotted companion walked in silence. They hadn't exchanged a word since they left the building, and not just because they were scared.

That bloody Kennedy. Michelle had preferred it when she was being shy and skittish.

Jen had rallied them all, given them a sense of purpose, which made the situation feel marginally less hopeless than it had a few minutes before. They were all on board for her plan, even though it involved splitting up and leaving the comparative safety of the house, but there had remained one outstanding concern. They had all looked up from the map, glancing at each other and asking themselves the same question.

It was Michelle who voiced it. 'So, who's going with who?'

Nobody seemed in a hurry to answer, then Kennedy stepped up, muttering something about being used to picking suitable doubles pairings.

Michelle would have taken anybody other than who she got. But that was the point.

'Helena and Michelle, you two take the southern path. Check the ruined cottages and then see if you can find this RIB.'

Before either of them could object, she had outlined her reasoning. 'Whatever issues you've got going on between you now, I'm betting you know each other's strengths and weaknesses better than anyone else's.'

Kennedy didn't seem intimidated by Michelle's celebrity any more. It was a sobering reminder how quickly status could become meaningless when something real was at stake. Michelle had felt an instinctive anger towards the girl for ordering her about, but maybe she was just shooting the messenger for delivering the chilling truth that tonight, her fame would count for nothing. Tonight, Michelle wasn't special.

The path began to rise, taking them around the side of a hill, trees clinging to the slope and extending westwards. They would soon be out of sight of the house, which somehow made it scarier. The fear was like the dead guy himself: a dominant, horrifying presence that you could neither ignore nor afford to focus on. It was like the time she played a sell-out show at Sydney Opera House while her mum was having cancer surgery ten thousand miles away in Glasgow. The worry was permanently on the edge of her thoughts, threatening to overwhelm her, while the task in hand was both intolerable under the circumstances and yet the one thing that would get her through.

There was a fork in the path ahead, a tributary heading towards the coast while the main thrust continued into the forest. Lauren had said something about the land's former owners planting pines back in the eighties for some kind of tax break. She implied that the island's woodland had not been well maintained after that as the owner's fortunes declined. It looked dense in there, quite forebodingly dark beneath the cover of the trees. It would disguise their approach, but that cut both ways. It was the kind of place Michelle would have found scary even without knowing what might be out here tonight.

'If we veer left, can we skirt around the woods and still get to the cottages?' Michelle asked, the silence finally broken by sheer necessity.

Helena stopped, frowning as she looked ahead and to the east. 'I don't think the path goes around. Hang on, let me check my phone.'

Everybody had taken photos of the map. Helena called up the image and zoomed in. 'No,' she said. 'This goes down to the water. I mean, the map is literally about a hundred years old, but it's not like the topography will have changed.'

Helena pinched to zoom out again, showing the whole map to get a sense of scale. Something struck Michelle about the shape of it.

'It's kind of like a Jazzmaster's body,' she said. 'We're around about the pickup switch. These woods are like the tone and volume controls, and we need to get to the power jack.'

She tried to make it sound like a casual observation, rather than the conversational gambit that it really was. She also thought it might be a useful term of reference for discussing their location, but in truth that was a secondary consideration. What she was finding hardest about being around Helena was the blankness, the refusal to acknowledge that they once had a rapport.

'Hmm,' was all she got back.

'Did you ever have a Jazzmaster? I can't remember.'

Helena made a disdainful tutting sound. 'No. Fucking poser's guitar.'

And with that, it wasn't merely like she was dismissing the suggestion, but rejecting any attempt to raise a discussion of those days.

They resumed walking, and with it their silence. Michelle wasn't ready to let that happen quite yet though.

'Is this it, then?' she asked. 'Are you going to be pissed off at me for the rest of your life?'

Helena didn't break her stride, didn't turn to look at her. 'I don't have anything I want to say to you beyond what we need to communicate for the purposes of the task in hand.'

'Yeah, and I think the whole problem is that you've got a whole lot that you want to say to me.'

Helena made that same disdainful sound again but offered no further response.

Michelle glanced at their shadows, impossibly stretched and spindly extensions of themselves on the coarse grass. She worried that they were so conspicuous. Anyone would see them coming literally a mile off. That worked both ways, though. As long as she saw nobody else, she was safe, which made it tempting to find some remote and sheltered spot and just lie low. Unfortunately, the same could not be said for Samira.

There was a horrible part of her, a self-preserving instinct, that was angry at Samira: for getting drunk, for mouthing off, for wandering away and getting abducted. It told her Samira's predicament was of her own making, so it wouldn't be Michelle's fault if she didn't find her. It wouldn't be Michelle's fault if something bad happened. She was able to silence that part by reminding herself that Samira's problems were still hers until she knew what, and specifically who, this shit was all about.

Michelle could understand why Helena might assume it was to do with Michelle, and not just because of her own grudges, but there were six other candidates here tonight, and there was reassurance to be found in the idea that it might be about someone else.

Her own first thought had been of Lauren, because if there was one business dirtier than the music industry, it was property development. But it was always easiest to believe something bad of the people you didn't know. So though it made her feel disloyal to Jen, she had to wonder whether Beattie was on to something, albeit in a ham-fisted way. Jen always played her cards close, especially about what Jason had been involved with.

Maybe that was just Michelle trying to alleviate her own guilt, though: wondering if there was something about Jen that made her less of an innocent victim in her relationship with a man whose dark side Michelle had failed to warn her about.

As they drew nearer, it became clear how dense the forestry was, the regimented rows of pine trees planted closer together than would have happened in any natural woodland. The ever-falling angle of the sun meant that even the track was in gloom, winding away out of sight. Helena slowed down, no less reluctant than Michelle to proceed, and the prospect finally prompted her to venture something.

'How about we skirt the edge of the woods,' she said. 'Then we can see out, but it would be harder for anyone to see in.'

'Gets my vote.'

They soon discovered that the path would have been easier, and far quicker. Even just staying one or two trees in from the edge meant negotiating an endless pattern of undulations, as well as the hazards of exposed roots, loose soil and ankle-snapping holes. It felt safer, though, and – though neither of them would acknowledge it – slow was good. Slow meant they weren't getting there, weren't finding anything, weren't having to make a decision.

Sheltered from the breeze, Michelle could now hear the constant sound of the waves. Land was visible across the calm water, a fading haze in the distance. She wasn't sure if it was the mainland, or maybe Skye, but either way it didn't look that far. She thought of this RIB they had been tasked with locating. Michelle had driven plenty of watercraft in her time, so she knew what she was doing behind the helm or at a tiller.

The question that had been gnawing at her since she was handed this particular task was, if they did get hold of the RIB, wasn't there something to be said for just firing it up and motoring out of there right away? Getting to civilisation and raising the alarm? And yes, full disclosure, getting herself to safety?

She knew Helena would argue that the Reaper had threatened to kill Samira if someone left the island. But as Kennedy pointed out, it might be precisely what the Reaper was afraid of. Who was to say Samira didn't stand a better chance if Michelle got the authorities involved and they sent a helicopter over here? Especially if it was Mica who was calling. The police would be shitting themselves about the bad press if they didn't get on it sharpish.

They were able to increase their pace because they had come to a place where the track through the woods wound close enough to the edge that it made little difference. They walked for maybe a couple of hundred metres. Michelle couldn't see the cottages yet, but she knew this meant they must be getting close, because where else would the path be going?

She caught a first glimpse of piled stone as the track turned more sharply towards the coast. It looked like a partially collapsed boundary wall. She never thought such a mundane sight could be so gut-tightening. They slipped back among the trees so as not to make their approach visible, finding a spot where they could view their destination unseen by crouching in a dip.

The nearest of the cottages was barely an outline of rubble, none of it more than a couple of feet high. Of the other two, only one still had a few beams holding up a remnant of roof, though in both cases the walls were high enough that they couldn't see what was on the other side. There was nobody outside keeping watch, though. The place appeared deserted.

'If Samira is there, wouldn't there be artificial light?' asked Helena, her voice low. 'You know, for filming her. Like a portable photographer's light, with a battery pack.'

'It's still bright out,' Michelle observed. 'And I don't think there's actually a proper roof on any of these things.'

'It's getting darker though, and Kennedy suggested they would want to send us more videos.'

'A light would mean she's definitely there,' Michelle acknowledged. 'The problem is, we can't deduce anything from a lack of one.'

'There would be someone outside keeping an eye, though, wouldn't there?'

Helena was seeking justification for not getting closer. Michelle understood because she was making the same calculations.

'I would refer you to my previous statement.'

Helena nodded in grave acknowledgement. 'We have to get closer,' she said.

They both looked at the cottages. Once you were out of the tree-line, it was still fifty or sixty metres to the ruins, across open land.

The moon was huge in the blue sky, so clear as to give a sense of being spherical rather than a flat disc. It seemed nearer than usual, and somehow this served to remind Michelle that she was just a creature clinging to a rock in space and nobody was here to protect her. Nature would not blink if she died tonight, and no amount of ticket sales, downloads or followers could alter that.

She reached into her bag for the radio. Her initial thought was that she should have it handy to call for help if they were spotted and someone came at them. Then she realised how pointless this would be. The radio, in fact, posed a greater threat if it made a sudden noise.

'What are you doing with that?' Helena asked.

'Switching it off. This is going to be all about stealth.' She didn't add the flipside, that if they were detected, it would be a fight for their lives, and the image of the murdered chef told her how that was likely to pan out.

They both looked again at the exposed stretch of meadow between them and the cottages. The coarse grass underfoot would be an ally, letting them approach in silence. But all it would take was somebody popping out from behind a wall and the whole game would change.

They turned to each other. There was finally a sense of commonality, of something shared, but it wasn't anything good.

'Fuck,' Michelle said. 'I don't think I can do this.'

Helena didn't reply, tears forming in her fear.

They would never know what shameful pact might have been born in that moment were it not for a horrifying cry that pierced the night. It reverberated around them, the strangulated sound echoing through the trees, but there was no doubt that it had come from the cottages.

Beattie

The first quarter mile felt like an incongruous calm before the storm, a stroll across gentle undulations as easy underfoot as it was possible to get on grass. This was because the route took them along two of the fairways on the six-hole golf course.

Looking at the map, Beattie had questioned why she and Jen were being given what looked a far longer trek than Lauren and Nicolette. Lauren had replied that although the journey to the croft on the west coast was shorter as the crow flies, the route over that hill was treacherous if you didn't know where you were going, especially with the light getting low. Beattie wasn't about to argue the point, especially given how steep the supposedly less treacherous hill ahead of her looked.

Beattie thought the greens were looking a little long, but she had heard Lauren say the groundskeeper had not been brought in ahead of this weekend because Jen hadn't requested it. Someone had been laying groundwork in advance of their visit, however. Someone had been planning for this trip meticulously and at length, and though their identity remained shrouded, Beattie had little doubt who their sights were trained on.

She could see that now, though when she first saw the Reaper's message she had jumped to a very different conclusion. It had all replayed instantly in her mind. Little Xander's screams. Her hand reaching for him. The moment of understanding that there was no time to swerve. The crunch of collision. The blood on the windscreen.

The body in the road.

She had read that the widow's family were wealthy. They had political connections down south. Their firm had a PPE contract worth tens of millions. They were swimming in cash, and had the kind of resources this would take.

But once the initial panic passed, Beattie's more rational self could see that this was merely survivor's guilt manifesting as paranoia. There was a far more plausible candidate for the Reaper's ire: someone with murky connections far closer to home. And that, inevitably, was who she had been paired up with.

'I know you've had your differences, but you guys are family,' Kennedy had said. 'That counts above everything else.'

And she was right. Beattie valued nothing more than family. But some family counted more than others. There was something about Jen that Beattie had instinctively not trusted. That could be true of many people, just an initial feeling that can be washed away by experience. But in Jen's case she vividly remembered the moment it crystallised, and nothing since had shifted that perception.

It was her nephew Calum's fifth birthday party. His birthday had been on the Friday, but as that was a school day they had planned a party in the garden for the Saturday, complete with a bouncy castle Jason had hired.

It was early June. It had been raining most of the morning and Beattie thought they were looking at a classic Glasgow barbecue: everybody huddled indoors while Jason worked the grill in the back garden under a golf umbrella. But no, the sun came out just before twelve and there wasn't a cloud after that.

Beattie stood on the patio sipping a spritzer, listening to the tinkle and screech of children's laughter as they played on the big inflatable and skooshed each other with super-soakers. Beattie's own kids were still at the age where they weren't too old to join in the fun. Beattie was ten years older than her brother, but there wasn't the same age gap between the kids because Beattie had Kathleen when she was twenty-five and Jen had her first when she was twenty-one. It was a joy to see them all playing together. Jason's two looked up to Kathleen and Scott, as most kids did to their big cousins.

Jason had looked so happy. Everyone did. All the grandparents had been there: Jen's mother and father, and Beattie and Jason's mum.

Beattie could never quite relax around Jen's father, though. He had the most scrutinising stare, eyes that seemed to penetrate the skin. She heard it said this was from decades of looking at punters from behind a bar, that he had learned to size people up rapidly so that he knew who might start trouble. Beattie just thought there was something shifty about him, like all the time his eyes were on you he was searching for your weaknesses, your secrets.

In that garden, though, he was the perfect grandfather, full of nonsense and mischief and sadly the only grandad they had, as her and Jason's father had died three years before.

Jen was being the perfect host, though Beattie was pretty sure she was hungover. She knew the signs. She was moving delicately, that headachey way when you were just a little too conscious of the impact of every footfall.

Jason had later hinted that Jen might have a problem but

swore Beattie to secrecy. It had been at another family do, their sister Maureen's wedding, when Jen had been moving a wee bit gingerly if you knew what to look for. 'Don't tell anyone,' Jason had pleaded. 'I really shouldn't have said anything to you. I think it's just a phase. She's been stressed by having more responsibility at work, and balancing that with childcare.'

Beattie was acutely conscious of the danger: someone with a drink problem who was involved in running a nightclub, but Jason had urged her to stay out of it. She had respected his wish, and he hadn't expressed any further concern on the matter. Jen was on Irn-Bru at the garden party, ostensibly the responsible mum but actually a sign she had overdone it the night before.

Everybody was in shorts and T-shirts, peely-wally Scots baring their vitamin-D-deprived flesh at the first opportunity. Jen was the exception, in linen trousers and a long-sleeved blouse that looked like a recent purchase. She must have bought it for the occasion and was determined to show it off, no matter the weather. From the way Jason was gazing at her, why not? She was looking good, and Beattie guessed she knew it.

Beattie had never quite seen why Jason fell for Jen, but she would have to admit she could never see past Michelle. And by the time Michelle was back in his social orbit, Jen thoroughly had her hooks in Jason.

They got married young. Barely twenty-one, in fact, the pair of them. Beattie had tried subtly to warn Jason off. Too subtly, perhaps. 'Are you sure you want to be tying the knot already?' she had asked him, when what she wanted to say was that she thought he could do better.

Beattie was not surprised to learn that Jen was pregnant, the development she had privately predicted by way of Jen sealing the deal. What did surprise her was how sanguine Jason had been about the prospect, indeed how happy he was about being a dad and having a family.

Jason seemed so content that day, sitting in his own back garden with his kids running around the place, Jen gazing adoringly at him, bringing him beers, insisting on working the barbecue herself. Maybe that was what he saw in Jen: someone who adored him, who spoiled him like she and her sisters always had. Someone who smiled whenever he walked into a room. And dear God, was Jen smiling that day; smiling and issuing a little chuckle on the end of everything she said.

But some nagging instinct told Beattie those smiles were just a front; that there was something in the background Jen didn't want anybody to see. She was hiding something, and not just a hangover or even a drink problem. It was the kind of smile that concealed deception, that masked a scheming mind at work.

Or perhaps she was smiling because she had already pulled off her great scheme. Michelle was long gone. Jen had ended up with Jason. And the con was that Jason only got her.

Nicolette

Nicolette's skin was crawling inside the hideous grey sweatshirt she had been loaned, some golfer's abomination that was left behind by a previous guest. When Lauren produced it from the cupboard, Michelle had been about to say she wouldn't be seen dead in it, before it struck her that she shouldn't be tempting fate. And as the cover of trees and bushes gave way to just heather and gorse, Nicolette was grateful for the sweatshirt's drabness making her less conspicuous on the open hillside. She was starting to understand what it must feel like to be a stag when the royal family were loose in your postcode. She was grateful also for the insulation, as the wind was growing stronger the higher they went, and there was more of a bite to it too.

Nicolette wasn't the only one who had needed to change. Everybody had gone off to grab more suitable gear, but her problem was that the stuff she had brought by way of outdoor wear had been light and colourful. She had chosen it for a leisurely afternoon stroll; camouflage had not been a consideration. Even then, she wondered whether advance notice of being hunted would have been enough motivation to shop in Trespass.

Though the climb was steep, it was nothing taxing for someone who played tennis three times a week and went running or hit the gym in the intervening evenings. Nicolette wasn't complaining, but it struck her that so far she hadn't encountered anything that could be described as treacherous, and certainly nothing that only Lauren with her local knowledge could navigate.

Her instincts were telling her that Lauren had another agenda. She had first tried to dismiss the croft, then become adamant that she should be the one who checked it out.

Kennedy had picked the pairings, something that admittedly she was pretty good at when it came to tennis. She totally got people's chemistry, but sometimes she put folk together out of devilment, a thought that had gone through Nicolette's head even though she and Lauren were all that was left.

Kennedy had offered reasons why she was making the other two pairings.

'And what do we have in common?' Nicolette asked.

'No reason not to trust each other,' Kennedy had replied.

It sounded reassuring at the time, but on a night like this you needed reasons to trust somebody, not an absence of reasons not to. This whole thing was about secrets, after all: things unsaid, true faces kept hidden. And there *wasn't* an absence of reasons not to trust each other. For one thing, there was the fact that as far as each of them knew, the other could be the person the Reaper was talking about.

There was another thing troubling her about Lauren, but that didn't bear thinking about. Not high on a lonely hillside, far from help and hidden from witnesses.

Nicolette tugged again at the sleeves of the bogging sweatshirt, as if trying to minimise its contact with her skin.

'It *has* been washed,' Lauren said, noticing.

'Oh, no, sorry, I wasn't implying anything,' Nicolette rushed to clarify. 'And I'm grateful for it. It's just that it's somebody else's. A man's.'

'I know. But I just thought I'd make it clear at the very least that it's clean. Though it has probably been sitting in that cupboard for a good six months or more. I could tell you it belonged to someone really cool and famous, if that helps.'

Nicolette felt her eyes widen with interest.

'I'd be lying, though,' Lauren went on. 'I think it was some tech-biz exec. I can see why he left it behind, to be honest.'

Lauren smiled as she said this, acknowledging the fuck-awfulness of the garment, which somehow made Nicolette feel better about wearing it.

'It must have fair lowered the tone, aesthetically,' Nicolette said. 'Everything in your house is totally stunning. Those Paladin radiators, the positioning of that claw-foot bath in my room. It's all, like, actual oh-my-God.'

There was a glow about Lauren's face. 'That means a lot coming from you,' Lauren told her.

'Why?'

'Because I can tell you have taste. As in, properly have taste. I liked your outfit tonight. It was a shame to cover it up, especially with that monstrosity of a sweatshirt. Was the blouse from Whistles?'

'Reiss. But Whistles do one very similar, a Pantone darker with a Peter Pan collar. I totally stanned your suit. Jacquemus, right?'

'Well spotted. You could identify that at a glance?'

'Professional eye.'

Nicolette didn't know why she said that. It hadn't so much slipped out as she couldn't stop herself. She had felt a desire to be seen by someone like Lauren as being on her level.

'Are you in fashion?' Lauren asked.

'I work for Reiss.'

'Oh, wow. Are you a buyer?'

Nicolette looked down, an action given cover by the constant need to check the underfoot terrain. 'More of a seller, really.'

'Marketing?'

'That kind of area, yes.' She felt her cheeks flush. She decided to turn things back to her host. 'I'm really taken with your eye for what works in terms of interior design, I mean from the fixtures right down to the fine details of furnishing. It's a gift.'

Why was she being so gushy? It was like she was back at school, trying to impress the popular lassie, desperate to be liked by her. To be friends with her. There felt like a legit rapport, though. She guessed that as host Lauren had to be good at getting along with folk, but Nicolette was feeling a warmth towards her that was unexpected. And troubling.

'When I started flipping houses I was on my own,' Lauren said. 'So it was just about what I liked personally. You come to realise that can be hit-and-miss. And you can fall into the trap of buying expensive stuff because you want to have it, when really you should be buying cheaper stuff that makes the place look good just long enough to sell it.'

'But that's not the case with Clachan Geal, surely.'

'No, that's been a different business altogether. I'm still developing properties purely for sale, but I'm on the lookout for other places where I might do something like here. It's far more of an endeavour, though, and I'm conscious of how much time I spend away from my daughter. She won't be home that much longer, so I shouldn't waste it.'

'What age is she?'

For a second Nicolette thought Lauren was ignoring the

question. Then she stopped and gestured Nicolette to do the same.

Nicolette froze, instantly on edge, though she didn't know what Lauren was reacting to.

'What is it?'

Lauren was still scanning the landscape. She gave a brief shake of the head, as though dismissing whatever had triggered her.

'Thought I heard something, like an engine. A boat, maybe. Problem is the way the wind carries sound out here. You never know where it's coming from. Sorry, what were you asking me?'

'How old your daughter is.'

'Sixteen. She often comes here with me. Thank God she didn't this time. She's with her dad this weekend.'

The way Lauren put this implied an arrangement. If she had just said 'She's with her dad', there would have been nothing more to infer. And no invitation to infer it.

'You two aren't together, then?'

Lauren gave a hollow laugh. 'We were never really together. It was kind of a holiday romance, or more like a holiday one-night stand that sputtered on longer than it should. When I realised I was pregnant, we both knew for sure we didn't want to be together, but I did want a baby. He's an okay guy, and a good father, no question. It wasn't particularly about him, more that I don't think I'm cut out to be with anybody long term. What about you? Married? Kids?'

Lauren was glancing at Nicolette's ring, which answered the first question even as she asked it.

'Married, twice,' she replied, wondering why she volunteered the latter detail. 'No kids, though.'

She tensed in anticipation of the follow-up so many people felt entitled to ask. *Did you not want them, or . . .*

Or, indeed.

She headed off the possibility by adding: 'Married. Just, I should say.'

'You're just married? Congratulations.'

'No. I mean I'm just about still married.'

Lauren turned to meet her eye, checking to see if this was a joke or something more.

'He's cheating on me,' Nicolette said. The words were out before she was conscious of saying them. To a stranger. WTF?

'Sorry to hear that. Is it a suspicion, or . . .'

'I'm sure.' Nicolette was surprised by how good it felt to say that out loud to someone. It had been too difficult to tell Jen because Jen knew her, so there was more of a sense of embarrassment to overcome.

'It's weird we only say cheating when we're talking about sex. I can say he's been cheating, but I also know I'm the one who wasn't playing fair.'

'How so?'

'I neglected him. I don't just mean sexually, though obviously there is that. But deep down I know I shouldn't have married him. He's decent but . . . I settled. We're not a match. I should have known that even from his job.'

'What does he do?'

'He's in IT. I met him at a time when I was maybe more vulnerable than I realised. Though in my defence, when we first met he acted like he had always been one of the cool kids, you know? When in fact I think he had always been a bit of a geek. Once you're married, the real you comes out, the stuff you can't hide; or maybe you just stop trying to hide it. Put it this way, if we had both known each other when we were teenagers, we'd have understood there was no way it would work.'

'How long have you been married?'

'Six years now.'

'How long were you married the first time?'

Nicolette winced. 'That one didn't last at all. Painful subject.'

'Doesn't sound like you've had a lot of luck.'

Nicolette sighed, conscious of how much she had been talking. 'Sorry for laying this on you. Maybe it's my mind distracting me from . . . you know. But it's pure TMI and I don't know why it's all spilling out. We've only just met.'

'Not at all,' said Lauren. She halted for a moment and produced a bottle of water, offering it to Nicolette. They were almost at the top. 'Sometimes it's easier to talk to a stranger,' she said. 'Why the Yanks all go in for therapy. It must be very painful for you.'

Nicolette took a sip. It was only now they had stopped that she realised how warm she was from the climb. 'It stings, but maybe not in the way I'd expected. I'm like, "How dare he?" Like, he should be so grateful to have me, how could he possibly think he'd do better?'

'Do you know who he's cheating with?'

'No. And I can't decide if I want to know or if ignorance is bliss. I'm assuming somebody more his speed. His problem is insecurity. He doesn't love me – he can't love me – because he doesn't believe I could love him. He married me for my looks but didn't examine the rest of the package. Or maybe projected something onto the package.'

Lauren hit her with a challenging stare. 'And what did you project onto him?'

It was refreshing to be called out, a splash of cold water to the face that made her see what should have been obvious.

'That's a fair point. Maybe it wasn't me that he didn't measure up to, but someone else.'

'The one that got away?'

'You said it.'

Except he hadn't got away. Not like that.

Helena

Helena felt her skin turn to gooseflesh and every hair react as though the sound had electrified the air around her. It was startling in its pitch, yet at the same time strangulated and muffled: the sound of someone screaming as a noose tightened around their neck, or just maybe of someone who had heard voices nearby and was crying out for help through a gag.

What overcame her fear was not so much courage as the fact that she was with Michelle. She wanted to look stronger than her. Better than her.

Helena broke first, running from the trees, the golf club clutched in her hand, though she had no notion of how she might wield it. She soon heard the soft pummelling of Michelle's feet behind her, catching up fast. She remembered that Michelle had been the faster runner, languid and athletic in her stride. She was soon alongside but did not overtake. Helena could not decide if it was solidarity or fear.

They heard the cry again. Shrill, urgent. It was coming from the central of the three cottages, the one that still had a partial roof structure. It covered less than half the building but enough that its open narrow doorway led into darkness.

Helena was conscious that they were both slowing the nearer they got.

She shouted. She couldn't stop herself. 'Samira, we're coming!'

But it wasn't Samira she was calling to. If there was someone else in there, she wanted to give notice. She wanted them to come out here. She didn't want to meet anyone in the dark.

She and Michelle were side by side as they climbed the boundary wall, gazes focused on the blackness of the doorway. Once across it, they were like pursuit cyclists, edging forward together, neither wishing to take the lead.

They would never find out which of them had the nerve to go into the cottage first, because at that moment something else came tearing out of it. Two things, in fact.

'Fucking foxes!' Michelle said. 'Literally. That's what the screams were.'

Helena felt a curious mixture of relief and disappointment. As soon as she had seen the animals, she understood. She had occasionally been woken by them at home in the night, startled by what sounded like screams in the darkness.

'Wee bastards,' she muttered. 'Such a horrible noise.'

'I just hope *I* don't sound like that when I'm at it,' said Michelle. 'Maybe I should check the tape.'

Helena looked at her in mortification for a moment, wondering if Michelle was implying she had seen it.

For what it was worth, Helena went inside the cottage first, taking the initiative while admittedly knowing there was little chance of anybody being there; certainly nobody who posed a threat. The place smelled of damp and of animals, moss and ivy covering the walls. It felt more like being in a cave than a derelict dwelling. She thought of Samira coming to and finding herself in such a ghastly hovel, lonely and afraid. A bleak and horrible place to die.

Samira wasn't here, though. That was the main thing.

Michelle had followed her inside. She stood there with one hand on her hip, the tote slung over her shoulder, looking around casually like she was assessing it as a potential fixer-upper. How did she do that? How did she always manage to look graceful and at ease with her surroundings?

Maybe it was primarily about being at ease with herself. Helena used to love that about her, before she came to despise it. But even that came from the same place: seeing something special and knowing you could never have it, never *be* it. It started as warm admiration then curdled into something poisonous.

For just a moment she glimpsed the girl she had known when she was five years old. Could they ever be those people to each other again? She could still picture Michelle standing in Helena's living room after school, making it seem that bit brighter by being there. Making Helena seem that bit brighter by being next to her.

It felt special to have Michelle in her house, in her bedroom. She kind of wanted to show her off to her mum. This is my friend, this amazing girl who everyone likes, and she likes *me*.

The downside was, when Michelle was in the house, Helena became more self-conscious about her mum's fuddy-duddy ornaments and worn furniture. The ratty bits at the edge of the rug, the frayed and peeling join in that section of the wallpaper, it all seemed so much more conspicuous.

Helena would never forget the first time she went to Michelle's house. It was Primary Two, after she started being allowed to walk home from school alone. They played with her Barbie and Sindy dolls, and her Tiny Tears. Then Michelle had opened a wardrobe and almost ceremonially pulled a cardboard box from it. 'Because you're my most special friend, I'll show you my most special doll.'

Helena was wondering what could possibly be so special, given how cool all her other stuff was. Maybe it was some kind of electronic baby that did things itself, or some new Barbie from America that hadn't come out here yet.

It turned out to be entirely the opposite. Michelle placed the box delicately on the floor and slowly opened a hinged lid. The figure inside was very old. It had a dress on that looked like a real dress, not like the flimsy patches of nylon covering other dolls, even the Barbies. This was a miniature version of a proper garment, albeit one from a long time ago.

'She belonged to my Aunt Meg. Aunt Meg is my dad's sister. When she gave it to me, she said I was to have it because it was special and I was special.'

'What's the dolly's name?' Helena asked.

Michelle shook her head regretfully. 'I can't tell you.'

'Why not?'

'Because I can't tell anybody. My Aunt Meg said she never told anybody else, and now I have to do the same. It's my most special secret.'

Michelle didn't take the doll out of the box. Helena watched her put it back as carefully as she had removed it.

Helena didn't care that she hadn't been told its name. Being shown it was enough, because Michelle had said she was her most special friend. They were each other's most special friends.

Jen

The path zigzagged up the hill, slaloming between rock outcrops, bracken and gorse. If Jen had been on her own, she would have been tempted to make a more direct ascent, but Beattie was struggling enough as it was.

Her labouring breaths were the only sound to have issued from her since they left the house, other than the odd grunt of acknowledgement when Jen said 'I think it's this way' or 'Mind the pothole.'

You could disguise anything in a crowd. Jen knew that better than most. The true nature of a relationship is starker when it's just the two of you. In her and Beattie's case right then, it was quite literally out in the open. She couldn't say it was an awkward silence, though. Not when she knew conversation would be far more uncomfortable.

Jen became aware of a buzzing sound, realising that she had been hearing it for a few seconds. It had come and gone on the breeze, but as it got steadily louder she realised it was an engine.

She looked down the slope but couldn't see anything, then a black shape came into view around the foot of the hill. It was Lauren's stolen quad bike. It was being ridden by a figure in a ski mask.

Jen put two hands on Beattie's shoulder and urged, 'Get down!' as she hauled her to the ground.

'What the—' Beattie began, but Jen clamped a hand over her mouth. The engine noise was unmistakable now, and explanation enough. Beattie gave a curt nod and Jen released her hand.

Jen raised her head as high as she dared. The steady sound of the engine indicated that the rider hadn't slowed in response to anything he might have seen, but she needed the reassurance of seeing him pass.

Jen looked at the hillside to the west, searching the slope for movement and reassuring herself that she could see none. If she couldn't see Lauren and Nicolette, that meant she and Beattie were not visible from a distance either.

She glanced across to Beattie, who was also peeking over the gorse. Her unblinking gaze was focused on the quad bike, as though she dared not take her eyes off it until it was gone. She looked hyper-alert, unquestionably afraid. Jen couldn't help wondering whether she was generally afraid or specifically afraid, though she could ask the same about everybody here tonight.

Despite the content of the Reaper's message, her initial thought had been that this was something to do with Zaki, because it was his sister who had been taken. Jen couldn't get the video of Samira out of her mind: tied to that chair, so tiny, so fragile, with twin babies who would be left motherless. Whoever was behind it knew that, Jen suspected. Samira hadn't been chosen at random.

Except Jen had no evidence for this. Only her own paranoia.

She knew Zaki had endured business failures, but she didn't know the details. It wasn't that he was secretive, he just didn't like to talk about it, preferring to be focused on the future, always upbeat and positive. That infectious optimism was one of the

148

reasons Jen was drawn to him. But a part of her was suspicious of it, thinking maybe that was in fact how he *concealed* his secretiveness. Still another part thought that was why his businesses had failed. You needed a bit of paranoia and pessimism as part of your due diligence. *If you assume people are out to scam you, you won't be caught off-guard*, she once told him. *It's my sworn mission to cure you of this, Jennifer*, Zaki had replied.

That's exactly what someone trying to scam me would say to get my guard down, she had responded.

He thought she was joking.

She wanted him to be right. She wanted him to cure her. She wanted to surrender all her trust to him. That was what made her most afraid. How could she trust her own instincts in falling for Zaki, when they had failed her so badly in falling for Jason?

Christ. There had been a time when she had seen Jason as a catch. But that was embarrassing enough, but what lay behind it was worse. It was because he had once been Michelle's. She could admit that in retrospect. It was like a celebrity endorsement, even before Michelle was a celebrity. Like it said something about her if she could have the guy everybody wanted when she was at school.

She should have trusted her dad's instincts, as he was such an astute judge of character. He was never sold on Jason, but he didn't press the point in the early days, probably because he didn't think it would last. As their relationship endured, his concerns were gradually lessened, but that was because Jen was working so hard to conceal the truth.

That was one of Jason's great talents: getting other people to sell his lies, thereby making them complicit in what was being concealed. What people seldom understand about an abusive marriage is that the abused becomes invested in the deceit. You don't want to believe that what you've poured your whole life into is all fake, a dangerous lie. When you do see the awful truth, it comes not in a dramatic reveal, but a little at a time, and by that point you are in way too deep.

It was a long time before Jen admitted to herself that she was afraid of her husband, scared of what he *might* do before he finally did it.

It happened the night before Calum's fifth birthday party.

She was always tense around the kids' birthdays, and even her own, having long understood they were a potential trigger for Jason. It was because other people's birthdays weren't about him.

Not all narcissists are sociopaths, but all sociopaths are narcissists.

She could just sense it from him when he came in from work, arriving home after the kids were in bed though she knew he had been on an early shift. She didn't say anything about that, even though it was actually Calum's birthday that day. Survival instinct had taught her to be alert to his temper, and to find ways of heading it off. But there were times when it was like he had already decided he was going to kick off, and he would just go around in circles looking for a reason. It had been crackling off him the previous evening too, early warning signs, because all the talk had been about arrangements for Saturday's party. But there were times when it was like he had already decided he was going to kick off, and he would just go around in circles looking for a reason. It could be anything. One time she had put a Beatles album on while they ate. Jason's face had twisted into a familiar sneer.

'The Beatles? They're not even the best band to come out

of Liverpool. Never mind the best band in the world. One word – overrated!'

He didn't even believe what he was saying. He just wanted her to dare to disagree.

It had been crackling off him the previous evening too, early warning signs, because all the talk had been about arrangements for Saturday's party.

She had waited to eat, even though it was almost nine. She thought if she had eaten before he came in then that would provide a pretext for him to have a go. She put the plates on the table and then poured herself a glass of water. She didn't pour him one because she knew he would want a beer, and if she picked it herself, it would be the wrong kind.

He waited until she had finished pouring and then spoke. 'I wanted a Stella,' he said.

'Ste— Right, sure, let me just . . .'

'What are you giving me water for?'

'That was for me.' She let out a wee chuckle. *See, Jason, it's funny, just a silly misunderstanding.*

'No it wasn't. This was you pass-agg telling me not to have a drink because of this fuckin' party tomorrow or whatever. It's not like I'm going to get tanked up and hungover.'

She knew no words would be enough, so she opted for action instead, reaching for the fridge door. His hand shot out and grabbed her wrist. She was chilled by the strength of just his fingers. The quiet intensity of his stare.

'Is this you trying to tell me I've not to have any beers when everybody comes around tomorrow?'

'No, of course not.' *Chuckle. Of course I wouldn't. Let's laugh about it. Nothing to get upset about.*

'So why *were* you pouring me mineral water?'

'I wasn't pouring it for you—'. *Chuckle*. 'I just didn't—'

'Can a man not enjoy a wee drink at his own table the night of his own son's birthday? The table he puts food on?'

She felt like she was standing on the edge of a skyscraper and the fear of falling was so great that it felt easier to jump. That was why she said it.

'Well, I noticed his birthday didn't matter enough for you to make time to see him.'

He changed his grip, grabbing her by the forearm and twisting it up her back, her face pressed against the fridge. Then he punched her in the side, powerful jabs, little drawback and all follow-through. He knew precisely how hard to hit so that it was excruciatingly painful but didn't break anything, didn't leave external evidence. She wondered if he had learned it at work.

He hadn't quite mastered all the techniques, though. His grip was too hard and by the morning she had bruising on her forearm, which would be visible in a T-shirt. She had to wear a long-sleeved top even though the sun was splitting the sky by the time the guests arrived. She knew it would look stupid with shorts, the long sleeves all the more conspicuous, so she wore linen trousers.

It was her first act of complicity in covering up her own abuse, but far from her last. It wasn't even her last that day.

Throughout the afternoon she had endeavoured to disguise the lingering pain in her side. She caught herself walking on light feet because even a heavy step sent a wave through her, but she was concerned that it was noticeable, so she pretended to be hungover as a cover.

In service of this, she stuck to Irn-Bru when she could really have done with a drink to take the edge off the tension. She needed that edge, though. She had to stay straight and alert so that she kept up the illusion, fetching him drinks and gazing adoringly at him, concerned about how he would respond if she disappointed him.

She winced when she recalled that little chuckle she had started doing after every statement, ringing like a bell on the ends of her words. Let's laugh, it said. If I've said something you don't like, I didn't mean anything by it. How could I if I'm laughing? So there's no need to react. There's no need for rage.

She was always laughing around Jason, which meant that people thought she was happy. But she wasn't laughing because she was happy. She was laughing because she was scared.

It was hard to stomach Beattie's unwavering faith in the goodness of her saintly brother, but Jen knew it was wrong to hate her for it. If Beattie had never noticed anything amiss, that was because Jen had made damn sure of it.

Nicolette

Despite the body heat she had generated on the climb, Nicolette wasn't tempted to shed a layer once they had crested the summit. She could feel the sweat cooling and the wind was stronger on this side of the hill, coming in off the Atlantic.

She could see their destination below them, a low and ramshackle grey building with a path before it leading down to the sea. It was tiny at this distance, but the sight made her think of a cottage from a fairy story: the kind the hero was warned not to visit.

She was still going over their conversation. *The one that got away*, Lauren had called him. Nicolette wondered who Lauren was picturing, what kind of relationship. Someone who left her for another girl and who she still pined for, maybe. Or someone she broke up with and only came to appreciate once it was too late. But he had been neither of those things.

His name was Ryan.

They had known each other since Ryan was a student and she had her first job as an assistant in the home furnishings department at John Lewis in the Buchanan Galleries. They were flatmates, sharing a place in Woodlands Road with two other students, but it soon turned into something else. Flatmates to

154

soulmates, they used to say, though she hated hearing that word now, because people used it without really knowing what it meant. She had lived what it meant. She and Ryan just got each other. Which was to say she would have loved him even if he hadn't been on the path towards earning millions, although that was certainly a bonus.

He was head of a tech start-up, in what he called 'the second wave of internet development'. He had seen that smartphones were where everything was going to happen, at a time when everyone was still getting excited about all-in-one iMacs.

They got married in September 2004. They both wanted kids, though not immediately. She was under no illusions regarding the demands Ryan's job would place on his time in these crucial early years, but she was going to be his rock, his anchor. She would be waiting for him whenever he came home, and a very nice home it was going to be. A home to raise a family in.

After the wedding they had a lovely but all-too-brief weekend in Prague because things were particularly hectic for the business around that time. They regarded their real honeymoon as merely delayed. They had the trip of a lifetime booked: a fortnight in the Maldives over Christmas.

Christmas 2004.

Nicolette and Lauren were about a quarter of the way down when they finally encountered a landslip: a dusty brown gouge out of the green hillside. There were patches of moss and tufts of grass growing out of it in places, and a path had been worn across it. It didn't exactly look recent, and hardly an obstacle either.

'Is this the treacherous bit?' Nicolette asked.

She meant it as a joke, acknowledging what other hazards might still be ahead, but Lauren's reaction betrayed her.

'It's a while since I've been up here,' she said defensively. 'I remember it being trickier.'

Nicolette once again got the sense that Lauren was hiding something.

'It's just that you mentioned heavy rains and it's clearly dry as a bone out here. Is there maybe another reason you wanted to be the one who took this route?'

Lauren drew to a halt, staring down towards the building at the foot of the hill. Then she turned to face Nicolette, an uncertain expression on her face. 'In keeping with our recent spirit of candour, there's something I ought to lay on you regarding the abandoned croft.'

Nicolette knew it. She bloody knew it. Her instincts had been bang-on. 'And what's that?' she asked.

'It isn't abandoned.'

Helena

They were standing on the far side of the cottages, looking at the coastline as it stretched south and west. A quarter of a mile ahead, the trees extended almost to the edge of a cliff that plunged twenty feet to the sea.

'I can't see that we have much choice but to go through the woods,' Michelle said.

Helena nodded in acknowledgement. She was still finding it difficult to bring herself to speak to Michelle, even though they were all each other had right now. A voice told her she was being childish, but it wasn't the child in her that was still hurt and angry. That stuff had all happened to a fully formed adult.

Michelle had been right when she said Helena's problem was that she had a whole lot to say to her. It felt like there was just so much she was afraid to tap into, wary of the pain it would revisit.

'We'd best get moving while there's light,' she managed to say.

They had searched the cottages and found no indication that anyone had been in them in decades, so their task now was all about the boat. She doubted anybody would be guarding that, so there was less to be afraid of once they reached the horseshoe bay. The same could not be said for getting there.

Staying on the edge of the tree-line again was not an option, and it was getting darker. Unlike before, the route did not follow a break in the trees, and it was not all that clear what was an actual path and what were merely negotiable gaps. After about ten minutes Helena had little confidence that they were even heading in the right direction.

She got out her phone.

'What are you doing?' Michelle asked.

'Google Maps.'

'Have you got a signal?' she inquired, suddenly optimistic. Helena guessed that when you'd had Michelle's life, it was easier to believe in miracles.

'No. It can't load the actual map data, but I can at least use it as a compass.'

'You always were the smart one,' Michelle said.

They proceeded with a little more urgency in their step, no longer hamstrung by the concern that every pace was a step further in the wrong direction. It was still slow going, and every time they heard a scurrying in the undergrowth they both stopped dead with fright.

'This reminds me of the time we were driving around in Madeleine's van,' Michelle said. 'Trying to find that festival site for T in the Park, back before everyone had sat-nav. Wondering why we hadn't seen any signs for it yet and it turned out we had taken the wrong road out of Perth and were about ten miles south of where we thought we were.'

Helena wondered why Michelle was making these overtures. Perhaps she wanted to act like nothing was wrong between them, because if Helena engaged on those terms then she could tell herself the past was the past and nothing needed to be acknowledged. In Michelle's mind, they would just be friends again, and nothing needed to be forgiven.

She had no notion how wrong she was.

'I think we should stay quiet,' Helena replied. 'So that nobody hears us coming.'

'Really? We're all about the stealth, are we? Why did you shout "Samira" then, back at the cottage?'

Having been rebuffed, Michelle's tone was less solicitous now. She never did like it when someone didn't give her what she wanted. Especially her loyal lapdog Helena.

'I thought I'd heard her scream. It was to let her know we were coming.'

It didn't sound convincing even to herself.

'Bullshit. You did it to let *them* know we were coming, so that we didn't surprise each other.'

'We're not supposed to be out here,' Helena argued.

'I'm not saying I'm not shit-scared of them too. But we're not breaking their *rules*, Helena,' Michelle replied, a dig at Helena's goody-two-shoes reputation.

Helena increased her pace despite the gloom, trying to forge ahead.

'Are you really so bitter about it all that we can't have a conversation?' Michelle asked. 'We were friends since we were five. We had good times. We did some amazing things together. That's got to count for something.'

Helena felt the hurt and anger boil up. This was what Michelle just didn't get. Those times Michelle wanted to reminisce about, they didn't give Helena a warm glow, they just reminded her of what she had lost. When Michelle dumped her like dead weight, she took away the best parts of her past as well as her future.

Some of her happiest memories were of Michelle's bedroom. She had a portable TV with a built-in VHS. They would watch tapes of *Top of the Pops* and *The Chart Show*. They used to dress up and sing and dance along. Michelle could dance properly. She had been to lessons. But she was amazed when she found out Helena could play actual tunes on this little electronic keyboard Michelle had.

Helena knew the chords for 'Too Many Broken Hearts' by Jason Donovan, and the keyboard had a very basic rhythm setting. It seemed to give Michelle a huge thrill to be able to sing along to Helena's playing, rather than just singing along with the video. It was a huge thrill for Helena too. Michelle had a lovely voice, and she could strike poses. Dancing along to the TV was still fun, but this felt like something else.

The first time they wrote a song together, they must have been ten or eleven. It was called 'Wet Playtime'. It was a very simple three-chord affair, the melody largely ripped off from Bananarama's 'Cruel Summer'. The pair of them kept having to stop because they were collapsing with laughter at the lyrics they were coming up with, all about their classmates and the teacher. Decades later Helena spotted a track on the second Mica album with the same title; that raised a bittersweet smile. Obviously that one was about something very different, though she was sure theirs would have got them into far more trouble had anyone else heard it.

It was around then that Helena decided to start learning the guitar. Looking back, she wondered if she had always been trying to make herself useful to Michelle: doing something she couldn't do herself, providing something Michelle needed. What was in no doubt was that once she was no longer useful, she was dropped.

'Okay, so what do you want to talk about?' Helena asked. 'Your new album? Your tour?'

'I want to talk about you,' Michelle replied, over-egging the sincerity. 'We haven't spoken in a lifetime. You've got daughters who've grown up without me even seeing them. I'm interested in what's going on with you. I know you teach music. Do you still play? I mean, *play* play.'

Helena wasn't sure which answer Michelle might prefer: that she had never been able to face picking up a guitar since the break-up, or that she had been strumming away sadly this whole time, dreaming of might-have-beens.

Yes, she did play. Not just play: she fucking *shredded*. She found it therapeutic. She would retreat to the music room and jam along to something just to feel the notes beneath her fingers and hear the sounds she could still make with a piece of wood and wire and steel.

She had been asked a few times to join cover bands, playing weddings and parties and the like, just for fun and company. She had been tempted but turned them all down because she never wanted to find out how it made her feel to be on stage in some cheesy function suite. She was also wary of how she might respond if someone in the band wanted to do a Mica song or, even worse, suggested a Cassidy number without realising she had been *in* bloody Cassidy.

She had been playing along to heavier stuff lately. It had never been her genre of choice, but metal was more technically challenging, and the harder it was to master, the more she could lose herself in the task. When your husband leaves you for a younger woman, you need to find a form of therapy.

For years her and Neil's relationship had been more like that of mutually indifferent housemates. She was never sure if they had been staying together for the kids or it was simply that neither of them had anywhere else to be. And then suddenly he did.

Helena had found another form of therapy more recently,

though you could say it came about as an indirect result of the first. She had developed an appreciation of certain bands through learning their music, and had gone to see them when they played in town. She went alone, which felt at once utterly sad and comfortingly indulgent.

She had met him at an Architects gig when they recognised each other in the foyer on the way out. She knew him through his wife. He was there alone too. They got the same train home as they lived only one stop apart. He had always been into this stuff, he explained, though his missus had never mentioned it. She seldom mentioned anything about him, in fact.

Helena started going to shows with him, a gig buddy. She never mentioned this to his wife, because he confided that he never mentioned who he was going with either. Then one night they went to see Opeth in Edinburgh. She met him at the venue because he had been working there during the day.

It was after that gig, when she was about to head for the station, that he mentioned he had booked a hotel room for the night.

How was that for following the rules, Michelle?

Helena was not the person everyone assumed her to be, and nobody knew what she was capable of. The Reaper's description matched that much about her, at least.

Beattie

They waited until the quad bike was out of sight and the sound of its engine fading into the distance before they climbed carefully to their feet, Beattie brushing tufts of moss from her clothes. Their eyes met in fleeting acknowledgement of their shared predicament, briefly bonded by fear – though what each of them was afraid of might be very different.

'Do you think he saw us?' Beattie asked.

'No. But I think I know where he's headed.'

'Same place we are,' Beattie acknowledged. He was taking the long way around, the hill route not being an option even on such a vehicle, but he would still get there first.

'Maybe that's a good thing,' Jen said. 'If we at least find out where Samira is, that would be a start. And if he's going to check on her, or shoot more video, then we could make our move after he's gone.'

'What's with the ski mask?' Beattie asked. 'Why would he be covering his face unless he already knows we're out here? In which case he knows what we're up to and he won't leave Samira unguarded.'

'We know nothing for sure,' Jen replied. 'But if they're worried about being identified later, at least it suggests they're not planning to kill us all as witnesses.'

Beattie became aware of another sudden sound and movement, but when she turned she saw only swallows whipping around the hillside, there and gone in a flash. She immediately thought of her grandson Xander, who got excited when he saw birds swoop from height or fly at speed. 'Burdies!' he would shout.

He was such a wee treasure, adorable and precocious. But at that age they could go from angelic to demonic in a blink. The sound of his crying always went to the heart of her, but it was so much worse these days, because it took her back to that moment, and the things she would have to carry with her forever.

That man's head hitting the windscreen on the passenger side, two feet from where Xander was strapped into his car seat. The sickening clatter as he bounced off the bonnet. The truth that only she knew.

Beattie had grown up to believe in an all-seeing God, which meant that there were always consequences when you did something wrong. That was what made it so hard to accept that she could do something terrible without anybody else finding out. But short of an all-seeing God, if anybody *was* going to find out it would be a family with connections at the highest level, who could requisition CCTV footage or computer data.

If that was the case, she had to think it would have happened by now. They wouldn't be coming for her this way, here tonight. Thinking rationally, the people she was worried about had official channels to go through. Whereas the people Jen had crossed were at the other end of the scale. Beattie's first instincts, head and heart, told her this was about her ex-sister-in-law, and so

164

far nothing external, nothing other than her own guilt, had given her reason to believe otherwise.

Jen knew this too. Beattie could tell by the way Jen had responded, because Beattie had seen this picture before.

A wet night more than a decade ago. Beattie knew it must have been after nine because she and Richard were watching *Ashes to Ashes*. Any time it was on, they joked about how Jason would love to be sent back in time to be a cop in the eighties, though in sunny Florida rather than a permanently grey London.

She noticed a car pull up outside and recognised it as Jen's. Beattie wasn't expecting her, and it was a weird time to visit. Weirder still, when she looked closer she saw that Jason was at the wheel, Jen in the passenger seat, and both the kids in the back.

Calum and Ailsa were normally tucked up in their beds by this time. They were very disciplined that way. Every way, in fact. The kids were polite and well turned out, if a little shy and quiet. Beattie had always thought that Calum would be more like Jason, bullishly full of himself, or even her own father, who had been very much the man in charge. Calum seemed timid by comparison, and Ailsa showed little sign of her mother's haughtiness. But they were young yet, and anyway, maybe it was no bad thing. Beattie had once complimented Calum on how well behaved he and his sister were. 'Mummy's the naughtiest,' he had replied. Which sounded about right to Beattie's ears.

Her first thought was that there was some kind of staffing issue to do with the nightclub. She was aware that Jen often had to do a lot of juggling over childcare arrangements. Jen and her father had rejigged their responsibilities so that she handled the administrative side, things that could be done during school hours, or daylight hours at least, such as organising staff rotas, ordering inventory and overseeing deliveries.

Jason was the one whose job took precedence, but that was just the way of things, wasn't it? Jason was proving successful in a career that he was cut out for and that he enjoyed. Between them, he and Jen seemed to have found the right balance. The money appeared to be rolling in too. Nicer cars, nicer holidays.

Beattie would admit that she was wary of how Jen had manipulated her way into Jason's life, but it all seemed to be working out for the best. She hadn't particularly trusted Jen, but she had never been suspicious of her, not with regard to anything truly sinister. Not until that night.

She watched Jen lean into the back seat of the car and emerge with wee Ailsa in her arms, the girl wrapped around her like a shawl. Calum appeared from the other side, looking pale. Something wasn't right.

Beattie hastened to the front door, opening it as they came down the path. 'What's happened?' she asked.

Jen looked to Jason to answer. Almost like whatever it was, it was his fault.

'There was a brick thrown through our living-room window,' he said.

'Good God.'

'The curtains caught most of the glass, but the brick landed where Ailsa had been sitting ten minutes before she went to brush her teeth. Calum often sits in that spot too while he's playing his PS3.'

Beattie ushered them all inside and put the kettle on. Jason and Jen told her they didn't want the kids in the house that night, but Jen's parents were on holiday in Tenerife. They had an apartment in Costa Adeje and seemed to be spending more and more of their time there.

Wee Ailsa looked dopey and confused, as befitting a child who had been set fair for the land of nod before all the sudden upheaval. Calum seemed more troubled, old enough to grasp the enormity of the incident and perhaps to speculate about consequences and implications. He had been in the room at the time, though mercifully curled up in a corner of the settee.

'I can't stay,' Jason said. 'I need to get back to the house. My colleagues are already on the scene.'

'What do you think it was about?' Richard asked. 'Something you're investigating?'

'It could be anything,' he replied. 'Probably an accident. Things can fly off of lorries,' he added, gesturing towards the kids to indicate that he didn't want to talk frankly about this in front of them.

Jason answered properly once Calum and Ailsa had been escorted away obligingly by their big cousins.

'We heard a car speed off. I'm not supposed to talk about ongoing inquiries, but it's possible our investigations are getting too close to certain individuals, and they're feeling threatened. As they should, because believe you me, we'll hit back hard. You don't do this to the polis, and you certainly don't bring it to their homes and families.'

Jason had seemed unsettled by the shock but fizzing with a determination to fight back. His response was precisely what Beattie would have expected of him. Jason never took anything lying down, and he bore grudges, sometimes for years, never letting them rest until he got his due.

Beattie didn't know Jen anything like as well, but it nonetheless struck her that there was something a little off about her response. It was hard to put a finger on it. It was like she was shaken up, but just not as much as she ought to have been.

As a mother you could surprise yourself with your own calm, how in the face of trauma you were able to hold it together because you needed your kids to feel that everything was going to be okay. This felt like something else, however.

It was noticeable that Jen wasn't looking to her husband for strength or solidarity. You could see it in her body language that this was not bringing them closer. Initially, Beattie assumed that it came down to her being angry at Jason for having brought this to their home, for putting her children in danger. That would have been understandable, if unfair: amid the shock and uncertainty, she needed someone to blame.

Eventually it dawned on Beattie what had been off. Jen didn't seem surprised. She had been expecting it.

What she later came to understand was that Jen's anger towards Jason had been a deliberate distraction. She was letting everyone jump to the conclusion that the attack was about his job, when in fact it was about hers. With her parents off in Tenerife half the time, she was increasingly in charge of the nightclub, and those places weren't about the drink any more.

She recalled an odd exchange with wee Calum.

'Is Mummy still the naughtiest?' she had asked.

'Yes. Daddy said if the other police knew how naughty Mummy is, they'd take her away.'

'What did she do?'

'I'm not allowed to say,' Calum replied. It didn't sound like he was joking.

Michelle

The scent of pine would normally be a source of simple pleasure, a smell that served to emphasise Michelle's distance from cities, from concrete, from exhaust fumes and schedules and commitments. Tonight it was a constant reminder of an unsettling remoteness, and of nature's cold indifference.

The carpet of brown needles beneath her feet cushioned her steps, but many of the trees that shed them looked diseased. She had passed several dead ones covered in ivy, like they had been strangled by it. The image made her think of Samira, the noose that would tighten with every melting drop. It was at once a motivation to succeed in her task and a reason to seek any way out that might present itself.

She had never seen a dead body before tonight, far less one that had died violently. And never mind corpses: fame and money had protected her from so many of the stresses other people dealt with as a matter of course. Mortgages, budgeting, waiting at bus stops, paperwork. She lived a life other people only read about with envy, never experienced. Was this the night it evened up, when she died a death other people only read about and gave thanks that they never experienced?

Every so often she would see a bird flashing out of sight,

gone before she could track the movement. Occasionally she would hear something louder. Something that could be a footfall. She thought of the foxes they had disturbed, where they might be now. It all contributed to a sense that there were eyes upon her.

Michelle had been paranoid about everything since the video leak. It wasn't just the awareness of her online vulnerability induced by the hack itself. The level of violation was so absolute that it completely destroyed all sense of personal security. It felt like anybody could get to her, any time.

The computer forensics investigator was called Shawn, turning up at Michelle's place in Santa Barbara within hours of being called. Money could buy that kind of haste. What it couldn't buy was to undo anything.

From the name and other assumptions, Michelle had been expecting a geeky young white dude. Shawn was instead a middle-aged black woman with the air of a schoolteacher – the kind whose homework assignment you never forgot to do.

'Had you turned on two-factor authentication?' Shawn asked.

Michelle felt a twist in her guts as she heard those words. It was something she had always been meaning to do, but every time she got an email prompt, she had thought: I'm busy, I'll sort that later.

Michelle could barely summon up any words in response, letting a shake of the head carry it.

'Don't beat yourself up,' Shawn told her. 'I'm not asking to tell you off. I need to know what level of sophistication was required to get through your security.'

Nonetheless, it burned Michelle to know that she could have closed the stable door.

'I used a unique password,' she explained, unsure whether it was herself or the investigator she was trying to reassure she was less of an idiot.

'Do you mean unique as in it wasn't a commonly recognisable word or phrase, or unique in that you never used it anywhere else?'

'Both,' she was minutely consoled to say.

Shawn kept telling her not to feel stupid, that anybody could be fooled. 'The reason so many high-profile people get their personal photos stolen and leaked isn't that they're easily duped. It's that it's worth the hackers' time and effort. In terms of the deed itself, they most likely got your username and password from a fake log-in screen, but getting you to that log-in screen takes highly sophisticated, bespoke strategies tailored to each specific target.'

'I do remember getting an email saying "Your account has been accessed from a new device. If this is you, blah blah blah." But I got that email when I had just stepped off a plane at LAX. I thought it was because I was using my phone in a different country so I ignored it.'

Shawn explained that it wouldn't have made any difference. 'Once the hackers accessed your cloud, no matter how quickly you shut things down, they could have downloaded what they wanted in minutes, seconds even.'

And once it was out there, there was no putting it back, no matter how many legal threats and take-down notices were issued, because proliferation was instant and infinite. The internet never forgets.

'What you got to remember is that this wasn't personal,' Shawn had said. 'This happened because of the job you do. Not because of who *you* are.'

Now, though, she wasn't so sure. She had to think this was

171

all linked. Jen's email had been hacked, and so had Lauren's. It couldn't be a coincidence, any more than *that* song coming on the moment they received the Reaper's message.

Helena slowed to check her phone again, frowning as she toggled between her photo of the old map and the blank screen she was using as a compass. They were passing through a clearing where some of the trees had been felled. Michelle could smell garlic, ransoms having grown around the stumps. There was something else in the air too, more aromatic, like perfume. With a jolt she thought it was maybe more like aftershave, but she only smelled it for a second then it was gone. It could have been anything.

They walked past two piles of logs covered in moss. They had evidently been felled and stacked years, conceivably decades, ago, but never moved, never put to any purpose: testament perhaps to some enterprise that came to nothing. It made her think about the songs Helena had been working on when she still thought there was going to be a third album. Michelle wondered whether she had written anything since.

It hurt that Helena wanted to act like none of this stuff had happened, retconning their shared past so that her memories were no longer canon.

She thought back to when she first heard 'She Knows'. It was a Thursday evening when she was twelve. She had gone around to Helena's house on a pretext about some textbook she needed to borrow. She found her in the living room, sitting cross-legged on the floor as she listened to her parents' Sanyo music centre, a gatefold sleeve open across her lap. As it was an LP, Michelle knew it was old. They were both starting to respond to music they had previously disdained as ancient and boring, finding unexpected treasures in their parents' album collections. In truth, the seeds of Mica were sown as much by listening to Dionne Warwick, the Drifters and even Helen Reddy as by the cooler acts she liked to cite in interviews.

'Who's this?' she asked.

It was guitar music: floaty and mysterious, sometimes menacing. What she would later know as goth, but somehow lighter, airier and irresistibly poppy.

'Balaam and the Angel. They're three brothers from Motherwell. My dad says they lived a couple of doors down from him on Reid Street when they were kids, which was why he took an interest.'

'I wish I had their hair,' Michelle said, looking at the band photo on the inside of the sleeve. The album was called *The Greatest Story Ever Told*.

'You've got to hear this one,' Helena said.

She dropped the needle carefully on the third track. What came from the speakers was a perfect combination of the guitar music they were starting to listen to and the catchy pop tunes that first made Michelle and Helena dance along to *Top of the Pops*.

Clockwork motion and magic potion.

It was the song that would change their lives, a moment that shaped their destinies. But if she had known that it would also begin a process that ultimately drove them apart and ended their friendship, would she still have taken the same path?

There was no point in pretending that was a hard question. Michelle knew herself too well. She wasn't going to hate herself for it either. There were enough people out there doing that for her. But it weighed heavily that one of them should be Helena.

Jen

Jen's eye was drawn briefly to the passing swallows, then her gaze returned to the headland, wary that the quad bike might appear again. She knew it was unlikely, though. He looked to be heading somewhere with a purpose rather than merely on the lookout. With that thought she reached for the walkie-talkie.

'This is Jen,' she said. 'We've just seen a guy in a ski mask on a quad bike, heading north. Not sure where he's going, but he was going there in a hurry. Anybody else got anything to report?'

There was a couple of seconds of silence, then a squelch of static.

'This is Lauren. Nothing so far but we've not reached the croft yet.'

Kennedy's voice was next. 'Nothing new on the chat app. Guess that's a good thing.'

Jen waited through a few more seconds of silence before she spoke again by way of a prompt. 'Michelle? Helena? Come in? Anything to report?'

There was still silence.

'Michelle? Helena, come in?'

Beattie sent Jen a concerned look at the lack of response.

'Don't worry about it,' Jen said. 'There's plenty of reasons they might not be responding: out of range, dead battery. Could be anything.'

But it was the unspoken reasons that remained at the forefront of Jen's mind. While she didn't know who this was about, she didn't know who was in the greatest danger.

Her mind was pulled back to what she had come to think of as the haunted playlist: the same songs played over and over, with intentional significance, but for whom? One seemed unmistakably directed at her, but even as she thought of why, she remembered that she wasn't the only woman present whose husband had disappeared never to be seen again. There was that Manic Street Preachers song which made her question whether the choices were by way of accusation or mere cruelty. 'Celebrity Skin', for instance, was clearly goading Michelle over her sex tape. She could only speculate as to the significance or intended targets of others, but suspected the Reaper knew things about all of them.

With that thought, it was as though two more of the songs suddenly revealed themselves.

'Drive' by the Cars.

'Crash' by the Primitives.

Perhaps that car accident of Beattie's wasn't as simple as it had appeared. The guy was found to be coked out of his tree and blind drunk, but maybe his family couldn't accept the official verdict. Beattie of all people should be familiar with that.

Jen knew she could go crazy thinking this way. It was as though her instinctive mistrust had spiralled her towards this ultimate moment of suspecting absolutely everybody, seeing even her closest friends as secretive and duplicitous, every one of them a possible threat.

Nonetheless, if there was one thing life had taught her, it was that just because you're paranoid doesn't mean someone isn't out to get you. It takes a long time to get over having a brick flung through your living-room window. It terrified Jen in a primal and fundamental way, reducing her to tears as she crouched on the carpet, throwing protective arms around Calum.

It was also the first time she glimpsed the possibility of a way out.

The moment of impact had felt strangely muted. Perhaps it was a subconscious alert response to the sound of a car pulling up at speed outside and the subsequent rapid thump of feet; a flash before the thunder that signalled danger and caused her to ready herself. Or maybe it was simply that she had been waiting for that brick to come through the window for a very long time.

After the unthinkable has befallen you once, you get that bit less astonished when another terrible thing happens, but that doesn't mean you aren't scared by it. The incident merely served to underline that Jason himself was no longer the only danger he had exposed her to. The world he was involved with had reached into her home, serving a warning to him by threatening his family.

She already knew how deep he was in. She had found drugs in the house and stashes of banknotes in thick rolls. She could picture him rolling them too, even if they had originally come as flat stacks. It was a running joke in Jason's family that he wanted to be a cop because he grew up fantasising about *Miami Vice*. It was truer than they realised, except what they got wrong was assuming that Jason wanted to be Crockett or Tubbs. It was the glamorous bad-boy villain lifestyle that he aspired to: money, drugs, sex and not a little danger.

She could literally smell the other women on him, and as for the drugs, he wasn't just selling. At times he was doing so much coke she was half hoping a heart attack would rescue her.

It was amazing how much she could compartmentalise her life. Getting the kids ready for school, going to work, going to the supermarket, cooking the dinner. She could retreat into the normality of it. She could tell herself that her life was mostly okay. She had a nice house, nice cars, expensive holidays. But when she got home to that nice house, she knew who would be coming through the door later, and she had no idea which version she was going to face.

For years after he disappeared, there were rumours of Jason having been spotted in various places abroad – Spain, the Balearics, Florida, even Australia – usually by someone who knew someone who saw something while on holiday. Jason had done a runner from Glasgow gangsters, they would speculate, and had stolen that money so he could create a new identity, start a new life. This would then be disputed by people saying there was no way he would leave his family behind.

They really didn't know Jason at all.

Not that Jen was under constant assault; not physically, anyway. But that was what people wouldn't understand: Jason got his way without making direct threats, because the threat was always there, in her mind. She had lived through ten thousand imagined altercations. Imagined scoldings. Imagined beatings. Coercive control is about what *might* happen.

The kids were afraid of him too. They could sense the energy coming off him sometimes, and knew to stay clear. Jason tried to keep the way he treated Jen hidden from them, but sometimes he was too coked up to be as discreet as he intended. And maybe he didn't always try that hard. Jen suspected he *liked* them being afraid of him.

That was another thing his family got wrong. They thought he joined the police because of the *Miami Vice* fantasy, but in fact Jason joined the police because he liked being in a position to push people around.

It crushed her to think of what the kids might have witnessed, but it hurt more when she learned how Jason dealt with that. Calum once told her what his father had said to him after he saw something he wasn't supposed to. 'Sometimes you're naughty, aren't you? And that makes Daddy angry. Sometimes Ailsa can be naughty too. But Mummy is the naughtiest. You mustn't tell anybody, though, because if the police find out how naughty Mummy has been, they'll take her away to jail.'

'But you're in the police, Daddy,' Calum had argued.

'Yes. That's why I'm trying to help her behave and not telling on her. But I'd get in trouble too if they found out.'

Back in her teens, when Jen heard stories of domestic abuse, she always thought the same thing: why didn't she just leave him? In Jen's case, it was a mixture of hope and shame that made her a traitor to herself. Shame because she didn't want anybody to find out; she wished she could even hide it from herself. Hope because she was already too invested, and she didn't want to throw it all away: this marriage, this family. That was why she believed his remorse, telling her it was something they could work on together. Asking her to help him deal with his overreactions, a subtle way of pushing the responsibility for his behaviour onto her.

Nonetheless, there were still moments of clarity. Moments when she understood the gravity of her situation, when she remembered that she did not deserve this.

In the aftermath of one of his explosions, she somehow found the courage to make a stand. She did not speak then, but chose her moment carefully. She waited until a couple of days after, when he was in the solicitous, remorseful stage.

'This can't go on,' she told him. 'Me being afraid of you.'

'I know, and I'm sorry,' he replied, eyes wide, nodding gently with sincerity. 'You deserve better. And I will do better. From here on—'

'No, listen to me,' she interrupted. 'I won't live like this. If you ever raise your hand to me again, I will leave you, and I will take the kids. But more than that, I'll tell everybody why.'

She was trembling as she said it, fighting back her tears but determined to get the words out. Desperate to make him believe she was serious.

Unfortunately, he did. His response was calm, collected and utterly sincere.

'If you take the kids away from me, I'll kill them.'

He wasn't coked up. He wasn't in a rage. She couldn't put it down to extremes of emotion or loss of control. He was absolutely in control, which was what terrified her.

'I'll kill them, and I'll make it look like you did it. That you went psychotic. I know how to stage it. I know how they investigate these things. You'll go to prison. You'll spend the rest of your days living with what you lost, and I'll move on.'

His voice was quiet, measured, coming from somewhere deep inside. It was the way Jason spoke on the rare occasions when he was telling the truth.

Kennedy

Kennedy's hands were trembling as she worked the keyboard. She held one up and examined it, trying to keep it steady, as though that would somehow convince her she wasn't as anxious as she felt. As if it could prevent her from contemplating just how badly this could end. It didn't work. Her fingers were shaking like she had the DTs, and her stomach was in knots.

She recalled the night before her first and only junior tour semi-final, the anxiety that had kept her from sleep, contributing to the sluggishness instrumental in her straight-sets defeat. She recalled also a final approach to Edinburgh Airport during a storm, stifled yelps and whimpers around her, the sight of white knuckles on seated cabin crew as they gripped their armrests.

Neither of those things came close to how she was feeling now.

She shuffled on the sofa, restive with the weight and stiffness of the ankle support on her left leg. The brace was removable, which was tempting while she wasn't going anywhere, but who could say when she might need to be on her feet? And besides, not going anywhere was more of a discomfort than the brace.

She knew there had been a couple of envious glances from those about to set off into the twilight while she stayed here, but for Kennedy, waiting was the hardest job. She wasn't someone who could be at ease relying on other people to help get her a result. It was complete anathema to her, in fact. That was why she had never been the greatest doubles partner. Just ask Kat Boniface.

Kennedy was good at being alone. Boarding schools, tennis camps, tennis tournaments, junior tour. She learned to pack light, emotionally: to never travel without a disposable version of herself, one she could quickly discard and leave behind when she had to move on.

She always told herself that was the way she liked it. She couldn't say she was liking it right now.

She returned her trembling fingers to the laptop, but had barely managed a keystroke when she was shaken by a thump from somewhere above. It was followed less than a second later by another, then several more at decreasing intervals. She realised it was just the plumbing, but the flight reflex of that first moment triggered a further lurching sensation, as it struck her that she had forgotten to ask Lauren for the keys.

There had been a lot going on at the time, but still, how could she have been so stupid? She couldn't remember if all the outside doors had deadlatches, the kind that locked automatically. She was pretty sure the front one did, but there were others. Including a back door exiting from the kitchen.

It wasn't an enticing prospect, but she decided to go there first, get that over with. At least there was nobody in there she needed to be afraid of.

She pulled herself to her feet, slowly and reluctantly at first, then jerking sharply upright in response to her radio.

'This is Jen. We've just seen a guy in a ski mask on a quad bike, heading north. Not sure where he's going, but he was going there in a hurry. Anybody else got anything to report?'

'This is Lauren. Nothing so far but we've not reached the croft yet.'

Startlement aside, Kennedy was grateful to hear their voices. She reached for the radio. 'Nothing new on the chat app. Guess that's a good thing.'

She stepped out into the hallway. With the music stopped, there was an unsettling sense of stillness about it. The place was dripping luxury but the décor was no mitigation against her dread. It might as well have been abandoned and derelict. Anywhere feels creepy when you're alone and you know there's a killer out there.

It wasn't just the house that was creeping her out. It was the whole island. She couldn't stop the scenarios playing in her head. If someone ruthless and determined enough wanted to kill all of them, this was the perfect place. Their bodies could be buried in any number of hidden locations, or even dumped at sea. There would be no witnesses, no evidence, no clues left for anybody to find. She tried and failed to stop herself wondering: if her fears were founded, given her role here, would she die first or last?

It was not what she needed on her mind as she entered the kitchen. She trod carefully, trying not to step in the blood. The smell caught in her throat, causing her to picture more bodies with their throats cut and rolled into shallow graves.

She passed through the utility area with its Belfast sink, washing machines and pantry, all the way to the back door. She saw that the lock was disabled, the housing unscrewed from the doorframe.

There was no refuge to be had here, no security. She would be no safer than anyone else.

Beattie

Beattie watched Jen slip the radio back into a zipped pocket, an overture to resuming their descent. The appearance of the quad bike had at least allowed her a breather. Prior to that, Jen had been setting a punishing pace, and Beattie had no doubt who the punishment was intended for.

Whether they wanted to move as fast again was up for debate.

Beattie remained troubled by the image of that ski mask. She took some comfort in the logic that it meant he didn't have the direst plans for witnesses, but she was struck by a different implication. What if he wasn't worried about being identified later, but about being identified now?

The Reaper's message stated that he was seeking retribution. That meant all of this had to be about a grudge between two people who had crossed swords in the past. And suddenly Beattie understood who both of them were.

If Jen had seemed strangely calm over a brick being chucked through her family's front window, then that reaction resembled a conniption fit compared to how sanguine she seemed when her husband went missing.

Beattie had been cleaning the oven when Jen rang. She had never been able to do it since without remembering that moment.

'I'm phoning to let you know that Jason has been reported missing. The police are looking into it.'

The passivity of it. Not 'I don't know where he is and I'm worried sick', but 'has been reported missing'. Beattie would have been justified in asking whether Jen had even been the one who made the report.

She gave few details and seemed in a hurry to get off the phone.

Beattie dropped everything and drove to Jen and Jason's house, where she found the family gone. Jen hadn't even told her that. The house wasn't empty, though. It was crawling with police. It looked like they were taking the place apart, which struck her as worryingly excessive for a missing persons inquiry, even when it was a fellow officer.

Beattie tracked Jen down at her parents' place, and it did feel like she was tracking her down. When she got to Mr and Mrs Dunne's house in Hamilton, she expected to find Jen in bits, as Beattie would have been. As Beattie *was*, in fact. Nerves frayed, jumping at the telephone, starting at the sound of every car door outside.

Jen was a little on edge for sure. She looked like she hadn't slept much, and she seemed extra fussy and protective around the kids. But Beattie would have expected to see more anxiety in the face of someone whose dog was missing.

Beattie had to coax out of her the time Jason was reported missing and how long he might have been missing for. That was when Jen told her that by that point Jason hadn't been seen for at least forty-eight hours.

'Why did you wait?' she had asked in dismay. 'Aren't the first twenty-four hours crucial?'

'That's just shite they say on the telly,' Jen replied.

'Was he out on a shift? When did you expect him home?'

'He *was* home. We were supposed to be going out for dinner. We had a table booked. Then he checked his phone and suddenly he left. I assumed it was work but he didn't say.'

'But he'd have told you if he wasn't going to be home all night, surely.'

Jen had laughed at that. Actually laughed, dry and bitter.

'So when did you last try calling him?' Beattie asked.

'I didn't. Jason doesn't like being checked up on.'

'And he wasn't at work, then?'

'Depends what you call work,' Jen replied, but she refused to be drawn on what she meant by that.

In such a horrible situation, it was reasonable to assume that the longer they went without positive news, the worse the outcome was likely to be.

A few days later, Jen came to Beattie's mum's house to tell them that the police had found Jason's car. It was discovered in a field off a single-track road between Blantyre and Uddingston, burned out.

It seemed a solicitous touch, visiting to deliver the news in person, as the implications were clearly bleak. But it felt as though Jen was concerned for Beattie and her mum rather than herself; as though she felt bad for them but had no personal stake in it.

Jen didn't stay for long. She wouldn't even accept a cup of tea. She said she had to get back for the kids.

Beattie followed her out to her car and spoke to her on the driveway, out of earshot of her mum. 'Jesus God, Jen, I know we all deal with these things in different ways, but he's been gone almost a week now. You're acting like he's nipped out for a pint and you're not bothered if he never comes back.'

Jen spun on her heel. 'If I don't seem on tenterhooks it's

because I've been waiting for something like this to happen for a while. It hasn't come out of the blue. Jason is not the person that you think, Beattie. You've never let yourself see it, but you'll find out soon enough.'

There was an odd combination of anger and apology in Jen's expression, as though she was sorry to have to break this to her but annoyed that Beattie hadn't already cottoned on.

'What are you talking about?'

'There's money missing from the club's accounts. A lot of money. That's the only part of it I can disclose because the rest is a police matter.'

'Jason *is* the police,' Beattie replied. It sounded feeble in her own mouth.

Jen opened the car door but didn't climb in quite yet. 'Remember when our window got put in?' she asked. 'When Jason said he was getting too close to someone he was investigating? I think he spoke a bit more truth there than he intended. That's all I'm prepared to say.'

Then she drove off, leaving Beattie to deal with a world that was about to crumble all around her, the coming nightmare of Jason being torn apart piece by piece when he wasn't there to defend himself.

There were accusations that he had been involved with drug dealers, talk of conspiring with other corrupt officers. Beattie just could not believe it, and yet the image of the police searching his family home lingered in her mind.

Jen wasn't lying about money going missing. The Fraud Squad combed through the nightclub's finances and found that almost £60,000 had been siphoned off over a period of months, but they were unable to trace how or where. They concluded that it had been Jason, but Beattie reckoned it was more likely to have been Jen or her father pulling some kind of tax or money-laundering scam, with Jason the scapegoat.

Not long after that, Jen's dad sold the nightclub. He and Jen's mum moved to Tenerife, where he had bought a bar.

Around the same time, Jen set up her own business.

Nobody was ever prosecuted in relation to these matters. According to Jen, the police were happy for it all to quietly go away, but it struck Beattie that it also suited Jen for the whole matter to be buried. She said she didn't want her kids reading about what their father had done, which Beattie could understand, but it always troubled her that Jen was determined never to give him the benefit of the doubt.

Then a few months ago a police corruption scandal going back more than a decade finally made it to trial. Darren Kyle, a former colleague of Jason's, had obviously cut a plea deal to spill his guts. Beattie remembered hearing the name, and faintly recalled meeting him a couple of times: once when she bumped into Jason in town, and the second time after Jason went missing. He had been at the house, directing the search.

Kyle told the court how he and Jason had been 'investigating the movement of high-value goods as a means of circumventing the Proceeds of Crime Act'. At the time, high-end designer watches were used by Glasgow drug lords as a way of storing wealth, as they could change hands without a paper trail. Kyle said that an informant tipped him and Jason off that a quantity of such watches was about to be sold by Sammy Finnegan, a major drug dealer who had a sudden need for cash. Finnegan had deputised a fixer to handle the exchange, a man by the name of Ronnie Bryceland. The haul was valued at close to £300,000.

Kyle said that he thought they were tailing the fixer so that they could interrupt the handover and confiscate the goods. He claimed that, instead, Jason had murdered Bryceland and drawn Kyle into a conspiracy to disappear the body so that it would be assumed the fixer had run off with the watches. Kyle told the court that Jason bought his cooperation with the offer of an even split. Instead, Jason had disappeared, and the cache of watches was never found.

That, Beattie understood, was why they had been tearing the house apart.

Again, here was someone who found it convenient to blame Jason when he wasn't there to give his side of the story. She thought it more likely the other way around: that Kyle had murdered the fixer and then murdered Jason, tearing his house apart as a further act of misdirection.

Then she understood what had been in front of her the whole time. She refused to see it at first, because of what it required her to accept about her brother. But once she allowed herself to admit that Jason was not the person she always believed, she was able to see that Jen was something far worse than she ever feared.

By whatever means they had come into Jason's possession, Jen must have found the watches in their house and recognised them as her ticket to a different life. The whole point was that they were easily moved, in cash transactions that were all but untraceable. And nobody would come looking for them if everyone thought her husband had disappeared with the lot.

That was why Jen had been slightly on edge in the aftermath, yet not remotely worried about Jason.

She had murdered him.

There had been times down the years when Beattie entertained the notion that Jen had killed Jason for the insurance or a police widow's pension. She had never been able to quite make herself believe it, though. For one thing, there would need to have been a body, and probably a patsy too. And though they said the most ruthless con artists ran a long game, seven years was a hell of a wait for a payout.

It had never quite added up, never quite felt right. But this, this made perfect sense of everything. Jen had murdered Jason, hidden his body and set fire to his car to cover up the evidence. Then her parents suddenly had the funds to buy themselves a nice bar in Tenerife, while Jen had the start-up capital she needed for her bakery.

And a great success she had made of it too. She had done a deal last year to sell the company, though she would still be in charge. It was in the papers, and not just the business section. Beattie had seen Jen's photograph in the *Daily Record*, holding a box of her products in each hand. The headline read: 'Muffin succeeds like success'.

It all sounded so sweet and innocent, like a fantasy from a Jenny Colgan novel. But Beattie had deduced that the whole thing had been built on her brother's blood and the proceeds from a Glasgow gangster's drug empire.

That was why she knew what was really happening on this island tonight. Beattie was not the only one who had seen the newspapers and worked out where Jen's seed money must have come from.

The Reaper was Sammy Finnegan, and he wanted his watches back. With interest.

Lauren

Lauren had thought she could somehow get away with this. She could come up with a reason why she was the only one who could or should go inside the cottage. Maybe tell her appointed companion she had to stay outside and keep lookout in case anyone was approaching. But that had all felt more plausible as they stood in the drawing room and discussed hypotheticals. It was a different story out here on the hillside looking down on the croft itself, not knowing what might be waiting inside.

The cottage was tiny from up here, but its very sight troubled her, less as a threat than an accusation.

'Someone lives there?' Nicolette asked.

Lauren felt herself grimace even as she nodded. 'Someone with a landline,' she admitted. 'But it's delicate. My relationship with this woman is strained to say the least.'

Nicolette looked like she was trying to be understanding, but she had a right to ask questions. Lauren had been correct in anticipating it would be easier to field them from just one person.

'Then why not send somebody else? She's not going to turn us away in an emergency.'

'First of all, I wouldn't make any assumptions on that score. But mainly it was because I didn't want to have to share this with everybody. It's my mess and I ought to be the one who cleans it up, but not in public, you know?'

'You're going to need to give me more than that,' Nicolette said.

They resumed their progress, walking as briskly as they dared. Given the gradient and the underfoot conditions, too much momentum in certain places could have them making a far swifter descent than intended, and Lauren wanted both her legs working at the bottom of it.

'That map I took from the wall. It's actually a recent print, a replica. The original is in some archival depository. Clachan Gael means White Stones. The island was named for the pebble beaches here. But what it says on the map is altogether less marketable.'

'How so?'

'Claiggean Geal means White Skulls.'

Nicolette broke her stride. People tended to have that reaction. Lauren certainly had.

'What's that got to do with whoever is in the cottage?' Nicolette asked, her tone suggesting she wasn't sure she wanted to know.

Lauren glanced down again. They were a long way from cover, so she could still see the croft. There were no lights on, but that didn't mean nobody was home.

'I'll give you the quick version. I was in and out of care from the age of eleven. My mum was a bit of a shambles. She had what they'd now politely call addiction and mental-health issues. She couldn't hold down a job for any length of time, and I know she loved me but . . . Anyway, I kept getting taken into care because of her drinking, and then permanently because she couldn't provide a safe home environment. Or any home at all.'

Lauren saw glimpses like she was flipping through a scrapbook, the yellowing Polaroids of the mind. Bittersweet memories, images only of her mum in happy times, because you only got the camera out for happy times.

'When I was eleven, we were evicted from this really scuzzy flat. The whole tenement should have been condemned. A death trap in terms of the wiring, miserable with damp, and the heating barely worked even when Mum had paid the bill. Mum got behind with the rent, and let's just say the landlord showed no mercy. I say landlord, but technically landlady, who was represented by this factor-cum-rent collector.'

Lauren could still picture the man: barrel-chested, awkward in his gait, reeking of cigarettes and stale beer. He was self-important yet faintly ridiculous, but nobody would have dared laugh at him.

'He liked to tell us how his employers, the McPhee family, had owned land and property for centuries. And he liked to tell us about the Highland Clearances, how they had brutally evicted tenants because sheep were more profitable. On one particular island, the McPhees sent in their own private militia, and the brutality of what they did there was intended as an example. They ensured word got around. The local people started referring to the island as Claiggean Geal, and it meant that the tenants in other places went meekly when their time—'

Lauren was interrupted mid-flow by her radio bursting into life.

'This is Jen. We've just seen a guy in a ski mask on a quad bike, heading north. Not sure where he's going, but he was going there in a hurry. Anybody else got anything to report?'

'This is Lauren,' she replied, scanning the view for the quad bike. One more thing to be worrying about. 'Nothing so far but we've not reached the croft yet.'

She listened to the ensuing exchange. Nobody had any news

of Samira, and in the case of Michelle and Helena, there was no news at all.

They came to a steep section of the path, a scattering of loose scree calling for careful steps. Lauren found herself losing control, breaking into a run to regain her balance but fearful she wouldn't be able to stop herself at the bottom where the path turned. Fortunately, Nicolette was alert to it, planting a strong back foot and grabbing Lauren with firm hands.

'Thank you,' she said.

Nicolette looked oddly embarrassed by her gratitude. 'It's nothing. I'd hate to miss the end of the story.'

There was something unconvincing about the sentiment, like she was using it to cover something else, but Lauren couldn't dwell on what that might be.

Picking her steps more cautiously, she returned to what she had been saying. 'Fast forward twenty-five years or so and I'm in a very different position. Clachan Geal comes on the market and the seller is none other than Moira McPhee, the landlady who evicted us when I was eleven. She had been a widow forty years, apparently, but not before having a son, Gordon. He was a spoiled arsehole who never learned from his own mistakes, and his business dealings just about bankrupted the old cow. By the time she was selling the ancestral home, it was because she was desperate. Gordon had run up huge debts and the place was dilapidated.

'To be clear, I didn't seek the place out to buy it because of who owned it. But when I found out, it felt like karma. She had no option but to sell, and I showed as much mercy as she showed my mother. I pulled every tactic from my repertoire to drive the price down. I think it barely covered the debts.'

Nicolette glanced towards the foot of the hill again. The croft was still just about visible, though they were getting closer to the trees.

'And that's who lives in the cottage?'

'The son wanted her to sell that too and put her in a home. I offered to buy it but she's a stubborn old witch. She said she had lived on this island her whole life and she wasn't leaving until she was carried off. That was fine by me. I wasn't her landlady, but I was the queen of the castle, formerly *her* castle, and she was just a pauper on my land.'

Nicolette's face took on a dark expression, anticipating where this was going. 'She knows, doesn't she? You told her.'

'I was still angry over what happened to my mother, what happened to me. So once the contracts were signed and she couldn't back out, yes. I told her who I was and what she had done to me.'

'How did she take it?'

'She wasn't remotely shamed or repentant, and I felt like I'd demeaned myself. She looked at me like she was still better than me. She's fucking horrible, believe me. She's from centuries of horrible.'

'What age is she?'

Lauren took a moment. She knew how this sounded. Nicolette didn't understand, couldn't understand.

'She's in her eighties. But still fully compos mentis and capable of looking after herself, believe me. She has deliveries coming regularly from the mainland. Probably has a chest freezer you could keep a whole cow in too. She could last out the zombie apocalypse here, so don't be worrying about her.'

'But she's a woman in her eighties, living alone in an old cottage on the edge of nowhere. What about the winters?'

'It's her choice to live here. And she didn't care too much

what the winters did to those of us living in freezing, damp flats.' As she spoke, Lauren could hear her own bitterness. These were things she had never said aloud to anybody.

'Do you look in on her at least?' Nicolette asked. It sounded like she was trying to keep a tone of accusation from her voice.

'I've walked past a few times, and I know she's seen me, but I didn't knock on the door. I couldn't bring myself to speak to her. We're not talking about some adorable old granny here. Moira McPhee is—'

Lauren silenced herself as she noticed a buzzing, just becoming audible over the white noise of the breeze. It took a costly moment to recognise what it was, but Nicolette was ahead of her.

'The quad bike,' she said.

Lauren looked north to where the coastal track disappeared around the headland. She couldn't see anything yet, but the sound was getting closer.

'Run.'

They hastened towards the cover of the bushes that would screen them from below. Lauren abandoned the more gently sloping path and scrambled straight down the slope, gravity and momentum pushing her too fast for her feet to control. She felt her left foot kick her right ankle and she tumbled painfully, bounding and rolling briefly before coming to an abrupt stop.

The fall was a mercy in that, with Nicolette crouching to help her, they were both low to the ground when the quad bike came into view, ridden by a man in a black ski mask.

They both remained perfectly still, eyes fixed upon him for any indication that he had noticed them.

He's just on patrol, Lauren told herself. It looked like he was doing a perimeter check of the whole island, but that wasn't good news either. What had sent him out? Who was he looking for? And who might he have already found?

She had felt something tear around her thigh as she came to a halt. She allowed herself the briefest glimpse, taking her eyes fleetingly from the rider. To her relief it was only the material of her jeans, though there was a cut. It wasn't deep but it was surrounded by angry abrasions, and it was going to sting.

The rider slowed and turned, directing his bike along the narrower path leading to the cottage. Neither of them dared breathe as he got off the vehicle, approached the door and disappeared inside.

'Oh Christ,' Nicolette said, her voice a dry whisper. 'If she's in there . . .'

But Lauren's fear was reserved for another possibility, one that should have been obvious all along.

Moira McPhee was the Reaper.

Jen

The sound of the quad bike was still fresh in her memory as Jen crested the hill, the sun getting ever lower towards the water. The golf club in her hand felt like a pointless burden. What kind of defence would it offer against a man who could take down the chef without his victim emitting so much as a cry?

Having reached the top, she stopped and looked at her phone. Despite Lauren's suggestion that this was the most likely place, the device had been stubbornly refusing to show any signal. Then her heart fluttered as she noticed a flicker at the icon, but it was just the screen refreshing itself as it went from zero bars to the 'no network' symbol.

She wondered if maybe it was only her network that didn't have coverage.

'You got anything?' she asked.

Beattie was already looking at her phone. She frowned. 'No network.'

It had been agreed that, despite the Reaper's warning, if Jen got the chance she should call the police, but her worry was how long any signal would stay connected. What if there wasn't time to convey the full nature of the threat, the fact that there was a hostage situation and therefore a need for stealth and caution?

So far it was proving moot anyway. She would keep checking but she wasn't holding out much hope. Lauren had probably said it simply because it was worth knowing, rather than something to realistically pin any plans on.

It mattered little. Jen had known that a phone call to the emergency services was never going to be the solution to this. Nobody had ridden to Jen's rescue before, so she knew that when you recognise the reality of your predicament, you don't waste time kidding yourself.

A couple of months after Jason went missing, Jen got a visitor at the club. Normally she would have clocked what he was right away. Being in the licensed trade, she had encountered a few of his kind, usually guys in expensive suits that served only to make them look like they were due in court.

This one was nothing like that, though. His clothes were tailored, the cut and the material veering somewhere between old-fashioned and timeless. There was something almost effete about him, and in some other context she might have thought he was an art critic or a theatre director. But Jen didn't know him, and her instincts told her what was beneath the cloth, regardless of the aesthetic.

'My name is Sam,' he said. 'Sam Finnegan. I'm an associate of your husband's. I was sorry to learn that he's gone missing. I can't imagine how distressing that must be for you.'

He was softly spoken, his diction precise. He was polite and deferential, charming even. But Jason could be all those things too.

'How is it that you know Jason?' she had asked. She was tempted to add, 'Was he investigating you?' but she knew it would serve her best to be equally polite and diplomatic.

He ignored the question anyway. 'I'm sure the police are doing their best, but I was wondering if they had all the information they might need.'

'Is there something you know that you would prefer to tell me than tell them?' she asked.

'No. But the reason I'm here is to ask you the same question.'

'What do you mean?'

'There are things a husband might tell his wife that he wouldn't tell anybody else. Reasons why a man might decide to make himself scarce. Reasons that a wife might understand.'

'Why are you so keen to find him? Or are you just concerned about his welfare?'

'Naturally. Yours too. I'm also concerned about the welfare of a chap named Ronnie Bryceland, another associate of mine. See, he's disappeared as well, along with a whole load of merchandise.'

'Are we talking about . . . ?' Jen ran a finger under her nose.

'Timepieces,' corrected Finnegan. 'By Audemars Piguet, if that means anything to you.'

He said this neutrally, as though inviting her to infer no judgement on his part if it did not.

'I know they don't sell many in Argos,' she replied.

'Then you'll understand my concern. The thing is, Ronnie was a loyal and trustworthy individual. He knew what side his bread was buttered. So I'm finding it difficult to believe he would abscond with articles belonging to someone else.'

He gazed deep into Jen, a man used to staring down a liar. She felt something inside her stiffen.

'You didn't happen to see anything like that around the house prior to your husband's wee impromptu vanish?'

Jen stared back, holding his eye for a long time before she answered.

'I'll tell you two things, Mr Finnegan, and then I'll tell you

199

to leave. Number one, Jason put my family in danger, and if I never see him again I won't be sorry. He trusted me with nothing, and I am only beginning to understand how much he was keeping from me, which brings me to number two. He quietly leeched sixty grand out of this place before he disappeared, and my father's retirement plans are all on hold because of him. So, if you are impatient to recover what Jason owes you, then get in the queue.'

Finnegan had left a card bearing the details of an art dealership on Great Western Road. He had left with good grace, but Jen read that as part of his image. Her husband wasn't the only one projecting a different persona to the watching world.

Jason had always been adept at keeping people guessing. It was how he managed to play so many angles. And once he was gone, nobody knew what to think. There were those in the police who thought he had been murdered by one of his underworld connections, others thinking he had been killed by someone in the police because he knew too much about *their* underworld connections. Then there were those, like Finnegan, who believed he had faked his own disappearance. Even that threw up confusion about which way around it worked. Some assumed Jason had gone on the run because he stole the watches, aware Finnegan had seen through his attempt to pin it on Bryceland. Others thought he had already decided to disappear, and swiped the watches to finance going on the run. There were even rumours that Bryceland had indeed made off with the watches, and that he had killed Jason to provide cover for his own disappearance.

They were all wrong.

Michelle

There was a dip ahead, a V-shaped trench far wider and deeper than the undulations between the rows of pines. Michelle heard it before she got close enough to see the stream at the bottom. The pine forest might only have been planted in the eighties, but this was a reminder that they were in a very old place.

She couldn't stop picturing the chef. She had been sure he was still breathing, even as he bled out. In a way that was worse than if he had been hours cold. It meant she had been there at the moment death took him. It made her feel that death was close by, had laid eyes upon her.

Michelle wondered how big a story it would be if she died here tonight. A top item worldwide. Trending for days. She'd be bigger than Adele for a while after that. She just wouldn't be around to enjoy it.

As she stepped carefully across the water, Michelle's eye was drawn once again to a flash of movement, a black shape disappearing between the trees.

'Did you see that?' she asked.

'No. See what?'

'Something moved. Definitely. Something big.'

'Another fox?'

'Bigger than that. Darker too.'

'Maybe there's deer. Could be Lauren offers hunting to some of the corporate wankers.'

Helena sounded like she was casting about for a preferable explanation rather than one she actually gave any credence. She was speaking quite loudly too. If there was someone flanking them, she wanted him to know exactly where they were, and how little threat they posed.

For the same reason, Michelle was not about to ask her to keep her voice down.

Despite her rebuffing any attempt at casual conversation, and despite her air of simmering resentment, Michelle was glad it was Helena she was with. Kennedy had been right about that much. Michelle felt, while obviously far from safe, at least safer than she would have with anybody else – except perhaps Jen. Maybe even including Jen. They had always been close, always been warm, but she had never known what it was to rely on Jen like she had once relied on Helena.

In Michelle's first year at Strathclyde, at the start of her abandoned law degree, it felt like everyone was starting a band. She auditioned for a couple of them, but they just didn't click. It didn't feel right, and she knew the problem was her. Then in second year she ran into Helena again. They had kind of lost touch for a couple of years. Michelle's family had had to move away, and then she had got her head down and made sure she got the Highers she needed.

They bumped into each other in Central Station. It turned out Helena was at the Royal Scottish Academy of Music and Drama. They hung out together for less than a fortnight before deciding to start a band.

It was completely different once Helena was part of the set-up.

Michelle was completely different. When she had tried out with other people, she was nervous and self-conscious, retreating into herself when she should have been leaving it all out there. When she jammed with Helena, though, she felt safe because part of her was still playing at pop stars in her bedroom. And as long as you were only playing, you were having fun. Nothing bad could happen.

Their band was called Echo Shells, a combination of both their names. Helena's surname was Eckhart, so she got nick-named Ecko at school. It was what they had always said they would call a band if they formed one, invoking the effect when you put a big seashell to your ear. They had both loved that when the teacher showed them it, how you could hear the sound of the sea, even as you sat in a classroom in Lanarkshire.

No matter what Helena had chosen to believe, the renaming was an accident. They rehearsed as Echo Shells and played a few gigs under that name in bars and student venues in Glasgow and Edinburgh. Helena had recruited a girl she knew from the Academy to play bass, a cellist named Daisy Wu. She wore the guitar down almost at her knees, presenting an air of nonchalant carelessness that utterly belied her precise musicianship.

The line-up was completed by a drummer calling herself Madeleine Smith, who had answered an ad Michelle left on a noticeboard in a music shop. Her real name was Jane Smith, but she chose Madeleine as an alias, after the notorious Glasgow poisoner. She had as many tattoos as the average docker and a filthier mouth to go with them. Everybody was terrified of her. She mostly listened to hardcore, but she had absolutely no problem playing whatever she was told. Perhaps for that reason more than most, she was still Michelle's drummer to this day.

There was a showcase night at the Garage, a battle of the

bands thing that had been set up as a kind of fuck-you to *Pop Idol*. There was a cash prize, but the main incentive was that there were going to be A&R people there.

Helena always believed it was an ego thing, a power play. She could never accept that it was just an accident, an administrative error. Michelle wasn't even the one who screwed up. She had to submit a form along with their demo CD. It asked for the name of the band, the names of the members, and the name of their representation, which was effectively just her. Whoever was processing it must have keyed one entry into the wrong field.

When it came to their slot, the host introduced them as Cassidy. He was reading off a print-out, but it wasn't only his notes that contained the mistake. The tech people had got the same sheet, so that was also the name projected onto a huge screen behind them on stage.

Michelle remembered mumbling 'We're actually Echo Shells' into the mic, but Madeleine was already clicking her sticks for the count-in.

By the end of their three-song set, a section of the audience was chanting 'Cassidy, Cassidy, Cassidy!' looking for an encore.

Some insipid bunch of Libertines-wannabes won the vote, but only because they had papered the house. They got the money, but it was Cassidy who walked out of there with everybody talking about them. That included the A&R men, one of whom was offering a record deal on the spot. At that point, a woman named Mairi Lafferty had intervened, swooping in from nowhere and telling them not to sign anything.

'This chancer is small-time,' she told them quietly. 'Don't be in a hurry. A wee bit of finesse and you'll have the major labels forming an orderly queue.'

It turned out she managed the venue. By the end of the night, she was managing the band too.

When Michelle corrected her about the name - and it *was* Michelle who corrected her about the name – Mairi said: 'I prefer Cassidy.'

If Helena had a problem with that, she kept her mouth shut at the time, perhaps because Mairi was as impressive as she was convincing.

Michelle didn't know if it had been gnawing away at Helena ever since, or if it was only after things went sour that she came to believe Michelle had engineered the name change. It wasn't true, but that said, Michelle had never been uncomfortable with people thinking Cassidy primarily referred to her. Time had certainly proven who the real star was.

Nicolette

Nicolette's heart was thumping so hard against her chest that she was sure it must be audible down the hill. She was more scared in this moment than when they had found the chef, because up until this point the threat had been unseen. Now it was rendered in muscle and bone, and it was inside that cottage doing God knows what to God knows who. It wasn't just the old woman who might be in there. Samira could be too.

She glanced across at Lauren. There was an intensity about her as she stared down at the croft, but for all that, she looked even more afraid than Nicolette.

She felt paralysed. As long as he was in there, they couldn't move. But shouldn't they? There were two of them and only one of him. Then she thought of Joaquin, the ripped physique she had been fantasising about. None of that had helped him against a man with a knife.

They should radio, at least: let the others know they had a situation here.

Before she could suggest this, they saw him emerge. He had only been in there for a minute; two at the most. He strode casually back into view, stopping next to the bike and holding something to his face. A radio. Then he climbed on board and rode off, heading south.

Nicolette got to her feet once he was out of sight, brushing grass from her clothes. Another reason to be grateful for the horrible sweatshirt. She was about to return to the path and continue her descent, but sensed reluctance from her companion. Lauren was back on her feet but remaining in place, still staring down at the cottage.

Nicolette noticed that Lauren was bleeding from her thigh. 'Are you okay? Can you walk?'

'It's nothing. I'm fine.' She didn't sound fine.

Nicolette looked at the cottage too. 'He was barely in there any time,' she said. 'Just long enough to check up on something and now he's gone. Samira could be in there, plus a landline. This could be the whole game, set and match.'

Lauren remained unmoving. 'He wasn't checking up on anything,' she said gravely. 'He was checking *in* with someone. With her.'

'Moira McPhee? You're saying you reckon *she's* behind all this?'

'I was in denial. I should have sussed it sooner. I hadn't seen her in a while, and I was starting to wonder why not. I realise now it's because she's been busy.'

Nicolette suspected the old woman loomed so large in Lauren's mind that she had lost perspective. 'I get that she might be a bitter old hag, but wouldn't she be sneaking in to put prawns behind your boiler before she escalated to something like this?'

'You don't know her. As I say, she's still got all her marbles, still got connections, and I'm pretty sure she's still got some money squirrelled away that the idiot son didn't know about.'

'Could it be him, somehow?'

'Gordon's got the brains of a hamster. He's too thick to even know I chiselled the deal. He was grateful for my money. No, this took planning and commitment. This took real hatred.'

Then she said it, her words sending a chill right through Nicolette. 'I've been receiving death threats.'

'From her?'

Lauren sighed. She looked suddenly paler, older. 'To make money in this game, you buy low and sell high, and the best way to buy low is from people who don't have time to wait for a better offer. I make no apologies. You can't blame the buyer when you're forced to sell. But after one of those profile pieces ran in the media, I started getting anonymous messages from someone saying I had ruined his life. He called himself the Punisher, had that skull logo. He said his parents had been forced to sell their home because his father had cancer and his mother had to give up her job to look after him. I got their house for a song and put them in a negative equity situation. The father died, the mother ended up having a stroke.'

Nicolette felt a woozy sensation, as though the hill was growing steeper.

'Christ,' Lauren said. 'I didn't give the guy cancer. I didn't know. How could I?'

'You couldn't,' Nicolette managed, her own voice threatening to break too.

'He said he had joined the army to build a new life and to pay for his mum's care, but then she had died too. Now he was out, and he hadn't forgotten or forgiven. He told me he had the training he needed, and one day he would be coming for me.

'I tried to ignore it, thinking this was just somebody who was angry at how their life had gone and taking it out on me. I told myself that sending death threats is a kind of impotent rage. If

208

he was actually going to do something, he wouldn't be warning me in advance. Then tonight happened.'

'But what has this to do with Moira McPhee?' Nicolette asked, though she was afraid she already knew.

'*One of the messages said: "I know I'm not the only one you've done this to. When you get what's coming to you, understand it's coming from all of us."* It wouldn't have been difficult for him to find out what other property deals I had done, certainly not to find out who I bought this place from. When I saw the guy in the mask walk up to the cottage, I put it all together. He found himself a sponsor, and Moira found herself a trained and willing pair of hands.'

Lauren looked down at the croft once more. 'We can't go in there,' she said. 'We'd be walking into a trap. The old bitch knew I would come here if they cut the phone lines.'

But Nicolette was already trapped. And the hardest part was that to spring Lauren's would be to slam the jaws shut forever on her own.

Maybe there was another way, though.

'If she's in there, she's on her own now. I think we can take her.' She offered an encouraging smile, trying to convey how much she fancied their chances. She just couldn't say why she knew that Moira McPhee wasn't part of this.

'We're not the only ones with walkie-talkies,' Lauren responded. 'If she sees us coming, she'll call him back here.'

'But we have to do something. Samira could be in there.'

'If she is, it's because she's the bait. *I'm* the prey. Don't you get it? Forget all that talk of reparation. These people want to fucking kill me.'

Lauren looked as scared as she was distraught, convinced she had worked out the awful truth. But there was a worse truth yet. A bill becoming due, with Samira's life being held as collateral.

Nicolette knew what sins she could and couldn't live with. What crimes she deserved to pay for.

The time had come. She swallowed, cleared her throat. 'This isn't about you, Lauren,' she said, struggling to keep her voice steady. 'It's not about Moira McPhee and it's not about the death threats you received.'

'How do you figure that?'

'Because I'm the one who sent them.'

Beattie

The descent was another zigzagging path, but this time narrower and the earth looser underfoot. Beattie often found herself moving faster than intended, driven by her own weight under gravity. It felt harder than the climb, not to mention scarier. At least on the way up she could always see what was ahead of her. Now it was difficult to see beyond the bushes, with the path only revealing itself one switchback at a time.

With every treacherous step, she found herself getting angrier at the sight of Jen a few feet ahead. She couldn't hold her tongue any longer.

'How long can you keep this up?' she asked.

'It's all the tennis. Keeps my legs strong.'

'I'm not talking about that. I mean how long can you keep pretending you don't know what's going on here tonight?'

Jen stopped and turned. 'I don't know any better than you what's going on here tonight, so if you have a theory, I am very much open to hearing it.'

Beattie met her eye. 'It's about Jason.'

Jen sighed and turned away again. 'Jesus Christ, Beattie,' she said, resuming her progress. 'To you, everything is about Jason. But allow me to humour you. Do tell me how the hell *this* is about Jason.'

'Jason's colleague, Darren Kyle,' Beattie said. 'I'm sure you followed his trial carefully in case the witness statements contradicted the rubbish you've been peddling down the years.'

'Actually, no, I didn't follow it closely. I've invested a lot of effort in putting all of that behind me and I didn't relish a trip down memory lane. But of what I did hear, precious little came as a surprise.'

'Oh, I'll bet it didn't. Not least regarding the watches. I bet you knew all about those.'

'I did, but only because Sam Finnegan told me about them when he came to intimidate me after Jason went missing. I'll tell you the same as I told him: I never set eyes on any watches. All I know is that they were worth a lot of money, and that they disappeared around the same time as both Jason and Ronnie Bryceland.'

Beattie could only see Jen's back, couldn't look her in the eye to face down her lying. 'It was also about the same time your father bought himself a bar and moved to Tenerife, and you suddenly had all the money you needed to start your new business.'

Jen gave out a dismissive laugh, as bitter as it was patronising. 'My dad sold his nightclub. Did you forget that? *That's* how he paid for the fucking bar, Beattie. And that wasn't the plan: he was going to retire, properly retire to Tenerife, not go there to run another business, and I was going to take over the club. But your beloved and saintly Jason changed all those plans when we found out he had stolen sixty thousand pounds from it.'

'What about the capital for expanding? Where did that suddenly come from? You went from one little shop to opening all over the place.'

'A private investor came along because they liked what I was doing. That's what happens when you run a successful business and nobody's secretly got their hand in the till.'

'Who was this investor?'

'That's confidential.'

'That's convenient.'

Jen stopped and turned once more, just short of another sharp bend. Her face looked flushed, and it wasn't from the effort of the descent.

'What is it you think happened, Beattie? Eh? Why don't you tell me? What is it that you want from me?'

'I want you to tell me the truth about my brother.'

'Believe me, hen, that's the last thing you want. I haven't been hiding the truth from you, Beattie. I've been sparing you from it.' And with that, she walked away again.

Beattie followed a few yards behind, feeling the strain in her thighs as she controlled her speed. She felt her hands tighten around the golf club as the fury continued to rise inside her, fury that had been building for years.

'And do you know what?' Jen called back. 'I'm getting a very strong "she who smelled it dealt it" energy coming off of this. You seem very keen to make out this Reaper business is about me. Maybe that's because you're afraid that it's about you. Is there maybe something you haven't told anybody about your wee accident?'

Beattie's anger now mingled with icy fear as Jen rounded the next hairpin bend. Given her past, Jen had to have connections on both sides of the law. Was she just speculating here, or did she know something?

Beattie felt she needed to say something soon because her silence sounded guilty as hell.

Before she could, Jen stopped again and extended a hand,

palm out. 'Hold on,' she said, her tone different: cautious rather than abrasive.

Beattie's eyes flitted back and forth, searching for a figure in a ski mask, but she soon saw that wasn't the problem.

Lauren had mentioned the danger of landslips on the route she and Nicolette were taking, but there was one in front of them right here. It looked like a section had been quarried out of the hillside, a sheer wall of rock and dried mud that plunged thirty or forty feet. Down below was a bed of more dried mud that looked hard as concrete.

Flanked by grass and scrub, a remnant of the path remained, roughly the width and depth of a large window ledge. Above it, the wall of rock bulged slightly outwards, meaning they couldn't lean against it if they were to try to cross.

Beattie might otherwise have embraced it as a reason to turn back, an excuse not to face whatever might await them at the cave. But in her anger, she saw a different opportunity, one she had been waiting years for.

'We can cross it,' she said. 'We can use the golf clubs for balance. One of us holds the club at the side for the one who's crossing to grip onto.'

Beattie held her club out to demonstrate, showing how it could form a guardrail part of the way across.

'Seriously, you're game for this?' Jen asked dubiously.

'I am if you are. Otherwise we'd have to go all the way back and take the long way round: the route the quad bike was on.'

Jen leaned closer, looking again at the ledge and at what lay beneath. As she did so, Beattie took out her phone and held it up as though checking one more time for a signal. Her thumb was busy doing something else: setting it to record.

'I'll go first, then,' Jen said. Like Beattie knew she would.

Beattie held out the club once more, gripping it by the handle and extending the head a couple of feet out above the drop. Jen inched into position, her back to the wall, hands gripping the shaft. She shifted her balance tentatively, taking an increasing weight on her left heel before fully lifting her right from the solid ground.

Once both of her feet were on the ledge, Beattie began to gradually pull the club outwards. It was just a little, but it was enough to send a message: Jen's life was in her hands, and she knew it.

'What the fuck are you doing?' Jen asked.

'I want to know what happened to Jason. You're going to tell me this truth you're "sparing" me from. Speak now or you *will* forever hold your peace.'

Lauren

Lauren's initial reaction was to assume Nicolette was lying, because at that point she was still thinking in terms of her own paranoid logic. Nicolette was saying this because she needed to believe that inside that cottage lay Samira, a working phone line and at most a harmless old woman, and to reach them she had to defuse the source of Lauren's fear. But as she looked at the tears welling up in Nicolette's eyes, the shame in her quivering expression, she could see that she was telling the truth.

That still didn't mean it made any sense, though.

There was a tiny voice telling Lauren she ought to be relieved, but it was lost amid the cacophony of contradictions that was raging in her mind, to say nothing of the baying anger.

Despite the volume with which she wanted to scream it, the question came out in a strangled whisper. 'Why?'

Nicolette just stared back, lip trembling.

'You didn't even know me,' Lauren said.

Then it struck her that maybe that wasn't true. She was trying to do the arithmetic. She and Nicolette were around the same age.

'Did I buy somewhere from your family? Your parents?'

Nicolette shook her head, swallowing to help herself form the words. 'I made it all up.'

'But it was so detailed, so involved.'

And so painfully plausible, she knew.

'It wasn't personal,' Nicolette offered.

'Wasn't personal? It was a death threat. How much more fucking personal can you get?'

'What I mean is, you weren't exactly unique in being a target.'

Nicolette wiped a tear with the sleeve of her borrowed sweatshirt. 'I'm a troll. I've sent hate messages and death threats to dozens of people. Messages tailor-made to be upsetting in as specific a way as I could imagine. I hate myself after I've done it, but I can't help myself, and nobody else can help me either. It's not like there's Trolls Anonymous. We're anonymous already – that's the problem.

'It was exactly what you said: somebody angry at how their life has turned out. I see someone happy and successful and I want to tear them down. I want to show them how scary and randomly unfair the world can be.'

'Are you kidding me? I don't need any lessons in how unfair the world can be.'

'I know that. It's not about you. It was never about any of the women I wrote to. And they were always women, I guess because I compared myself to them. I sent abuse to actresses, sports stars, pop stars, businesswomen.

'I read about how you bought places that were under foreclosure. I thought up a scenario that would be the worst thing you *hadn't* imagined. Because that's what happened to me with my husband: the worst thing I hadn't imagined.'

'An unsatisfying marriage and a bloke cheating on you? That's hardly an unimaginable fate.'

'I was talking about my first husband.'

Lauren sensed they had reached the heart of the matter. She made an effort to rein in her anger. 'What about him?'

Nicolette swallowed again. 'His name was Ryan. He died in the Boxing Day tsunami in 2004, on our postponed honeymoon. We had been married three months. He went for a swim while I stayed in our hotel room drying my hair, and everything fell apart.

'Now I'm married to a man I treat like a consolation prize because he can never measure up to what I lost. I feel this anger about everything that was stolen from me, the life I was supposed to have, and I take it out on people I've never met. I'm sorry, I'm just so sorry.'

Lauren felt the wind whip around them. It seemed for a moment like they were the only two people in the world. She looked again at this woman who had put her through such fear, who had conjured a terrifying phantom in her mind. She looked pathetic.

'I could kill you. Right now, on this hillside. I could fucking kill you. There's a real death threat.'

Nicolette met her gaze. 'And I would deserve it. But Moira McPhee is not in cahoots with some ex-military mercenary. And given that the guy in the mask has just been in her house, I don't think it's only Samira's safety we need to worry about.'

They approached cautiously and silently through the trees, Lauren aware that any time the cottage was visible to her, then so she was from it. The man on the bike was gone, but he might still have been checking in with someone, even if it wasn't Moira. They had no way of knowing how many of them there were.

Finally they reached the edge of open ground, an unkempt

stretch of lawn between the tree-line and the house. Nobody had cut the grass or tended to the weeding in a long time. At this distance she couldn't make out much through the back window, as there didn't appear to be any lights on. She thought of how the masked man had just walked in, emerging again two minutes later.

There was nobody here, she told herself. Moira must have gone to the mainland, got some friend with a boat to collect her, if she had any of those. She might even have moved into a care home like her son wanted. That was why Lauren hadn't seen her in so long. It wasn't as though she would have popped in to say her farewells.

But something about Nicolette's confession was troubling her. Lauren had so readily believed the story those messages spun. Because no matter how often she said she made no apologies, it wasn't that she felt there was nothing to apologise for; rather that she had anaesthetised her conscience. Nicolette was the first person she had really spoken to about her relationship with Moira McPhee: all she had done to Lauren and all Lauren had done in return. What she had seen in Nicolette's response was everything she had lost sight of. Yes, Moira was a callous woman who had exploited people's weakness and vulnerability in order to make money. But didn't that make two of them?

Lauren had got the better of Moira McPhee, but that didn't mean she had been better *than* her. To do that, Lauren would need to have forgiven her.

The back door proved unlocked, the only impediment the clunky stiffness of the ancient mechanism. Lauren entered a small utility area dominated by an ancient twin tub washing machine, the edges flaked with rust. She tentatively opened a second door revealing the kitchen, which was functioning but filthy. There was a smell in the air of something damp, something rotten: the smell of disuse, emptiness. And something else, something far nastier.

If it had been Lauren's intention to condemn Moira McPhee to living in reduced circumstances, then she could not have reduced them much further.

There was a door ajar leading out of the kitchen, through which she could see into part of a sitting room. As in the kitchen, the wallpaper was peeling and mildewed, but there *was* wallpaper, which meant this place could not have provided the backdrop against which Samira had been filmed. Not unless the cottage had a cellar, but she didn't think it likely they had excavated deep beneath ground level when they were building a place like this.

Lauren's eye was drawn to just left of the sink, where a museum-piece telephone was bracketed to the wall. She was in the act of grabbing the handset when she noticed that the cable had been neatly snipped. She suspected that was what the man in the ski mask had been here to do.

Nicolette was already making straight for the living room, in search of Samira.

'Oh Jesus! Oh Jesus Christ.'

For a moment Lauren thought Nicolette had found her. But she had found someone else.

Moira McPhee's body was lying in a contorted posture on the frayed carpet.

Nicolette looked from the corpse to Lauren as she stepped into the room. 'How long do you think she's been here?'

Lauren was no expert, but she estimated Moira had been dead for weeks, possibly months. She'd had a heart attack or a stroke or something, maybe both. And there had been nobody there to help her.

'No idea,' she mumbled.

'When did you last see her?'

Lauren was asking herself the same question. How often had she been to the island since she last saw Moira out and about? Ten bookings? Twelve? And the last time Lauren had physically set eyes upon the cottage had been almost a year ago, standing out on the path and glimpsing Moira scowling back from the window.

'I'm guessing her son wasn't exactly doting or dutiful,' Nicolette suggested, but Lauren was finding it difficult to think worse of him than of herself.

'I've got to get out of here,' she said, hurrying through the front door into the night air.

She stood in front of the cottage, feeling crushed by shame. She willed tears to come but they wouldn't, perhaps her newly woken conscience denying her the catharsis.

A few moments later, Nicolette appeared at her side. 'You okay?'

'No.'

Lauren stared out to sea, where the sun had still not quite set over the water. 'The map in the drawing room,' she said. 'I had that version made to order, with the name amended to Claiggean Geal, as a reminder of what this place symbolised for me. Turned out it was bollocks. The factor must have made it up to intimidate people. There were never even any sheep here. Moira McPhee *was* my landlady, that part is true: the slum landlady who turfed my mum out onto the street with a kid. I believed the White Skulls part when I was young because I was scared of the factor, and I believed it later because I wanted to. I needed it to justify what I had done. Everything I had done.'

She turned to look Nicolette in the eye. 'Your messages, your death threats . . .'

'I'm so sorry, Lauren, it was—'

'I forgive you.'

Jen

Jen's centre of gravity had shifted just too far forward. For a moment she had thought maybe she could push back suddenly and then let go of the shaft, before inching her way to the other side. But even if that was true, when you're standing on a ledge next to a bampot holding a golf club, pulling it away from you is not the only thing they can do if they mean you harm.

This wasn't the first time Jen had found herself trapped. After Jason made his threat, she had felt imprisoned. But when that brick came through the window, she saw that it had also damaged the walls of her cell. That was when she realised what she could do. What she *had* to do, because one way or the other, Jason represented a deadly danger to her children.

Like any prison break, it took time and planning. For one thing, she had to wait for winter and the dark nights. She also had to wait a suitable interval after making a certain purchase. She had gone through layers of intermediaries, telling her direct point of contact that she needed it to zonk herself out on a long-haul flight. Even then she had to give it a couple of months for them to forget her face; a couple of months spent talking herself in and out of it, rehearsing it in her mind, never quite sure she was capable of going through with it.

She did it on a Friday night. It was the 23rd of November, the anniversary of when Jason first asked her out, and Jen had arranged for the kids to go to her parents' house overnight. She didn't choose the date for its significance, at least not consciously, but sometimes fate threw in its own flourishes. Jason always made time for this occasion because it was part of his self-image as a romantic husband, which was another way of saying not only that he expected sex, but he also expected Jen to act like the sex was *his* treat to her.

As anticipated, because it was a special night he had come home direct from his shift, leaving his car in the drive. It was a Porsche Boxster, something he hadn't bought with his police salary. Jen put it in the garage while he was in the shower, closing the living-room curtains so he wouldn't notice, and hoping he hadn't left anything in it that might cause him to spot the car had been moved. She didn't want to answer any awkward questions.

'Where the fuck's the motor?'

Like that one.

It was as his voice reverberated down the stairs that she remembered she had left the curtains open in the bedroom. Though they had a double garage with an internal connecting door off the kitchen, Jason liked to have his ostentatious vehicle out on display.

'I put it in the garage for you,' she replied, that little chuckle tinkling on the end. Nervous, pleading.

'Why?'

Jen feared she would dry up, giving herself away at the first hurdle. Then something in her brain clicked into gear. 'Helena said there's been a few break-ins round her way lately, CD players getting nicked. As there's going to be nobody home, I thought . . .'

'Aye, fair enough.'

Once he was dressed, she fixed him a beer in front of the TV while she was getting herself ready. She went upstairs to the bedroom, where she called his mobile on a pre-paid burner. When he answered, she held it up to the clock radio so that he would hear some muffled background music. She heard him say hello a few times before he decided it must be a butt-dial, then he hung up. The call would be logged, though, its duration plausibly long enough.

Then she waited, practising breathing exercises to keep her heart from pounding.

Normally Jason would hover at the doorway as soon as his beer was finished, impatient over how long it was taking her to get ready (though he would also be pissed off if he thought she hadn't made enough of an effort, especially for their anniversary). There was no hovering that night, though.

The breathing exercises could only do so much. Jen's heart was thumping as she descended the stairs, terrified that the Rohypnol in his beer hadn't worked. Terrified that it had.

She found him slumped in his favoured armchair, unmoving, his eyes almost but not quite closed. She stood in front of him, blocking his view of the TV. That would usually be enough to elicit an impatient reaction.

'Jason,' she said firmly. 'Jason. Jason.'

There was no response. She clicked her fingers in front of his face. Still nothing. Then she pinched his earlobe, which his sister Beattie said nurses did to people they suspected of pretending to be unconscious.

Jason remained unresponsive, which simultaneously filled her with relief and dread. Relief because her plan was working, dread because she now had to go through with it. If she didn't, how was she going to explain why he had suddenly passed out? As a cop, he would have no doubt what the after-effect symptoms indicated. And if he suspected she had drugged him, she didn't want to think how far he might go by way of retaliation.

There was no turning back, and no time to waste either.

That was when the doorbell rang.

Helena

Helena stopped dead at another sudden sound, startled by a rush of noise and movement before she identified it as the flap of wings as a bird took off from one of the trees. It seemed so disproportionately loud, but out here everything did because the silence in between was overwhelming. It was the dense, enveloping quiet of a soundproof studio combined with the eerie emptiness of being in an expansive void, and it felt like she and Michelle were utterly isolated here. They were all each other had to rely upon, and given Michelle's track record, Helena found that far from comforting.

Kylie said better the devil you know, but Helena would rather have been out here with literally any of the others. Even Beattie. She could be a miserable old cow, but Jen always maintained that much of what made her such a pain in the arse was that she had a profound sense of duty and obligation.

The thought prompted a realisation.

'We haven't heard anything from the others,' she said.

'Shit. That's because the radio is still off.'

Michelle pulled the device from her bag and switched it on. 'Hello? This is Michelle. Any news?'

There was a long delay, or maybe it just felt long because

every second of silence unleashed worse possibilities. Then there was a static burst and a voice.

'This is Kennedy. Where the hell have you guys been? You weren't responding.'

'Our radio was off for stealth purposes. Forgot to switch it on again. Sorry.'

'Any news?'

'No. We checked the ruined cottages. We're trying to find the boat now.'

Michelle was putting the radio back in her bag when the static sounded out again, followed by Kennedy's voice. 'Oh fuck oh fuck oh fuck!'

'What?'

'I just got another video on the app. I think we're running out of time.'

There was an excruciating silence.

'Kennedy, you still there?' Michelle asked.

'Sorry.' Kennedy's voice was faltering. 'This is difficult. The ice is melting. I don't know how long we've got. I think you need to all get back here. We need to make a decision.'

There was another painful silence as they took it in.

'I hear you,' said Michelle. This time she did put the radio away.

Helena turned, trying to gauge what might be the most direct route back towards the house.

'We're almost at the boat,' Michelle said. 'We have to be.'

'Didn't you hear? We're running out of time.'

'We've come this far. And for one thing, if we get hold of the boat, it means we can get back quicker.'

Helena thought of the time it had taken to get here. What Michelle said made sense. It was worth the gamble, though she was far from eager to face the discussion that awaited them on their return. Somebody was going to have to give the Reaper what he wanted.

'Okay,' Helena replied. 'Though I think at this point it's fifty-fifty whether we end up heading towards the bay or back towards the house. I've lost my bearings in this bloody forest.' She looked at her phone again. 'I know that's north, but I can't relate it to the map.'

'I can't even hear the sea now,' said Michelle. 'I've a feeling we've been heading away from it.'

That was the danger when you were disoriented in the woods: every pace could take you further from where you intended, or even around in a circle. Helena asked herself how she might know they had done that, what feature they would recognise. That was when she saw what they had missed before.

'The stream!' she said. 'We double back and follow that. It's got to go down to the sea.'

Michelle flashed her a huge grin, full of relief, gratitude and something that could have been affection. Helena didn't immediately identify it as such because she was reluctant to admit what it was.

'You're a genius.'

'Hardly,' Helena muttered. Part of her didn't want to let Michelle have the moment she was trying to turn it into. And part of Helena knew *she* didn't deserve that either.

Christ, how did it get to this?

She had been left with conflict where once there had been affection; mixed feelings about even her most treasured memories. One in particular left her all churned up.

It was Michelle's seventh birthday. Michelle's mum took her and Helena to the cinema to see *The NeverEnding Story* at the

ABC in town, then they went out for food at Back Alley in the West End. They had burgers and milkshakes and desserts, all with crazy names. The film was amazing, the food like something out of a movie, but the best part was that afterwards she got to go back to Michelle's for the evening, because Helena's parents were out somewhere.

They were up in Michelle's room, playing with the Barbie StarCycle scooter she had got for one of her birthday presents. Then Michelle had gone into her wardrobe and taken out the special doll.

'I'm going to tell you her name,' she said. 'Because you're my best friend. Only you and I will know.'

Michelle let Helena hold the doll, and it felt like something sacred. Not the object itself, but to be trusted by the most amazing girl in the world. The doll's name was strange, something that sounded made-up, but that was beside the point. It was Michelle's birthday, but it felt like the best day of Helena's life.

That was why it hurt all the more, eighteen years later, when Michelle jettisoned her like ballast that was holding her back.

That was why she could never forgive her.

Jen

The doorbell rang a second time. It had never sounded so loud.

Jen thought about ignoring it, but the lights were on and the TV was probably audible from the doorstep. She peeped through the curtains. It was Alastair, who lived a few doors down. And he had seen her looking.

She hurried to the door.

'Is Jason in?' he asked.

She realised he knew the answer was yes. He had probably come round after noticing Jason's car going past on his way home.

She felt like the whole thing was about to unravel then and there from one simple question. But she coached herself: this wasn't the last test of nerve she would have to face tonight.

'He's in the shower,' she said.

'It's just that he borrowed the charger for my motorised caddy. I think he'd lost his. I can come in and wait.'

Alastair was about to step inside, where she had invited him a dozen times before. Jason would be in his line of sight through the living-room door as soon as he stepped into the hall.

'I don't know how long he'll be, but the thing is, he's running late and we're due out for dinner just as soon as he's changed.

I'll get him to pop round with it first thing in the morning, is that okay?'

'Well, the thing is, I need to charge it overnight.'

Jesus.

'On our way out to dinner, then.'

'That would be great.'

As she watched him walk away, her relief was replaced by the fear of what he might later tell the police. Then she realised that it would work in her favour. Alastair was a witness for the timeline. Jason was here, they were about to go for dinner, they had a table booked. Then Jason had got a phone call and had to go out. Alastair didn't know where the phone call came in that sequence.

She had got lucky, but it had cost her time. She was past the point of no return, so this was entirely about survival now.

She went to the garage, where she had stored a hand-truck they used at the club for shifting crates of beer. She had replaced the one from the club with a near-identical model, taking the old one because its purchase could not be traced if it was ever found.

She laid it flat on the living-room floor and manoeuvred Jason's unconscious body onto it. Lifting at a shallow angle, she slowly wheeled him backwards into the garage, where she laid out a length of old carpet on the concrete floor. She rolled him up in it, tying it in place with two lengths of cord. Then she hauled him across the back seat of the Porsche, making him the first person ever to have travelled in the rear – there wasn't legroom for an adult and it was too tight for kids' car seats. The boot hadn't been an option as it was so small, though it was at least big enough to hold the can of petrol she would need later. It was so like Jason to have bought a car that was totally unsuited to those typical family needs, like ferrying kids around, going to the supermarket, or murdering your husband.

She pulled on some of Jason's clothes: a dark sweatshirt, a pair of jogging pants, and a baseball cap he had bought on holiday. She wasn't sure how good the definition was on traffic cameras, but she figured that in the dark it would at least not be obvious that it wasn't him driving.

She kept doing those breathing exercises, slowing it down so that her heart might do the same. She had read that it was a physiological rather than psychological response, though ironically, knowing this helped convince her it was working.

She took the Porsche out along the back road from Uddingston towards Blantyre, then turned off down a single-track farm road that went all the way to the banks of the Clyde.

When she killed the engine, the dark was both daunting and reassuring. There was heavy cloud and a light drizzle, no moon or stars penetrating the gloom, though there was some light each time a train passed over the nearby railway bridge, as well as the sodium glow of streetlights from Uddingston on the other side of the water.

Jen pulled the hand-truck from the rear footwell and laid it on the grass to receive the bundle from the back seat. She used the burner phone as a light, placing the handset on the bonnet of the Porsche. It would have been easier to see what she was doing if she put the headlights back on, but that increased the risk of being seen.

Once the bundle was in position, she got two more lengths of cord from the boot and tied the bundle to the truck. Then she began hauling it the last few yards to the edge of the river.

Then her own mobile rang, causing her to drop the truck's handles. She hurried to fish the handset from her pocket so that she could kill the noise, even though there was nobody within half a mile.

It was the restaurant, asking if they still wanted the table. She had forgotten she was supposed to call and cancel. Now was as good a time as any.

'I'm really sorry,' she said. 'My husband got a call from work and now he's a bit tied up.'

Christ. The words had come out before she could think.

As she pocketed the phone and grabbed the handles again, she tried to forget what was wrapped in the carpet. *Who* was wrapped in it. Her mind tormented her with images of good times. Those seductive thoughts that it could all still be okay. They could work it out. He hadn't meant what he said, and this wasn't who she was.

Then the bundle began to move. He was starting to come to.

You only know what you really want when the choice is about to be taken from you, and Jen knew what would happen if Jason got free. It was enough to dispel all her delusions.

Jason had absolutely meant what he said, and as for who she was, there was no doubt there either. She was no longer a victim. That's who she was.

Jen levered the truck upright and tipped it into the river. It made a startlingly loud splash but then there was silence as it disappeared beneath the surface. The water here was cold and deep, and though it was black in the night, she knew that it was coppery and opaque even in the height of summer.

He would not be found. She had needed to make absolutely sure of that. If his drowned body was ever examined, a post-mortem that revealed traces of Rohypnol would not suggest a very gangland style of killing; far more a battered-wife style of killing.

And it had worked. Time proved that she had fooled the police, fooled the gangsters, fooled everyone who knew Jason. Everyone except the woman who now had her balanced on the edge of a precipice.

'You killed him, didn't you?'

Jen didn't see how either answer was going to improve her situation. She had to offer Beattie something, though. And given what Beattie had just done, she deserved to get what she was asking for.

'Jason terrorised me for years. He terrorised all three of us. I hid it from everybody, and that was my real crime. When I finally threatened to leave him, he said he would kill the kids. He would kill Calum and Ailsa, and frame me for it. Then he would move on, like we never existed.'

'Lies,' Beattie said. 'More lies.' But her expression suggested she wasn't so sure, and consciously or not, she brought the golf club back in just enough for Jen to regain her balance and scramble to safety.

They eyed each other from opposite sides of the drop, so close yet separated by a chasm.

'But you did kill him, didn't you?' Beattie said. 'That's what happened to him? You're admitting that?'

'Yes, I killed him. I did what I had to do as a mother. And my conscience is clear: I've slept fine every night since because I don't have to live in fear any more.'

Beattie turned away, looking at the ground. Jen couldn't see her face. Neither of them said anything for a few seconds. When Beattie spoke again, Jen saw the anguish in her expression, the tears already running.

'You don't know what it's like,' Beattie said. 'To not know.'

Suddenly Jen felt the full weight of guilt she had been forced to suppress. All she had ever seen was Beattie's anger and suspicion. She had never allowed herself to see the agony Beattie and her family had endured, because it was the only way she could live with what she had done. It was hard enough confronting the confusion her own kids were dealing with. They had been scared of Jason half the time, but he was still their daddy, and she had taken him away.

The only mercy was knowing that she hadn't made him suffer at the end. Because of the Rohypnol, Jason wouldn't have been aware of anything. But that was not the kind of detail she was planning to share with Beattie.

'I'm sorry,' Jen said, her head bowed. 'I can barely begin to imagine how painful this has been for you and your family. Nobody should go through that.'

Then she met Beattie's eye once again. 'But nobody should go through what he did to me either.'

Beattie stared at her across the gap, a familiar coldness visible through the tears. 'What you *say* he did to you.'

Jen had allowed herself to truly feel Beattie's pain, but that didn't mean she was taking her shit.

'Why would I do something like that unless I had absolutely no choice?'

'I can think of a few reasons more plausible than what you're claiming about Jason.'

Jen bit back her anger, held fire for a moment to collect herself. It was time for both of them to lay down their cards.

'I saw you messing with your phone,' she said. 'I'm guessing you've got me on audio.'

Beattie's expression confirmed it. Wary but defiant.

'What you do with that is up to you. But you played this wrong by letting me cross first, because now you're stuck with a choice. Do you turn back by yourself and prove you never really cared about Samira, or do you put your life in my hands right here, knowing that I could do what you did to me? I could wait until you're halfway across and demand you toss me your phone. Or I could help you cross. Just depends on what kind of person you really think I am.'

Jen made sure she had a firm footing on the grass, then held out her golf club.

'I've admitted what I did, and I've told you why I did it. But now you need to decide if there's a difference between what you actually believe, and what you'd just *like* to believe.'

Michelle

It seemed to take longer to find their way back to the stream, probably because this time they were looking for it. Michelle was worried that if they didn't find it soon, Helena would suggest they turn back, though turning anywhere implied they already knew which direction they were going.

She was relieved that she had made Helena see that if they found the boat, they had options. The next stage was going to be getting her to understand what some of those options were. Helena thought that the selfless thing was always the right thing. It was one of the reasons why she was a music teacher and Michelle was a star.

Finally they made it back to the stream, and Michelle almost lost her footing in her eagerness to clamber down. She skidded a little, stopping just before her right foot was about to slip into the water. She watched Helena make a more controlled descent, only for her to slide at the last moment when her head turned in response to a noise. It sounded like a burst of radio static.

'Was that a message?' Helena asked, righting herself at the bottom of the slope.

Michelle feared that if it was, it wasn't meant for them.

'It didn't come from my radio. It sounded like it came from over there.'

They glanced towards the source of the sound, seeing only trees. They shared a look.

Michelle pulled out the radio from the bag. 'Did anybody just try to broadcast? We heard static but no message.'

There were a few moments of silence, then Kennedy replied. 'I said nothing and heard nothing.'

'Okay, don't worry about it,' Michelle said.

Helena was looking at her with dismay. 'Don't worry about it? There's someone stalking us.'

Kennedy's voice broke over the radio again. 'Are you guys on your way back now?'

'Copy that,' Michelle replied. She got a look from Helena, who understood she had no intention of diverging from her present course.

'Why are you so dead set on finding this boat? If they see us taking it, we don't know what they'll do to Samira.'

'They're not going to expend their only leverage just like that.'

'She's not "leverage". She's a person. We were told not to leave the island.'

'And if we do as we're told, if we just go back right now, we're entirely in their control. Whereas if we get hold of this boat there are possibilities open to us.'

Helena looked certain she had read Michelle's thoughts. She had a high-minded expression on her face.

'Possibilities? Yeah, I can just imagine. But I guess taking the main chance for yourself and leaving everybody else behind is kind of your thing.'

Michelle felt a surge of anger and wondered if it was because there was a ring of truth to what Helena said. You tend to scream louder when a blow hits a sensitive spot.

'So, it comes down to that,' Michelle said. 'My great betrayal. The fact that there was an opportunity offered to me and I was single-minded enough, *selfish* enough to take it. Is that about the size of it?'

'It's not about what you took for yourself,' Helena replied. 'It's about what you took from me: the career I could have had.'

'I took nothing from you, Helena. That part's all in your head. You're angry about not getting something you only *think* you wanted. An imagined version of this that edits out all the elements you wouldn't be able to handle.'

'You changed the name to Cassidy so that people would assume you were the star, but even that wasn't enough. You wanted to be Mica, so you didn't have to share the spotlight.'

'I never had to share the spotlight, Helena, because I wasn't the one who was hiding from it. That was why they only wanted me. They wanted a pop diva singing commercial, radio-friendly songs. You were never going to be happy going along with that, were you? Whereas I just wanted to sing. Like Madeleine just wants to play drums and Daisy is happy playing bass. You're holding on to a grudge about not getting something you never wanted anyway.'

It felt good to have finally told her this, face to face. Then Helena hit her with the thing that had bothered Michelle all these years.

'How do you know if you never asked?'

Michelle could still see Anders from the record label as he walked across the lobby of her hotel on that fateful afternoon in Lisbon. She was there for a short break because at the time she was dating a DJ who was playing in the city that weekend.

She figured Anders showing up was not a coincidence. He was with someone she vaguely recognised but couldn't place. Michelle thought he might be from the label's parent company, so she was convinced they had come to break it to her that they were dropping the band: doing it in pleasant circumstances then leaving it to her to tell everybody else.

Anders introduced his companion as Alan Devine. That was when it dawned on Michelle what was really going on. He wasn't from the record company. He was in management, and his roster contained some very big names. Alan Devine was here in Lisbon with Anders, while Mairi Lafferty, Cassidy's manager, was God knows where.

It was all on the table before the drinks even arrived. It was the end of the band, she had been right about that much, but the beginning of something else. New management, new record deal, new look, and new money: an awful lot more of it. Money she wouldn't have to share with anybody, because there was the catch, if you could call it that: it was only her that they wanted.

Michelle liked to tell herself it had been a difficult decision, but it wasn't.

She didn't even ask, 'Can Helena stay on board as a songwriter?' She knew Anders blamed their indulgence of Helena for the second album's failure. Emboldened by the first record's success, they had let her have far more creative control, and it just hadn't worked.

'Helena is my best friend.'

She said that much. But mostly she said it so that she could tell herself she had said something.

'You don't do anybody any favours clinging on to the past once you've outgrown it,' Anders told her.

Alan put it far more eloquently. 'As your man Sting once sang, if you love somebody, set them free.'

She could absolutely feel the truth in that. But the person she loved most, the person she was setting free, was Michelle Cassidy.

Striding parallel to the stream, Helena spoke with an anger so fresh that it sounded like she was talking about something that happened this morning.

'You didn't ask me what I was and wasn't on board with. You just unilaterally ended Cassidy and announced it as a fait accompli.'

'Cassidy had already crashed and burned by that point,' Michelle replied, digging deep into the reserves of justification she had acquired over the years. 'And it crashed and burned because *you* weren't committed enough, not me. That second album, that was when it all got too real, and you didn't commit because you were scared. Scared you weren't good enough, scared to expose yourself, scared to fail.'

'That's bollocks. You were the one who was going through the motions. You couldn't wait for it to be over.'

Michelle knew she had no comeback for this, because it was true. But there was one thing that always sustained her whenever reverie gave way to pangs of conscience. She glanced back and looked Helena in the eye.

'Your eldest just turned seventeen, didn't she?'

'What's she got to do with it?'

Michelle returned her gaze to the front. She couldn't take her eyes off her footing for any length of time. The stream was widening, and she could occasionally spot a flash of something rippling through the trees, the sea's shimmering surface twinkling in the last rays of the dying sun.

'I did the arithmetic a long time ago, Helena. You were pregnant while we were on that final tour.'

There was a beat while Helena took this in, though Michelle didn't imagine she'd be long in formulating a response. When it came, it found its mark.

'Are you saying that if I was truly committed to my career, I'd have got rid of it?'

This cut deeper than Helena would ever, could ever know, all the way down to the scared girl, just turned fifteen, who still hid deep inside Michelle. She was glad they were walking in single file so that Helena couldn't see her face.

It took her a moment before she could reply. But she was not short of an answer.

'No,' Michelle said. 'I'm saying we all make choices, and you want to pretend I made this one for you. You make out like you married Neil and settled down because I took everything away. You were thinking of leaving anyway.'

'So a woman can't be a mother and have a career in music? Because that's a hell of a take from someone who likes to pose as a feminist.'

'I think you're the one who didn't believe you could do both, and you had already decided which one you wanted more. Even if you hadn't made a conscious choice, let's just say you were ambivalent in your contraceptive practices.'

'What the hell is that supposed to mean? And what business is it of yours?'

'It means I know you were careful when you needed to be. And it was none of my business, but there are fewer secrets in a band than you think, especially when hotel walls are so thin. You flung it about like God knows what on that first tour, and you didn't get pregnant then. But you started getting serious with Neil around about the same time as we were working on the second album.'

'So you're slut-shaming me now?'

'Says the woman who only hours ago implied I leaked my own sex tape to generate publicity. Yes, I overheard. You weren't speaking as quietly as you thought. But the sad part is, Helena, you're not angry at me for selling out. You're angry at *you* because you didn't, and now you're feeling like what you bought with your precious integrity wasn't worth it. So to make yourself better, you're calling me a whore.'

'I'm not calling you a whore, Michelle. I'm not saying you're prepared to do anything for fame and money. But I do know what you *were* prepared to do back then. You were prepared to leave me behind. You didn't trust me not to screw it all up for you.'

Another wellspring of anger suddenly turned into something else: a profound sense of loss, a longing for the bond they used to have. Michelle was not about to apologise, but there was something she needed Helena to understand.

'I always trusted you, Helena, and I always believed in you. More than you believed in yourself, but there was nothing I could do about that. I've trusted you since we were seven years old, remember?'

They proceeded in silence after that. The channel remained fairly straight for a hundred yards or so, then bent sharply to the left. After the turn Michelle could hear the lapping of the waves. They were getting closer, but it appeared that the passage was blocked. At first glance she assumed a tree had fallen. Drawing closer, she thought it looked like a section of plastic pipe: black and curved. Then she realised that it was the RIB.

It struck her how lucky they had been. It had been hidden there, deliberately tucked out of sight from the shore. If they had reached the bay by any other route, they wouldn't have seen it.

Michelle hurried towards it, driven forward by a surge of elation. The way off this place was in her own hands. Behind her, Helena upped the pace too. They chucked the golf clubs into the RIB along with Michelle's tote, then tested the weight, Michelle at the prow, Helena at the stern. It was going to be a struggle, but it was only about fifteen, twenty yards to the water. They could haul it between them.

'We're taking this back to the house, right?' Helena asked as they neared the lapping waves. Her voice was low, stripped of the insistence and certainty that had accompanied her earlier indignation. It was the first thing she had said since Michelle invoked that seventh birthday. She seemed sombre, all passion spent. There was something else in her demeanour too, something Michelle couldn't read. Regret, maybe: that same sense of loss Michelle had felt for the friends they had once been to each other, never more than when they had shared that secret.

It was a daft thing. It had meant a lot when Michelle's auntie Meg entrusted her with not only the doll, but the doll's name. Meg had invented it herself when she was a girl, combining the names of her own aunties. She told Michelle that this meant no other doll in the world could be called the same thing.

Making a secret of it had made her feel closer to Meg, sharing something special that only they knew. That was why, when she had felt such closeness to Helena on her seventh birthday, she wanted to share that same bond with her. So she had told Helena the made-up name that to this day she had never written down, and never spoken aloud to anybody else.

I used a unique password.

Do you mean unique as in it wasn't a commonly recognisable word or phrase, or unique in that you never used it anywhere else?

Both.

Suddenly she saw it. She could read Helena's expression now. Regretful, yes. And worried.

Guilty.

'Carriamolina,' Michelle said.

Helena looked up. Her eyes filled, but not before Michelle read a shame in them that left absolutely no doubt.

Michelle felt like she was experiencing the leak all over again, except this time the violation was nothing compared to the betrayal.

Before either of them could say anything, Michelle heard the sound of urgent footsteps crunching on pebbles. When she looked round, she saw a figure in black fatigues and a ski mask racing towards them.

Beattie

Neither Beattie nor Jen had uttered a word throughout the rest of the descent, the silence even more charged than during the climb. Beattie had thought she would feel vindicated now that her instincts had been proven right, but it was those same instincts that told her she could trust Jen to help her across the ledge. Instead of bringing a sense of clarity, the picture seemed muddier than ever.

She was hating herself for it, but she was starting to glimpse fragments of the past as though seeing them from outside herself. Moments with Jason and the kids that now seemed different: how well behaved they were, how shy and quiet, how unlike their father. The nervous tics that Calum sometimes exhibited.

Mummy is the naughtiest.

She saw flashes of Jen at that barbecue, supposedly hungover, walking in tender, careful steps. Jen's unnerving calm after the brick incident. And now she understood a horrible possibility. Jen had been so calm because it wasn't the worst thing to have happened to her. Or the most frightening.

She couldn't bring herself to believe what Jen was saying. But she couldn't quite bring herself to disbelieve it either.

The good thing was, she didn't have to make up her mind

now. What she had on her phone meant that, in time, all the evidence would come out. That was what she had always wanted, after all: that there should be a proper investigation. A murder trial. But most importantly for her, for her sisters, for her mum, there would be a body to bury.

Finally she was able to bring herself to speak again. 'Where is he?' she asked. 'You owe me that much. All of us. We deserve to know.'

'You do,' Jen conceded. 'And I'll tell you. But now is not the time.'

They had rounded the last of the hairpin bends and were now at the foot of the slope, in a wooded area in the lee of the hillside. The grass was longer here, sheltered from the wind. Only in its absence did Beattie realise she had become used to the white noise of it in her ears.

If there was any engine sound it would have been impossible to miss. Instead there was only silence. They proceeded at a cautious pace, peering through the foliage for signs of anything that should prompt them to halt and lie low. Despite their attempted stealth, they were upon it before they realised. Not a cave but, as Lauren had described, walls of bare rock, outcrops and overhangs.

There was no quad bike, no man in black, and no Samira.

Jen got out her phone, looking at the video again. 'The rock looks similar. The lichen and moss. She's somewhere like this, but . . .' She sighed. 'It could be any patch of live rock. We passed smaller sections like this on the way down.'

Jen's radio sounded again. It was a blessing to hear their voices, but what followed a few moments later reminded her there was no comfort to be had in this place.

'The ice is melting,' Kennedy said. 'I don't know how long

we've got. I think you all need to get back here. We need to make a decision.'

Perhaps the worst part was that it felt inevitable.

Jen looked at Beattie as she put the radio away. 'We need to get moving.'

Beattie felt relief that they were not having to confront anybody, but nobody had found anything and time was running out. She grasped at the narrative she was piecing together, in the hope that it could restore a sense of control.

'The guy on the quad bike. I reckon it could be Sammy Finnegan. That's why he was wearing a mask: not in case he got identified later, but because you already know what he looks like.'

'Why would it be Sammy Finnegan?' Jen asked.

'Because he thinks you took his watches.'

'If Sammy Finnegan really believed I had his watches, he wouldn't have waited ten years to make a move, and he wouldn't do it in some round-the-houses way. I told you: this isn't about me and it isn't about Jason.'

It had all made so much sense in her head, but as Jen spoke Beattie could see how flimsy her reasoning was. Jen's words at the landslip echoed in her mind.

There's a difference between what you actually believe, and what you'd just like *to believe.*

Darren Kyle's court case had happened shortly after the accident. Beattie couldn't say for sure which of the two had ramped up her feelings towards Jen, but she knew that when you've come to hate yourself, the only way you can feel better is if you can find somebody to hate more.

'Then maybe it's about me,' Beattie said. 'Or rather, the man I hit.'

'What about him?'

'As you said, his family have connections.'

'I was only lashing out, Beattie. I didn't mean—'

'You were right, though. There was more to it.'

Jen tilted her head, curious but wary. 'How much more?'

Beattie exhaled at length. She wasn't sure she should be saying this, but she was absolutely sure she needed to. Unlikely as it seemed, Jen was the one person she could talk to. Not least because what Beattie carried in her pocket gave her insurance.

'Wee Xander was kicking off. We had him overnight while Kathleen and Michael were at a hotel for their anniversary. He wouldn't go to sleep, and he just wouldn't stop crying. You know that way: over-tired and totally lost it, red-faced and screaming so much you feared he'd forget to breathe.'

'Been there,' Jen said, nodding.

'I think he was teething. I can see that now. But at the time you can't think straight, can you? Hence I put him in his car seat and took him out for a run at eleven o'clock at night.'

'Been there too,' Jen said. 'Cars were like anaesthetic to Ailsa.'

'Exactly, right? Normally Xander would be asleep in five minutes, but after driving for about three times that, I was on the Clydeside Expressway, and he was still howling. Then he started crying out for a song we play him on the car stereo, about the dingle dangle scarecrow. He's screaming that. "Dingle dangle, Gran! Dingle dangle!"

'I was trying to find it on the wee touchscreen but I'm useless with those things at the best of times, and when you're under pressure you hit the wrong buttons. It was late, so there was hardly any traffic and absolutely no pedestrians. But I was looking at the screen and not the road.'

Beattie swallowed, bracing herself to relive the impact. This was the most painful part to remember.

'When I looked up, I saw him step off the verge onto the tarmac right in front of me. I had no time to brake or swerve.'

She swallowed again, but it was too much. The tears welled up. 'He had a wife,' she said, her voice choking. Beattie had seen her picture. She had forced herself to look her up on Facebook, to confront the truth of what she had done. The lives that she had ruined.

'I know,' Jen said. 'I also know that he was found to be full of coke, ecstasy and booze. He had been on a two-day bender. You said yourself, you saw him step out from the verge. It's not like he was already in the road when you looked up.' Her voice softened. 'Or was he?'

Beattie shook her head. She had a vivid recollection of her disbelief that he was over the barrier and veering towards the road, but her mind had rewritten the moment so many times that she wasn't sure what she really remembered. One thing was for sure, though.

'If I hadn't been looking at the screen, I would have seen him sooner. Maybe I'd have noticed something about him that put me on edge, warned me to slow down.'

'And just as likely you'd have noticed nothing,' Jen said, her tone firm, almost stern. 'You're looking for a reason to blame yourself. It's a form of survivor's guilt. Like thinking how much worse it would have been if you'd hit a car when you were looking at the touchscreen, with Xander in the passenger seat.'

The tears spilled now, because these had been exactly her thoughts. For a moment she imagined Jen was about to step across and hold her. She couldn't even say for sure that she didn't want that. Jen held her ground, though she did offer a tissue.

'So what's this got to do with his family?'

Beattie wiped her cheeks and her nose. 'I'm afraid they might know something. Or that somebody does. There were no witnesses, no CCTV. But everything in the car is computerised. Everything is logged. The police checked my mobile records to make sure I wasn't on it at the time of the accident, but what if someone else checked the car data and it showed my activity at that moment?'

'I think they need reasonable grounds to be able to request that kind of information from the car manufacturer. And if that was going to happen, it would have happened by now.'

'But what if someone got hold of it independently, and that's what this is about: that they're going to blackmail me with it?'

'Then they would just blackmail you. They wouldn't do this. Besides, the data wouldn't prove anything. If it even records that kind of information, it would show that your last keystroke was before the car suddenly stopped, before he left the verge. Plus, if it ever came to court, we would just need to sit each member of the jury in a car with a wean that's been crying solidly for two hours. See how their judgement is at that point.'

Beattie was welling up again, this time with unexpected relief. She was seeing this clearly for the first time, and it was down to Jen. The harder part was the question of how many other things she could tolerate Jen being right about.

'So this isn't about me,' Beattie said, looking for affirmation.

'No,' Jen replied. 'As Zaki insists on telling me, not everybody is playing an angle all the time. This isn't about you and it's not about me either.'

'Then who *is* it about?'

Helena

The moment she heard that word, Helena knew she was undone. It was not merely that her shameful betrayal was exposed; it was as though decades of certainties had collapsed, self-serving delusions crumbling into dust and exposing the stark truths that lay behind them.

She had done it shortly after she found out Neil was leaving her. She could cope with him having an affair, but not him walking out, not him being the guy who *does* actually leave his wife for the mistress. But why wouldn't he? The kids were all grown up and the marriage was holed below the waterline. He had grabbed a lifeboat. Grabbed a life.

Michelle was right about how Cassidy had ended. It was exciting at first, but the whole thing had started to feel too big, too scary, and Helena couldn't handle it. Suddenly she didn't want to be in a band; she wanted to be back playing at pop stars in Michelle's bedroom. She had never been so happy as when she was a wee girl growing up in those safe suburban streets. She knew she couldn't have that again, but she also knew she could have the next best thing.

She had decided she wanted a quiet, normal life, and poured everything into being a wife and mother. Then her kids grew up and her husband left, and she found herself asking: Ever get the feeling you've been cheated? Michelle was right about that too.

Jen had forwarded a link to some scans of old photos Michelle must have unearthed. She would occasionally copy Helena and Michelle into email exchanges she was having with the other, part of her low-level long-term parent-trapping strategy. It meant Helena had Michelle's private email address, and the download link showed which cloud service she was using.

Helena had only tried that password out of curiosity, but it worked. Suddenly she was in. She had access to all Michelle's private stuff.

People talked about hate-watching shows that starred someone they didn't like. That's what this was. She was hate-scrolling through Michelle's personal photos, pictures of this perfect and amazing life that seemed to be going from one success to the next while Helena's was falling apart.

And then she came to the explicit stuff. The sex tape. And in her anger and bitterness she did something unforgivable.

She was utterly terrified when she came to see how big a story it was. There were computer forensics experts looking into it, making her think it was only a matter of time before she was discovered and what was left of her life would be destroyed. She had been lucky, though. At the time, her laptop had been running a VPN to spoof an American IP address so that she could watch US Netflix. It hadn't been her intention, but it meant they wouldn't be able to trace the source of the hack or her subsequent upload to a porn site.

She felt no pleasure or satisfaction over her revenge: that was the hollow truth those seeking vengeance only ever discovered too late. She retreated into denial about how damaged Michelle had been by the whole thing, telling herself Michelle was creating a drama to make herself the centre of attention as usual. She could not let herself feel any guilt or shame over what she had done, because if she felt even a little, she knew it would open the floodgates.

But then Michelle spoke the name of her doll, and that was when the dam broke. The inescapable enormity summed up in those same two words that had once changed their lives.

She knows.

Helena felt suddenly weak, fearing she would lose her grip and drop the boat, but it didn't matter. Michelle's feet were already in the water and the prow afloat.

Then she heard the thump of boots, and when she saw the man bearing down on them she understood that Michelle had been right about this too. Having the boat changed everything, which was why he was going to stop them taking it.

She had been wrong about so many things, and in her misguided anger she had betrayed her best friend. She couldn't make any of it right, but there *was* something she could still do.

She dropped her centre of gravity and pushed the boat forward until it was fully afloat, causing Michelle to fall into it over the prow.

'Go!' she urged. Then Helena turned, gripped the golf club and rushed towards her deserving fate.

Nicolette

Nicolette was still trembling as she stood alongside Lauren, looking west towards the glow of the horizon. She knew the rippling of the waters ought to be a calming sight, but she could vividly recall the calm of the surface on the morning her life fell apart. Terrifying forces can be silently and invisibly at work, never announcing themselves at the time. You only see the devastation afterwards.

The sight of the old woman's body had shaken her, but that it had clearly been there for some time was a source of relief. The face had been gaunt and rotten, but for all that, less horrific than had it been freshly dead.

It was not the first corpse she had seen. When they were evacuated from the Maldives, efforts had been made to shield the survivors – especially those who had lost people – from sights that might further distress them, but they had all glimpsed things. When death was so widespread, it was impossible to hide it.

Nicolette now understood that her problem wasn't just that she had been traumatised back in 2004. It was that she had been numb ever since.

Lauren saying 'I forgive you' seemed to turn on her feelings again.

Losing Ryan had made her stop appreciating what was truly valuable in her life, made her blasé about the possibility of losing that too. Her husband was having an affair, and she had been acting like it was merely another thing to be disappointed in him for, when it was actually a far bigger threat. What did she think was going to happen if he left? That someone better would come along?

Shamefully, deep down, yes. That had always been her delusion. That one day she'd trade up. It was pathetic. Who did she think was going to want her? She was a retail assistant approaching middle age.

She had lied about what she did for a living because she felt so inadequate. Jen had come into the shop once and she felt weirdly embarrassed, so she told her she was only there on a recce, and made something up about being in marketing. It had just come out and she had been stuck with it ever since.

For years Paul had been suggesting she do a degree. Design, marketing, whatever. He seemed to think she could handle anything. She told herself she wasn't smart enough, but the truth was she lacked the drive. She lacked the desire to make herself happy because she thought it was impossible for her to *be* happy. She thought there was only one model for happiness, and after it was washed away in the tsunami, everything else was a consolation prize.

Paul had loved her: she just told herself that he didn't in order to make herself feel better about not appreciating him. She told herself he didn't love her because of his insecurity about her being out of his league. In truth, he was the one who was out of her league.

She had never let herself see who he was because she had always told herself she deserved someone better. But Paul was

257

the one who deserved someone better. And if she got off this island, she was going to give him someone better.

Lauren looked exhausted, like a fire in her had burned out.

'I'm okay to go back inside,' Nicolette told her. 'I'll make the call.'

'The line's been cut. That's what the guy in the mask was here to do.'

Nicolette felt disappointed but not surprised. It was never going to be that simple. And even though they might try to convince themselves otherwise, she was aware that bringing in the authorities might doom Samira. Nicolette knew this because she had been asking herself whether she could live with that if it meant she was saved.

The jury was still out.

'The guy in the mask,' Nicolette said.

'What about him?'

'Got to be some kind of psycho to just walk in, cut the phone line and walk out again without having any response to finding a dead body in the living room.'

'I'm guessing corpses aren't such a rarity in his line of work,' Lauren replied grimly. 'When we were wondering why they killed the chef, I think we overlooked cold, calculating pragmatism. Joaquin was somebody big and strong who might be a bit handy, a variable they wanted out of the equation.'

'But if they're here to do a specific job, if this is just about one person, I don't get why they would kill only the chef. Why eliminate one risk while letting all the others run free?'

'How free have we been running, though? They've got us where they want us. See, I don't think it's purely about revenge on somebody who's pissed them off. The message talked about restitution. No matter how they dress it up, ultimately that's going to mean money. Somebody here is going to be forced to pay, and *everybody* else is being held as collateral, not just Samira.'

Nicolette couldn't dispute it. She had entertained paranoid thoughts that the Reaper could be one of her many trolling targets forcing her to own her shit, but quite frankly she just wasn't important enough. There were three people here who might be, but one of them had no connection to the rest. And if Lauren was the target, horrible as it was to contemplate, they'd have come when her daughter was here, not seven strangers.

'This has to be about Michelle or Jen,' Nicolette said.

'I can't see who else is in the picture, unless somebody here is a lot wealthier than they've been letting on.'

Something niggled at Nicolette when Lauren said this. It was a thought, an association that was just out of reach: vivid but fleeting, glimpsed and then gone.

'The message said she's not the person you believe her to be,' Lauren went on. 'That could be a smokescreen to keep everybody paranoid and suspicious of each other, but allowing for that, what do your instincts say?'

'My instincts are worth bugger all,' Nicolette replied. 'I've known Helena close to a decade and I never even knew she was in Cassidy. As for the rest – Jen, Michelle, Helena, Beattie – they've all known each other since the nineties, the eighties, even. The only ones none of us knew well were you and Samira.'

'How long have you all known Kennedy?'

'Six, seven months. But if it's about money, it's not going to be her. Not on what they pay her at the club.'

Even as Nicolette spoke she got that niggling feeling again, like a flash of a blurred image, still tantalisingly evasive. It was about Kennedy, though. Nicolette had tried to look her up, find out more about her tennis tour days. It was partly out of curiosity and partly looking to embarrass her with an old photo on the hen weekend. Without a surname to go on, she had spent ages trawling through pictures from the early 2000s in the archives of tennis tour websites. She had only been able to find one. Even after locating that, when she searched for Kat Boniface the same single image was all she found.

After Nicolette presented it, Kennedy claimed it was wrongly captioned, so maybe that had been the problem. But that being so, wouldn't she have found more pictures of the real Kat Boniface?

She thought of that grainy headshot, unquestionably Kennedy's youthful face staring back at the lens. Then it hit her: the thing she had glimpsed, why it was both vivid and fleeting.

Nicolette pulled out her phone. Lauren looked quizzically at her, perhaps thinking she had briefly forgotten there was no signal.

Nicolette opened her photo gallery. She scrolled back through shots of the house, the pool, her room, the views, the furniture, Barra airport, the beach they had landed on, the aircraft they had flown in. She stopped and zoomed in on the group selfie of everybody holding their drinks in the departure lounge at Glasgow. It was difficult to believe it had only been about twelve hours ago, everyone utterly oblivious of what was waiting for them. They all looked so happy, eyes wide and smiling as they gazed into the lens. All except Kennedy. Her face was hidden behind the glass she was holding up.

That was what was niggling her. There was something familiar about the image, or lack of it.

Nicolette opened up Facebook but it hung on loading, awaiting a signal that wouldn't come. She went back to the gallery, remembering that it automatically stored all the pictures that had been shared on WhatsApp. She scrolled through the endless grid of images, zooming in when she came to certain occasions – a night out for Helena's birthday; a group selfie taken on the outside courts when they opened again after winter – all the way back to the Christmas party, the first time Kennedy had socialised with them after joining the club.

In every last picture, Kennedy's face was obscured. She was wearing a baseball cap, head down. She had just ducked out of shot. Her face was hidden behind someone's outstretched hand.

Nicolette lifted her eyes from the screen and met Lauren's, confirming that she had seen the same thing.

'I mean, she could just be camera shy, but . . .'

'No,' Lauren stated. 'That girl is hiding from somebody.'

Michelle

Helena's sudden charge drove the RIB against Michelle's knees, tipping her forward into the boat. It was now fully afloat and driving forward with the momentum. She turned and watched Helena wade towards the onrushing figure. What the hell was she doing? Why wasn't she jumping in too? Then as Michelle scrambled to get hold of the outboard, she realised it was because Helena knew there wasn't time. The man in the ski mask would have been upon them before she could start the engine.

She gripped the outboard with a strong hand and pulled the ripcord, determined to get it first time. As she did so, she saw Helena swing her golf club. Neither of them got a result. The engine failed to start, while the man feinted and blocked the swing with a hand on Helena's wrist. A second later, the two of them were grappling in the shallows.

Michelle realised she had forgotten to set the motor to neutral. She flipped the lever then tugged the ripcord again. Still nothing. Then she noticed the dangling cable and realised the kill switch was unplugged.

The man was on top of Helena now. He was holding her under, trying to drown her. She was fighting, though. Her head came up again as Michelle pulled the ripcord a third time.

The engine sounded powerful, the waves gentle. There was still enough light. She could make it to the mainland in this thing no problem. She would raise the alarm, get help. By doing that, she could save the others, maybe even save Samira. But she would not save Helena. She would not save the bitch who had hacked her cloud and leaked her sex tape. Not the bitch who had rained down all this pain and anguish.

Not the girl she had trusted because they were best friends. Not the girl she had leaned on when she didn't feel strong enough alone.

Not the girl she had left behind.

For there was no denying it: Michelle *had* left her behind. Like with Cassidy, she had feared Helena would unconsciously sabotage the whole thing because she couldn't handle where it was taking her.

So yes, she chose career over Helena, she chose opportunity over friendship. Over *best* friendship, even. And the truth was, she knew she would do it again.

But not tonight.

Michelle killed the engine and grabbed her weapon. She clambered over the back of the RIB and splashed towards the masked man, swinging the golf club as she advanced. He heard her coming, but that was okay, because he had let go of Helena and that was what she wanted.

He turned, ducked the blow. He was quick and agile. Trained. She felt an explosion in her side as his fist drove into her, her legs simultaneously swept from beneath her by his foot. Then she was under, saltwater filling her mouth, her nose, her eyes. She waited for the grip upon her neck, the irresistible pressure from above, for him to do what he had been doing to Helena.

It did not come.

She turned around and sat up, spluttering. As she wiped the spray from her stinging eyes, she saw him scrambling onto the RIB. Then she heard the roar of the outboard, felt a blast of heat and smelled a sweet whiff of petrol. He was away. The boat was away.

Michelle climbed to her feet. Alongside her in the shallows, Helena was on her knees, bent over and coughing up seawater.

Michelle waited until she was done, then held out a hand to help her up.

Helena looked at it with incredulity at first, then grasped it tight and pulled herself upright.

They stood together for a moment, watching as the RIB disappeared around the headland.

'Well, you finally got what you wanted,' Michelle said. 'This time I did chuck away my big chance, just to end up in the same shit as you.'

'No good deed ever goes unpunished,' Helena replied weakly.

Michelle looked her in the eye. 'I'm glad you're here, though. This weekend, I mean.'

Helena looked like she didn't dare believe it. 'Honestly?'

'Honestly. I'd hate for you to have missed this.'

Kennedy

Kennedy had hauled herself up to the second floor, bringing the laptop and radio with her. None of the doors were locked, so she had gone into someone else's bedroom. She wasn't sure whose, but what mattered was that it was as high as she could reach and had dual-aspect windows. It wasn't exactly a lookout tower, but she had decided the absolute least she could do for herself was to try and see who might be approaching.

She scanned for movement, shadows, anything. She wasn't just on the lookout for danger: that was only part of it. She was a dog at the window, anxiously watching and waiting for the return of the people she cared about.

Kennedy had felt relieved to hear Jen's voice over the radio, then unnerved by how little it reassured her. Unnerved also by the depth of her feelings. She had survived this far by never letting herself care too much about anyone, because soon enough they were always gone. Or she was.

She recalled a conversation they had in a coffee shop a couple of weeks back. Jen had told Kennedy, 'I'm here if you ever need to talk,' but Kennedy wouldn't let herself believe it.

Jen had given the impression she knew Kennedy was putting on a mask, but that she cared for the person behind it anyway.

Even worse, the person behind the mask was starting to care about Jen.

Kennedy used to believe she was safe where nobody knew who she was. Life on the junior tour had prepared her for the nomadic existence that followed. She told herself she was happy on the move, content in her own company, and didn't need to put down roots.

So why did it feel like she'd been running half her life?

She glanced at her laptop, remembering the places she had taken it, and more importantly the places it had taken her. She wondered what the others would think of her inability to get past the Reaper's firewall if they knew about some of her past exploits; exploits being the operative word. But of course, if the Reaper was coming for a hacker, it made sense that he'd make sure to declaw that kitty.

Kennedy was adept at moving on without leaving anything of herself behind. But having once hacked a DNA database, she of all people knew that nobody can fully escape their past.

She kept telling herself she wasn't the one who had brought this down upon them all. The problem was, it didn't matter. Just ask Samira.

That second video was so much worse. At least in the first she was slumped so that her face wasn't fully visible. Seeing her head lifted by the rope as it began to tighten had made Kennedy feel she was about to throw up. But that had become a familiar feeling of late.

Looking out into the growing darkness, it was clear that despite her elevation she wasn't going to see danger coming. Nobody was. And the darker it got, the harder it became to think that everything was going to be okay.

You're a whole other person when you're scared, she thought.

All your most comforting beliefs crumble. Such as the idea that nothing terrible will happen to you because you've never done anything that bad.

It brought no sense of solidarity to know there were six other women who must be feeling the same way. To know she wouldn't be the only one asking herself difficult questions about how she had treated certain people – and who she had chosen to trust.

Jen

Jen glanced back at Beattie, making sure she wasn't leaving her straggling. The light was fading rapidly now, and her instinct was to push the pace. It wasn't like there were any streetlights to guide them, and she didn't want to be relying on phones and torches to navigate this kind of terrain.

Beattie was doing a decent job of keeping up, but it looked like she was feeling it. She had taken off her jacket and slung it over her shoulder, still gripping her golf club in her left hand. The jacket was a pack-a-mac thing, lightweight but waterproof, probably for the boat. Jen would bet her husband Richard had an identical one. They were that kind of couple. He was away at some medical conference this weekend, in Zurich. They were always flying him off to places to speak.

Beattie hadn't said anything for a while. This was not a good sign. All those doubts about who Jason really was would be fading again with every step she took back up the hill. The version of events she had always chosen to believe would soon be restored, except now she had proof.

When Beattie finally spoke, it wasn't about that, but Jen was still sure it was underpinning her perspective.

'I've been mulling over the question of who this is about,' she said. 'And no offence, Jen, but what if it *is* still about you? I don't mean to do with Jason or Finnegan or any of that stuff, but you've had media coverage, people know you've got money now. Nobody gets to be successful in business without making enemies.'

'I sell muffins, Beattie. Not drugs or weaponry. But I take your point. People can get jealous, or feel they deserve a slice of what you have.'

'There's nobody you're instinctively suspicious of, nobody who immediately leaps to mind?'

'No,' she replied. 'To know my plans for this weekend, and to put something like this together, it would take someone observing me to an obsessive level. I'd like to think I'd notice that.'

'But would you? You above all must know how carefully people can hide their intentions.'

Beattie's dig was about what Jen had done to Jason, but that was not whose face it summoned. Jen's mind flashed an image of her bedside drawer, when she was convinced Zaki had been looking through it. When she first saw the Reaper's message her initial thought had been that Samira wasn't taken at random: that this was somehow about her brother. And now another thought, a terrible thought, began forming in her head.

Not everybody's playing an angle all the time.

The Reaper's message was intended to put them at each other's throats, keep their focus away from what might otherwise be obvious. Jen had known Helena, Michelle and Beattie for decades, but tell them *one of you is not the person you believe her to be* and everybody starts conjuring reasons to be suspicious of each other. Kennedy was under suspicion as they had known her no more than seven months; Lauren all the more so, because they had only met her a few hours ago. They had only met Samira a few hours ago too, but nobody had thought of her because Samira was the hostage.

But what if she wasn't?

A calmer voice pointed out that Samira had spent the last few months a prisoner in her own home, overwhelmed by new motherhood. She was hardly a candidate for the sleeping partner in a long con. But then it struck Jen that she had never seen these twins in the flesh, only photos on Zaki's phone. How hard would it be to pose for a couple of pics with someone else's babies?

Jen had known Zaki for almost two years but had never met his sister before today. Even with the pandemic, wasn't that a little odd? How could she be sure Samira even *was* Zaki's sister?

It's probably just that all us brown people look the same, Samira had said to Michelle. She was messing with her, but was the real joke on Jen? Was another brown face enough to convince an ignorant white woman?

The calmer voice reminded Jen that Samira had been in no state to take part in some conspiracy tonight. She had been shit-faced.

Or pretending to be.

Don't let Samira drink too much. She can't handle it at the best of times, and this is her first time let loose in forever.

When Zaki told her this it had merely seemed annoying that he should task Jen with policing his sister's booze intake at her own hen party. But what if its purpose was to prime Jen for the deception by drawing attention to it?

Jen thought of Samira's remarks to Michelle and Helena.

My favourite is Almost Famous. *All that tension between the singer and the guitarist over which one is the star.*

Not to mention how she had been with Nicolette.

270

It's as well you don't have kids then, because they wouldn't stand a chance if they were being raised by a fucking stupid cow.

She was setting people on edge. Injecting bad feeling, readying them to be suspicious of each other.

No, the calmer voice insisted: this is insane. And with that she realised whose voice it was: Zaki's. This was the very paranoia and suspicion that he was trying to cure her of. It was the legacy of her years with Jason, as though he was striking back from beyond the grave by poisoning her relationship and preventing her from finding happiness with anybody else.

Except there was no grave, a thought which brought Jen back to the other great threat to her future happiness: one that was walking three or four yards behind her, and had Jen's confession on audio.

When she glanced back, she noticed how Beattie's jacket was swinging in time with her stride. The movement was indicative of a weight in one of the side pockets. That had to be her phone. It wasn't like she'd have packed her purse in case they passed a shop, though if anybody had it would be Beattie.

Jen stopped and bent to retie the laces on her trainers. They hadn't been loose: it was so that Beattie would overtake, and she could walk behind her for a bit.

It was better than she hoped. There was definitely something in the pocket, and the flap had been tucked in rather than folded over, which meant it was loose and unfastened.

Jen kept her eyes on it as it swung, moving closer. Then there it was: a flash of grey metal.

It would be better if she could do this subtly. If Beattie didn't notice, then she might assume that the phone had fallen out at some point. But that barely mattered. The main thing was

271

getting hold of it and making sure that audio recording disappeared forever.

Jen increased her pace as they approached another hairpin bend. She made it seem a natural coming together as she was overtaking. Her hand slipped into the pocket and pinched at the phone. She only got it between her middle and forefingers, her thumb snagging on the flap. The movement caused the phone to slip from her grasp as it cleared the pocket, tumbling onto the path at her feet.

Jen was down to it like a falcon, slipping the device swiftly into the front pocket of her jeans, but the hand is never quicker than the eye.

'What are you doing with that?' Beattie asked sharply. 'Did you take that from my cagoule?' She grabbed at the jacket, patting the pocket down. 'You did! What are you doing with it?'

'There's something on it that belongs to me,' Jen told her, backing away to give herself distance. 'It's not legal to record someone without their permission, Beattie.'

Beattie straightened her stance, thrusting out her jaw. 'It's not legal to murder your husband either.'

'It was self-defence. You know that, deep down.'

But from Beattie's expression, Jen knew that she was already back in denial.

'You say you sleep fine at night and your conscience is clear. If you can justify it to yourself, you should be able to justify it to a court.'

'Aye, because the authorities have always been very understanding towards women when it comes to that kind of thing. Especially when a policeman is involved. I'm not going to jail for that bastard. He made me a prisoner long enough.'

Jen gripped the device, winding up to chuck it down the hillside as far as she could throw.

'Wait!' Beattie urged, palms out. 'Before you do that, there's something you should know.'

'What?'

'That isn't my phone.'

Before Jen could even ask herself if she was bluffing, Beattie produced a second handset, one with a navy-blue shockproof cover. The kind of cover Beattie would put on her phone.

Jen looked at the mobile in her hand, a Samsung with a cracked screen. 'Whose is this?'

'Samira's. I found it when Nicolette and I got sent to look for her. It was just sitting by the sink in her room, not even charging. She must have gone to the loo and forgotten about it.'

At least this settled one question: Samira couldn't be part of this if she had taken off without her phone. Or couldn't she? Leaving it behind would provide further evidence of her apparent abduction. Plus there was no signal, so if Samira was part of this, she wouldn't be communicating by phone anyway. Not tonight at least. But there would have been prior communications. Like the kind of email you deleted if you were the one who made a show of sharing a laptop with the mark in a long con.

Jen pressed the button to wake it. It was locked.

This is insane, said that calmer voice. Zaki's voice. *You sound crazy.*

She thought about when she first saw him at that trade exhibition. She had been the one who walked up to him. But had he subtly placed himself in her path? And how many times might he have done that, waiting for her to stumble onto him? That was how long cons worked. They made sure you always

273

thought you were the one making the moves, while the con artist appeared the passive party.

She swiped to wake the screen again. It wasn't asking for a pin, but looking for a pattern.

It couldn't be, could it?

She drew a Z.

The phone unlocked.

Jen's heart surged.

She went straight to the email app. The main account was mostly shopping and admin stuff. Nothing older than seven days, auto-deleted after that. A second account was work-related. There was nothing in it, which tracked, as Samira wouldn't have been at work for months.

Jen scrolled down further, and there at the bottom was the account name that stopped her heart.

grimpox02@vapourmail.com.

Helena

Helena felt a surge of relief as she spied a break in the trees and recognised it as the main track through the woods. There was still just about light enough to see, but it was darker beneath the canopy, and even with the torch she worried it was only a matter of time before one of them took a spill.

They were both soaking from head to toe and starting to feel the cold, but she knew it could have been so much worse. Despite her relief, something about their encounter at the beach continued to trouble her.

'He could have killed me,' she said.

'I gathered that. It's why I so selflessly blew my chance of escape to come to your rescue, remember?'

'No, what I'm saying is, I was struggling but he was much stronger than me. He *let* me surface. He wanted you out of the boat. He knew you would come back and help if it looked like he was drowning me.'

'I'm not sure you can assume that. No offence, but in the early moments, *I* wasn't sure I was going to come back and help you.'

'What I mean is, he was primarily interested in the boat, or stopping anyone getting away on it. Because once you got out of it, he could have killed you if he'd wanted, killed both of us.'

'I see what you're saying,' Michelle replied. 'For all the threats and messages about rules, the bottom line is they want us stuck here, alive.'

Despite the cold, the return journey felt shorter, perhaps because they were talking more. It felt easier, if sad, but sad was better than hateful.

'I don't think there's any way I can ever make up for what I did,' Helena said. 'But if you think of something, let me know.'

'Maybe we should call it quits and move on. Besides, there's nothing so terrible that you can't get a song out of it.'

'You've written a song about the sex tape?'

'Yeah. It's called "Jerk-Offs". It's about all the jealous little nobodies out there, how they think they've put me down because they've watched me fuck, while they are literally just wankers.'

The thought of it hit Helena to the gut, all the implications she had been in denial over. Michelle sounded sincere about moving on, but Helena would be a lot longer in forgiving herself.

'My daughters are both big fans,' she admitted. 'They probably felt disloyal at first. I tiptoed around the subject, and they always knew you were a sore point, but they still bought your records.'

'I'm sorry I didn't get to know them growing up. I'd have liked to, but you know . . .'

'I think we both know I wouldn't have responded well had you reached out.'

Michelle shook her head. 'I would never have admitted it to myself, but there must have been a thousand times on tour or in the studio when I thought it would be easier if you were there; how you'd instantly get what I was trying for with a sound or a melody. I missed you. There, I said it out loud. I missed you.'

'I missed you too,' Helena replied, having to swallow to get the words out. 'Moments like when my daughters were born, all the milestones. I denied it to myself, but part of me wished you could be there to share them.'

'It's not too late,' Michelle told her. 'We've just wasted a few years, that's all. We're not dead yet.'

'Let's keep it that way.'

The rutted and dusty track turned to neatly raked gravel as they neared the house, heather and gorse to well-kept lawns. Looking at the care and attention lavished on the grounds, Helena remembered that Lauren's maintenance staff were due back here on Monday. It wasn't soon enough but it wasn't indefinite either.

She heard her phone chime as they approached the building, her device reconnecting to the wi-fi and receiving a new message on the Reaper's app. It was the video Kennedy had told them about, reminding Helena that the only time-frame that mattered was how long it took ice to melt.

'Don't watch it,' Michelle urged her. 'We all know what's on there.'

Kennedy hobbled out of the drawing room in response to the sound of Helena and Michelle entering the downstairs hallway. 'Thank God you're both okay.'

The poor girl hadn't gone anywhere and yet she looked wrung out. It only belatedly struck Helena that being left here alone might have been a scarier shift than the one anyone else had been handed.

'Okay is relative,' Michelle muttered, the two of them hurrying upstairs to get changed out of their wet clothes.

Helena stripped and patted herself from top to toe with a towel. She had seldom known cotton to feel so welcome against her skin, but it only served to emphasise how much had changed in a matter of hours. Luxury was meaningless. Everything now was reduced to function, to survival.

She could hear more voices as she re-emerged from her bedroom, Michelle appearing at the same time. She saw Nicolette and Lauren standing in the entrance hall. Everybody was asking if everybody else was okay, but nobody had any news that hadn't already been relayed over the radios.

'I'm starving, actually,' said Michelle, as though surprised by the revelation. 'I haven't eaten since late morning and I'm suddenly feeling it.'

Helena realised she was feeling it too, that she had been hungry for ages but too distracted to fully notice it.

Kennedy grimaced, indicating the closed door of the kitchen.

'I don't care,' Michelle said, striding past her and down the hall. 'I'm getting shaky, hypoglycaemic. I just need a hunk of bread, anything. I've seen him dead once. He's not going to get any scarier.'

Helena looked away as Michelle reached the door. She didn't want to see the body again.

'Fuck!'

Michelle's voice was loud with shock. She had stopped in the doorway again, like déjà vu.

Helena's heart surged as she looked up, fearing who else might be dead. Instead she saw that the body count had been altered in the opposite way.

The chef was gone.

Nicolette

'How in the name of Christ can he be gone?' Nicolette asked. She found herself moving down the hall despite the fear the kitchen held. Like the body itself, she had to see its absence with her own eyes to believe it. The chef's corpse had taken on such significance in her mind that it seemed impossible that it should have disappeared.

Michelle was right, though. The puddles of blood remained around and on top of the kitchen island, but the chef was no longer there.

'Is it possible he wasn't dead?' Michelle asked. 'I was sure I saw his chest move when I first found him.'

'He was dead,' said Kennedy sharply. 'He'd had his throat opened. You don't lie down for a minute then get up and walk it off.'

Nicolette ventured a few paces deeper into the kitchen alongside Michelle. She still felt an aversion despite the absence of the corpse, like the place was infused with menace from what had happened there.

Behind the island she could see streaks of blood trailing towards the back door.

'Someone dragged him out of here,' Michelle said.

'Didn't you hear anything?' Nicolette asked Kennedy.

'No. The walls are very thick,' she said. 'And I was upstairs – trying to keep a lookout.'

Lauren and Nicolette shared a look. They had speculated that Kennedy was hiding from someone. She was the one who had been alone here with the chef's body, and perhaps the one with reason to cover up what had happened to him. Joaquin had been secretly foisted upon them, with both Jen and Lauren assuming it was at the other's request. Had Kennedy recognised him? Had she killed him because she knew his true agenda here?

All eyes switched from the kitchen to the other end of the hallway as they heard the front door being opened. It struck Nicolette that there were killers on the loose, yet nobody had taken steps to establish any kind of security in the place where they were all holed up. Fortunately, it was just Jen and Beattie.

There was a distinctive energy to Jen's face. While everyone else looked drained and distraught, she looked on the verge of raging.

Jen took in the gathering around the kitchen door. 'What did we miss?'

'Joaquin's body is gone,' Michelle told her. 'We just found out.'

'Why would they do that?'

'Getting ready to cover their tracks, maybe,' suggested Lauren.

'Cover their tracks?' replied Michelle. 'There's seven witnesses that he was lying right there.'

'At this stage I don't see how it makes any odds,' Nicolette said. 'The fact is, we're back where we started. Literally. We didn't contact the authorities, we don't have a boat, and Samira's time is running out.' She looked Kennedy directly in the eye. 'Anybody feel like telling a secret?'

Kennedy met her gaze but there was an unfamiliar timidity about her expression, and she didn't reply.

Jen did, though. 'Well, I don't like to speak on someone else's behalf, but I suspect Samira has got a doozy.'

There was a moment of silence as everyone took this in, wrestling with the possible implications and getting nowhere.

Jen held up a mobile.

'This is Samira's phone. It unlocks using Z as a pattern. Z for Zaki. All this bullshit about someone not being who you think, all this "secrets and confessions" nonsense, it's intended as a distraction from the two people who are quite definitely not who we think. My so-called fiancé and his wee sister – if she even is his sister – are in this together. We're being played. The hostage videos are fake.'

'*Zaki?*' Helena asked, her tone suggesting Jen might be losing it. She wasn't the only one. Nicolette had thought Samira was for the watching, but she just meant in terms of being a two-faced snider. And as for Zaki, no way. Nicolette thought he was a bit sketchy but the two of them always seemed so loved up.

'I had this fear that he was too good to be true, that he was getting close to me because he was after my money. Turns out I was right.'

She showed them all an email from Zaki to Samira.

'"Subject: Our little secret",' Jen quoted. '"Message: All systems go. She doesn't suspect a thing." He was deleting emails last night. We argued about it.'

'Bloody hell,' said Lauren.

'That's not all. He's been working this for a long time. He made a big deal about having no password on his laptop, making out he was keeping no secrets from me. It was a bluff so that I didn't suspect he had *my* password and was rooting around in my accounts. I'm betting he's used my socials to research everybody who was going to be here. And just to drive it home, he was the one who insisted I invite Samira, even though I'd never met her before.'

'Christ, Jen,' said Helena, putting a supportive hand on her shoulder. 'What do you think he wants? And why would he kill the chef?'

'Money. This shit's always about money. I don't know what his next play is, but I do know the game has changed. People are due back here on Monday: staff, Michelle's boat back to Rum, our helicopter. We can fortify this place, wait it out. Now we know what's really going on, time is on our side.'

Kennedy had a weird look on her face. Nicolette was about to ask her about it when the hallway reverberated with the sounds of seven phones chiming. Nicolette reached for her handset. It showed the preview frame of a third video.

Jen glanced at it, wearing a look of grim vindication. 'Safe to say they've bugged us too,' she said. 'They're upping the stakes in response to me sussing them out. Well, I'm calling their bluff.'

Nicolette played the clip. The ice had melted further, and the rope was tightening. Samira's eyes were still closed but she looked like she might be starting to respond.

'I'm calling your bluff, you creepy fucking arseholes,' Jen shouted, her fury echoing around the walls. She didn't sound like herself. Jen had always been a bit paranoid, and this email from Zaki was unquestionably suss, but not enough to bet Samira's life on.

Nicolette had to say something. She held out the handset. 'Look at her, Jen. Are you telling me she's acting?'

'I'm telling you Zaki's been acting the whole time.'

'Pretending that he loves you? For two years?'

'That's how long cons work, Nicolette.'

'And what if you're wrong? How are you going to tell Zaki

you let his sister die because you thought he was a con artist?'

Jen was thinking about this at least, but Samira didn't have time for soul-searching. Nicolette looked around at the others. Everybody seemed paralysed. All eyes were on Jen, who had offered them something tempting to believe in, but a very dangerous kind of hope.

All eyes, that was, except Kennedy's. Hers were fixed on the floor, where they had been for some time. She hadn't said a word since claiming she'd heard nothing while someone entered the kitchen and took the chef's body away.

Nicolette had said her instincts were worth bugger all, but they had been right that Lauren had an agenda at the croft. Now they were screaming that Kennedy was hiding something.

Nicolette thrust her screen into Kennedy's view.

'I say again, do you feel like telling us anything, Kennedy? Fiona? Kat? Or whatever your real name is? Maybe something about why your face never appears in any photographs? Because now would be a really good time. Or do you not care who gets hurt as long as it keeps your secret?'

Kennedy's gaze met Nicolette's for the briefest moment, but long enough to see fear, shame and defeat. Tears filled the younger woman's eyes.

'I can't do this any more,' she said, her voice breaking. 'I can't fucking . . .'

She slid down the wall and fell into a crouch against the skirting board, where she began thumbing at her phone with a millennial's frantic dexterity.

A moment later, six phones chimed again.

Kennedy: I'll give u what u want. I'll admit to it all. Just cut her loose.

Jen

As Jen looked at the message, this stark and brief statement of confession, her first instinct was to ask herself what Zaki and Samira wanted with Kennedy, what could have brought them together in this conspiracy. Then it finally hit home just how far down the labyrinth she had gone: to believe her fiancé had been working her for years; to watch Samira's suffering and write it off as an act.

Not everyone is playing an angle.

The root of her paranoia was the inability to accept that someone like Zaki wanted to be with her, to believe she was good enough, and that she deserved to be happy.

Her phone chimed again and again. There were seven people in the hallway, none of them speaking, all of them staring at their screens, all of them in crisis, a remote presence firing poison into their midst.

It was truly a portrait of the age.

The reverberations made her conscious that the music was no longer playing, and hadn't been since they returned. She had been wrong about Zaki but suspected she was right about them being bugged. The timing of the Reaper sending that last video was too much of a coincidence. He had sent it in response to what was being said.

284

Kennedy: What do you want?

The Reaper: Tell everyone what you've done.

Kennedy: Cut her loose first. You still have your hostage.

There was a pause.

The Reaper: Type faster. ⬛

Kennedy looked up from the floor then returned her attention to her phone.

Kennedy: I'm a criminal. A blackmailer. Now cut her down.

The Reaper: Not until I get reparation.

Kennedy: What do u want?

The Reaper: What you took. ⬛

Jen felt a surge of fury. She tapped at her own screen.

Jen: You can only kill her once, arsehole. Once she dies you have no more leverage. Cut her down.

Jen's heart beat harder as she waited for a response. It felt loud enough to be audible amid the silence. Ten seconds became thirty, became a minute.

Two minutes.

She was starting to worry she had forced him to prove her wrong, that he could kill Samira and then take a new hostage.

Then finally the Reaper responded, in the form of another video. It lasted barely a second, long enough to show that while Samira was still strapped to the chair, the noose had been adjusted. It was a demonstration that he was granting more time but nothing more.

'You're a blackmailer?' Nicolette asked.

Kennedy bit her lip, looking up from where she was crouched against the skirting. She nodded. It appeared for a moment that she might not elaborate, but then she straightened her back and spoke.

'Let's just say when it became clear I wasn't going to make it as a pro, I had difficulty adjusting. I moved around Europe for a bit, mostly bar work and the odd bit of coaching. I was angry and messed up and I thought the world owed me something better. Long story short, I became pretty good at identity fraud.

'A few years ago, I managed to wangle a log-in to a DNA database. It was a very subtle breach, which meant I could keep dipping in for more information.'

'Blackmail material,' Jen said.

'There's a lot of money in knowing who somebody's real father is,' Kennedy replied. 'Sometimes it's cheaper to pay up than to be liable for paternity. But there can be other reasons you don't want the world to know you're somebody's daddy.'

'Who are we talking about here?' Jen asked. 'Who is the Reaper?'

'His name is Jordi Cabrera. As in the Cabrera scandal.'

Blank looks were exchanged. Kennedy frowned. 'It was a big story in Spain. Obviously not so much elsewhere. The Cabreras are – were – a political dynasty in Catalonia. They had a finger in everything until it came out that they were taking kickbacks on an incredible scale.'

Jen remembered the report she had glimpsed on TV in the departure lounge this morning. The Catalan Kardashians.

'They had major organised-crime connections too,' Kennedy went on, 'including Francisco Aguilar. He's a major player, originally from Mexico, with precisely what you think that entails.'

'That's who's coming after you?' Helena asked with a mixture of horror and incredulity. 'The cartels?'

'No. That's what I was leveraging. I had DNA proof that Jordi Cabrera is the biological father of Francisco Aguilar's youngest daughter. He had been shagging Aguilar's wife. I extorted money from him to keep that quiet.'

'When was this?' Michelle asked.

'About five years ago.'

'Why has he come now?'

'He was in jail for three years because of the scandal. When he got out, he would have been angry, broke and desperate. I thought I had covered my tracks better, but you always leave traces. He must have worked out who I was. As I said, identity fraud was my thing, so I've been on the move for years. I decided South Lanarkshire would be suitably low profile.'

Jen swallowed. She barely dared to ask, but she had to.

'How much?'

'It was around two million euros.'

'You've been sitting on two million euros?' Nicolette asked. From her tone Jen could imagine Nicolette's disdain for Kennedy's wardrobe choices becoming considerably deeper.

'I've been sitting on two tennis rackets and a laptop. I rent a one-bedroom flat in Hamilton. I've got the clothes on my back and a few hundred in cash in case I need to run again.'

'What happened to it all?'

'Let's just say I had a good couple of years. That might have contributed to them working out who I was. Spent about a quarter mil. The rest went into the ether.'

'How?'

'I took the blackmail pay-off in bitcoin. Untraceable. But crypto was the Wild West back then. The scammer got scammed. Somebody cleaned me out.'

'And now Cabrera wants his two million back,' Jen said.

'No,' Kennedy replied. 'He said he wants what I *took*. He means he wants what the bitcoin would be worth now.'

'Which would be what?'

Kennedy's voice cracked. She swallowed. 'Unless the bubble has finally burst since I last checked, around seven million euros.'

'Seven million?' Helena gasped. 'He can't possibly believe you have that.'

'He would if he assumes I've been pulling the same scams down the years.'

'This is the other reason they didn't cut the internet altogether,' Lauren observed. 'It's needed for money transfers.'

'You knew all along, didn't you?' said Nicolette, barely keeping the anger from her voice. 'When we got the Reaper's message, you knew everything. You sent us all out, hoping we might find Samira and that would buy you time to run. But they did this here on this island so you had nowhere to run to.'

Kennedy nodded.

'When I saw the message I was afraid it meant me, but I was still hoping it would be someone else. I mean, wasn't everybody?'

Then seven phones chimed once again.

The Reaper: Just to be clear, Kennedy, if I don't get what I am owed, I will not only kill Samira. I will kill you too. Not here, and not tonight, but soon. You will not know the

288

day or the hour. And if it is the only pleasure I am going to get from you, then I will make sure it lasts.

Kennedy closed her eyes, a tear streaking down her cheek. She sat crumpled on the floor with her hands hugging her legs, her left foot sheathed in its support brace. She was so fragile, so broken, nothing like the irrepressible figure who had brought so much light into Jen's life. She looked as though you could break her like a twig: scared, vulnerable and, Jen was sure, pregnant.

Jen thought of the confession on Beattie's phone. It had turned out to be Kennedy's crime that was being balanced against Samira's life, but it could just as easily have been Jen's. How much would she give to make sure her secret stayed beneath the dark waters of the Clyde? How much would she give to make it up to the ones she had caused such pain?

'Tell him you'll pay,' Jen said.

Kennedy looked up, uncomprehending.

'It'll hurt,' Jen told her. 'But not as much as losing Samira or losing you. I mean, I don't have seven million euros, but I've got money.'

She glanced at Michelle, who stared back for a moment and then gave a nod, subtle but definite.

'Me too,' she said. 'How much do you have that's liquid?'

Jen did some quick calculations. 'I can move maybe one and a quarter tonight at a push. You?'

'Two point five. I've got that in bitcoin already.'

'No. This isn't right,' said Kennedy. 'I can't—'

'But it is, though,' Jen replied. 'Because it's like you said. It could have been any of us.'

Jen looked at Beattie. 'I know what it is to have done something terrible, to have hurt somebody. I know what it is to need to pay a penance.'

Beattie's eyes flickered, a break in the permanent wall of cold neutrality she sent Jen's way.

'I hurt somebody too,' said Michelle. 'I dumped my best friend for the sake of my career.'

Everyone looked at Helena for a response to this admission.

'I leaked Michelle's sex tape,' she said.

That was a showstopper.

Michelle reached out and grasped Helena's hand. Squeezed it. They had been through this already.

'I'm an online troll,' said Nicolette. 'I sent abuse and death threats to Lauren. Her and a hundred others.'

This was clearly not news to Lauren, and she was not about to cast the first stone.

'I made my fortune exploiting people who were in debt,' Lauren confessed. 'I specialised in screwing the vulnerable.'

Beattie swallowed. 'I was distracted when I hit that drunk guy. I might not have killed him if I was paying proper attention.'

Jen wondered why Beattie still believed this, then realised she probably didn't. She had another motive for her confession. Everyone was looking at Jen, the only one who had not said what her secret was.

Jen cleared her throat. 'Jason terrorised me and my children for years, then when I threatened to leave, he said he would kill the kids and frame me for it.'

They all stared at her expectantly, aware that this was not a confession.

'I killed him,' she said. 'I drugged him and drowned him in the Clyde. I left Beattie and her family with the pain of not knowing.'

Nobody spoke. Even Kennedy looked gobsmacked, so Jen could be in no doubt who had won the Biggest Sinner trophy. That said, Kennedy had looked more shocked by what Jason had threatened to do than by Jen's actions in response, which made her feel a little better.

Jen's eyes met Beattie's again. Beattie gave a curt nod of acknowledgement; not exactly a thank you, but she could hardly expect that.

Jen looked at Kennedy. 'The bottom line is that we've all got something to atone for. So maybe this is justice.'

Michelle

There weren't many things Michelle would have thought could distract her from the prospect of handing over two and a half million euros to a psychotic extortionist. Learning that one of her oldest friends had murdered her husband was definitely one of them. There was barely time to process it, though it did make her realise that in volunteering what they each had to atone for, Michelle hadn't named her biggest sin.

Jen had never told her outright what it was like living with Jason, but Michelle had known enough to imagine. She knew also why Jen wouldn't have told her, wouldn't have told anybody. The shame. The denial. The self-recrimination.

It had taken years for her to understand that what Jason had done to Michelle was actually rape. She had the same misapprehension as everybody else: that it had been consensual, that boys were always going to be the ones who pushed things sexually. Now, as an adult, she could see that though there hadn't been violence at the time, nor an explicit threat of it, that didn't mean it wasn't always present. There had been a constant fear of what might happen if she didn't please Jason, and also of what would happen if she didn't go along with pretending it was what she wanted. That was what coercive control meant.

Michelle did not want to think about how bad it must have got before Jen did what she did. She wasn't sure Beattie would see it the same way, though. Beattie knew too: that much was clear from her lack of response to the revelation. Jen must have told her already. There was a vibe between them even tenser than normal when they came back from the cave. It wasn't the kind of thing you just got past.

'I recently sold a place,' said Lauren. 'I can move about eight hundred thousand.'

'What about you, Nicolette?' asked Jen.

Nicolette looked at the carpet a moment. 'I've got about six hundred,' she said.

'Thousand?' Jen clarified.

'Pounds.' Nicolette's cheeks flushed. 'One more confession. I'm not some high-flyer at Reiss. I made that up because when I first met all you guys you seemed so together and impressive. I'm a retail assistant in the Buchanan Galleries. I'm sorry. About everything.'

'Can you at least get us a discount next time we're in?' Jen asked.

Nicolette's eyes filled at this. Only Jen could put someone at ease like that, even in the worst circumstances.

'I don't have much now either,' said Helena. 'But I want to contribute. I can pay you back later. I've things I can sell. I've a 1965 Gibson Les Paul worth close to thirty.'

The past few hours had been a salutary exercise in understanding what Michelle was and wasn't prepared to lose. In a way it was a relief learning the price would just be money. She had seen one dead person tonight, and spent much of the time since fearing he would not be the last.

When she saw that bastard holding Helena under the water,

it erased all the bullshit between them. She had jumped from the boat without thinking about the consequences for herself. Of course, that changed the moment she felt his hands upon her, but for that brief moment all Michelle had cared about was that her friend needed help.

'Don't even think about it,' she insisted. 'The Les Paul stays.'

'But it's not fair that you—'

'Let's not turn this into an extreme version of who's paying for the coffee,' Jen told them all.

Michelle had often wondered at the trade-offs she made in life, asking herself would she be happier with less if it would make certain things right. Life didn't work that way though.

'We all know it's an ill-divided world,' she said. 'Some get over-rewarded for their success, some get over-punished for their mistakes. But what we give tonight, we give collectively. It doesn't matter who pays what. And it's the price of absolution for everybody, right?'

'Right,' they all replied.

All except Beattie, whose eyes went to her phone even though there had been no new message.

'By my arithmetic I reckon we can pull together about five million euros,' Jen said. 'Tell him that's the first and final offer, because we can't do any better tonight.'

Kennedy sent the message and again they waited.

Less than a minute later, the Reaper responded with a screen full of gobbledegook: numbers and codes.

Jen looked to Kennedy. 'You know what this is?'

Kennedy nodded solemnly, apologetically. 'It's for a bitcoin transfer, so that the money can't be traced.'

There was also a new video. The noose around Samira's neck had been tightened again. He was putting them back on the clock.

The Reaper: By my estimate you have half an hour to complete the transfer.

'I need my laptop,' Kennedy said. She climbed awkwardly to her feet and they all followed her into the drawing room.

'The fucker's biting our hands off,' Michelle observed. She wasn't complaining, but she was surprised he didn't push for more. Kennedy did mention he was desperate. 'Well, now that we know who he is we can track the bastard down.'

Jen was making crazy waving motions, then put a finger to her lips.

'What?' asked Michelle.

'I think he can hear us.'

'Shit.'

A few seconds later, she got confirmation.

The Reaper: I have your chef's body. I also have the murder weapon, bearing a set of prints transferred from one of you. Think of it like Russian roulette. If any of you go to the authorities, you will never know if it is your own prints that will be found on the box cutter. That is if you are insufficiently motivated by the fact that I will, of course, also kill my blackmailer.

There was an expectant silence in the room while Kennedy worked at the laptop. Michelle and Jen had supplied the necessary details, written on a notepad. Michelle felt sickened watching it, even though she knew she was doing the right thing, but the time to get angry was once everybody was safe. Starting with Samira.

Glancing at the empty glasses from what were supposed to be pre-dinner cocktails, Michelle realised that part of what she was feeling was hunger. She had been on her way to grab something to eat when she discovered the chef was gone.

'I'm starving,' she announced. 'I'm going to the kitchen.'

'I'll come with you,' said Jen. 'We'll bring back something for everybody.'

As they approached the kitchen door, they stopped, briefly looked at each other then fell into a hug.

'I'm so sorry,' Michelle said.

'For what?'

'Jason. What you went through. What you had to do. I knew what he was like, and I didn't warn you.'

'Don't be daft. How could you have known? You were what, fifteen?'

'There were signs.'

'Come on, Shell. If there's one thing that tonight's taught us, it's that we need to learn to forgive ourselves. Anyway, I'm the one who should apologise. You made the effort to come here for my hen do and you're walking away two and a half mil lighter.'

'I made almost that much investing in your business,' Michelle reminded her. 'Anyway, money is replaceable. People aren't. Neither's friendship. I think Helena and I are good again, so that's something. Admittedly I think we were good before I had to cough up, but sometimes it needs to hurt for you to learn a lesson. That said, I could use a drink. And I have *got* to eat something.'

They strode into the kitchen, where there was an unpleasant smell in the air; not overpowering, but noticeable. It was the blood. It reminded Michelle of a market she had visited in Bangkok where a recently slaughtered goat was being butchered in front of her. The sight of it had galvanised her recently acquired vegetarianism.

The aroma was mixed with something else, probably the spatchcocked quails the blood had spilled over on the island.

Taking care not to step on the pools and trails on the floor, Michelle opened a cupboard, hoping to find a loaf. There was no bread, and not much else in there either, just a bag of dried pasta and a box of porridge oats.

The next cupboards she tried held only crockery, but across the room Jen had slightly better luck. She opened a door to reveal a stack of cans: chopped tomatoes, chickpeas, cannellini beans, coconut milk. Still no bread, though.

'It's just standard storecupboard ingredients,' Jen said, with more confusion than disappointment. It had been a long time since Michelle had needed to worry about her own catering, so she didn't get the problem.

'I would settle for cold chickpeas right now,' she said. 'And I'd eat them from the tin.'

But Jen had stepped across a puddle and opened the fridge. There was some veg in there, enough to throw together a decent salad – if the worktop hadn't been covered in blood.

Jen stepped away but left the fridge door open. She had a troubled look on her face.

'What's wrong?'

'This looks like stuff left over from the previous guests.'

Michelle still didn't get it. 'So? Waste not, want not?' she suggested.

'We were signed up for three days of fine dining, and there's seven of us. Where's all the stuff?'

Jen opened more cupboards, revealing only glasses, mugs and a small stash of baking staples.

'It must all be somewhere,' Michelle said. 'It's not like the chef thought, Well, there's no point in bringing enough for three days if I'm going to be murdered on the Friday night.'

'Yes,' Jen said, looking intently at her. 'That's exactly what it's like. He only brought enough for one meal. Or maybe just the appearance of preparing one meal.'

'Come on, Jen. What are you saying? That he was in on it? He was lying on the floor with his throat cut.'

'He's not lying on the floor now, is he?'

Michelle recalled the moment of opening the door to find him there, the awful knowledge that she had seen his chest move, that she had witnessed him breathe his last.

Then Jen reminded her what had happened next. 'Kennedy checked his pulse. She was the one who told us he was dead.'

'Yes,' Michelle replied, 'and she was aggressively adamant about it just now when we found the body was gone.'

Jen leaned back against the draining board, colour rushing to her face. Blood. Energy. Anger.

'I've already convinced myself of something embarrassingly insane in the past hour,' she said. 'I want you to walk through this with me. Was all that stuff about corrupt Spanish politicos and Mexican gangsters just a bullshit back-story? Is my friend Kennedy, teary and frightened Kennedy, stealing five million euros from us in the sitting room right now?'

'I don't know,' Michelle admitted. 'Remember, this whole theory falls apart if we find we've missed a second fridge or a crate full of supplies at the back door.'

But the image of Kennedy tapping away at the laptop, getting ready to transfer all of Michelle's bitcoin, pulled something into focus.

'Identity fraud,' Michelle said. 'She as good as told us she's a scam artist. But she's more than that: she's a fucking hacker. She has to be. Whether the back-story is bullshit or not, you don't just "wangle" a log-in for a DNA database. She was fudging the term because she didn't want you making the connection that your and Lauren's emails were hacked.'

'Which was done to foist Joaquin onto us,' Jen replied. 'Her co-conspirator. Fuck, I just remembered. The previous tennis coach got fired for inappropriate use of a computer.'

'Creating a vacancy which was promptly filled by Kennedy?'

Jen nodded solemnly, like she was trying to keep herself in check. 'Kennedy, who just happened to injure herself a couple of days ago, meaning she could stay here at the house while we all ran about the island on a wild-goose chase. Teaming us up with people we bore grudges against, to increase the sense of paranoia and bad blood.'

'How did she know?'

'She's been getting close to us for the past seven months. I must have mentioned that things were strained with Beattie. And half the world knew about you and Helena.'

'But how could she know about all our, you know . . . our secrets?'

'Everybody's got a secret, Michelle, something they regret, something they would be mortified by if anyone knew. So she puts us in a situation where we're all forced to confront our guilt, so much so that we decide to help pay for her sins as an atonement for our own.'

'Christ.'

'So, am I crazy? What do you say?'

'I say we shut down that fucking laptop. Only problem is, we don't have proof of any of this. How are we going to convince the others?'

Jen wore a look of menace. 'Leave that to me,' she said. 'I'll make it music to their ears.'

Jen

Kennedy was perched on the central settee, hunching over the low table as she tapped the keyboard. She was so intent upon her screen that it was doubtful she noticed Michelle had remained at the door, blocking her possible exit.

Jen glanced down at her mobile as she approached, pressing send once she was at Kennedy's side.

All the phones chimed, prompting everyone to respond; everyone but Jen and Michelle. Jen watched Kennedy pick up her handset and unlock it with thumbprint recognition. That was when Jen snatched it from her grasp, slamming the laptop closed with her other hand.

'What the—?'

Jen put a finger to her lips. 'He's listening, remember?' she said in a whisper. 'Let me cover it up with some tunes.'

She toggled through the open apps on Kennedy's phone as she stepped away, Kennedy getting to her feet in response.

Jen paused, momentarily halted by what else she had just found, then hit play on the music-streaming app.

A familiar jangly intro played over the speakers.

'"She Knows",' Michelle said, staring triumphantly at Kennedy.

'What the hell's going on?' asked Helena.

'We've got good news and bad news,' Jen replied. 'The good news is that the chef isn't dead.'

'*What?*'

'The bad news is that he's the one who's been running around out there in a ski mask, so we didn't recognise him. He's in cahoots with Kennedy to kidnap Samira and extort our money. It was Kennedy who declared him dead, remember?'

Jen could tell the exact moment when what she was saying sank in, because that was when they all turned to look at the tennis coach.

Kennedy held up her hands in a gesture of exasperation and let out a mirthless chuckle. Her eyes went to the door, though, where Michelle stood gripping a golf club.

'This is insane. Come on, Jen, I get that we're all stressed out our boxes here, going nuts with paranoia, but come on. Half an hour ago you were convinced the Reaper was your own fiancé.'

Jen skipped to the next track, Manic Street Preachers' 'Tsunami'. She played a burst then skipped again. OMD's 'Secret'. Hole's 'Celebrity Skin'. 'Crash' by the Primitives.

'The playlist we couldn't change,' Jen said. 'She was controlling it from her phone. But that's not all she's controlling.'

Jen toggled to the app she had found a few moments before. Among the active fields were 'Signal strength', 'Distance to transmitter', 'Channel frequency' and 'Mute'.

She hit the last and held up the screen for the others to see.

'I said he was listening to us. Well, this is how. She's got an app that relays to a radio somewhere, so she can stay in contact.'

Kennedy looked around the room, gauging the response. Jen was doing the same. The jury hadn't needed to deliberate: nobody had any doubt once they heard the music. Helena looked hurt. Nicolette looked vindicated. Lauren looked furious. Only Beattie looked unperturbed, like it didn't matter who was doing this, because nothing mattered as much as what Jen had done to her brother.

Jen couldn't afford to think about that, though. 'You're blown, Kennedy. You're in the hole for fraud, extortion and kidnapping. Your best chance is to do the right thing. Where is Samira?'

Kennedy's voice was different when she responded, drained of its usual bubbly energy. She sounded immediately older, grimmer.

'Knowing won't help you,' she said.

'Then there's no reason not to tell us.'

Kennedy thought about it, then seemed to come to a decision. Sat back down. 'She's on the boat.'

'How can she be on the boat?' Helena asked. 'She's somewhere rocky and that last video only came in ten minutes ago.'

'She's on the boat,' Kennedy repeated. 'In front of a green sheet. There's no rock and no ice. That's all layered in by computer. It's all about adjusting the length of the noose.'

Everyone looked again at their phones, but Jen kept an eye on Kennedy in case she used the moment of distraction to do something drastic. She wasn't getting far with that brace, though. Jen doubted her injury was real, but she had been confronted before she had the chance to take off the boot.

Jen now understood why the image was so low-res, dark and grainy. It was so nobody noticed the special effects, even if they could bring themselves to look at it long enough.

'Who is he, the chef?' Lauren asked.

Kennedy shook her head. 'The less you know, the better.'

'It's not just the chef, though, is it?' said Michelle. 'I found him on the floor just before Samira went missing. Someone else had to have taken her to the boat. So there's three of you.'

Kennedy tried to look nonplussed by this deduction, but Jen could tell she was rattled. It was hardly a stunning revelation that there should be a third pair of hands, so there was something about this other person that Kennedy didn't want known.

'What was the plan once you got the money?' Jen asked. 'When we got back to the mainland, were you really banking on us not telling the cops because of the dead chef? There would be corroborative testimony from seven people about what really went down, so the first thing the cops would do is look into you and your supposed blackmail activities.

'You were going to disappear, weren't you? We'd never see you again. Maybe we'd think you were running from Cabrera, or maybe we'd suss your true role once it was too late. You'd have to disappear because you were the face of the operation, and that makes you its greatest liability. You can name both of your accomplices.'

Jen unmuted the relay app on Kennedy's phone.

'Listen, fucker. Yes, I'm talking to you, the prick who's got Samira. The ball's on the slates. We know Kennedy's in on this, which means she can identify you. So here's what's going to happen. You bring Samira back and we trade her for Kennedy. You still have the boat, so you'll have a head start before we can alert the authorities. Plenty of time for Kennedy to pack up her life and disappear.'

Jen waited for a response but was met with silence.

'Cut your losses,' she said. 'If the cops don't find her, they can't find you.'

Still she heard nothing. Then the phones all chimed.

The Reaper: Money first.

'Fuck,' Jen muttered.

He knew that as long as he held Samira, he could still dictate the terms. And Samira was all that mattered.

'Why isn't he just talking?' Nicolette asked. 'Why is he still sending text messages?'

'He doesn't want us to hear his voice,' Michelle replied. 'Nothing that might help us identify him later.'

'Complete the transfer,' Jen instructed Kennedy.

Kennedy opened the laptop again and resumed what she had been doing.

Nicolette was taking photos of her, presumably to give to the cops. The sight reminded Jen that it wouldn't be the only phone bearing incriminating evidence, but now it wasn't only Beattie who had heard her confession. Jen's whole world was falling apart because of this person who had somehow slipped under her paranoid defences.

'Why were you really crying in that café?' Jen asked. 'Was it all part of the act?'

Kennedy kept her eyes on the laptop and said nothing. Her lip did tremble though.

'It worked,' Jen told her. 'I felt so sorry for you. I even thought you were pregnant. I thought that must be the reason you weren't drinking on a hen do. But it was because you were on duty. Guess the Reaper wasn't kidding when he said we'd no idea what you were capable of.'

Jen crouched in front of her, forcing her to make eye contact. 'Why me?' Jen demanded. 'Don't I deserve to know that much?'

Kennedy met Jen's gaze, her voice a choked whisper. 'Because you've got money. Nothing personal.'

'It feels very personal, Kennedy. When it requires getting this close for this long, that's a commitment. How does it work? Do you join a health club and seek out a valuable mark? Or was I always the target, ever since you saw that I had sold my company?'

Kennedy's eyes flitted briefly to Michelle.

She had betrayed herself. Jen thought of how insistent Kennedy had been that Jen invite Michelle on the trip, how anxious she was to hear confirmation. Then she recalled how weird Kennedy had been around her at first.

'Was Michelle the target, and you used me as a route to get to her?'

Kennedy's eyes were filling. She wiped at them so that she could focus on the screen. Her fingers glided swiftly across the keys, entering codes. A sound emitted from Kennedy's phone, a different chime. Two-factor authentication for an account. Jen held up the handset so that she could see the code.

Kennedy keyed it in and hit return.

It was done.

Then she broke down.

'If this is a bid for sympathy,' said Michelle, 'I would warn you about the law of diminishing returns. We've already seen your waterworks routine once.'

Kennedy wiped her eyes again and shot Michelle a bitter smile. 'Maybe I'm crying with happiness.'

It didn't look like it. There was an unnerving intensity about her: drained, overwrought, clinging on by her fingernails. It was less a moment of triumph than a moment of unravelling.

Jen tried to make her tone as gentle as her anger allowed. 'What's wrong, Kennedy? You got what you wanted.'

Kennedy took the support brace off then stood up. She walked to the fireplace so that she was facing the whole room. Jen noted the theatricality of it, wary of what was coming.

Michelle stayed in place, blocking the door.

'The Cabrera story was bullshit,' Kennedy said. 'But I wasn't lying about hacking a DNA database. It's amazing the things you can discover in those sites. Like how Helena Eckhart wasn't the first person Michelle Cassidy abandoned to protect her own future.'

'What the fuck are you talking about?' Michelle asked.

'I'm talking about the real reason your family moved away when you were fifteen.'

Michelle looked anxious now.

'She was pregnant,' Kennedy said. 'With Jason's child.'

Michelle's reaction indicated that Kennedy wasn't lying. Jen and Helena shared a look as a missing part of their shared history fell into place.

'Being a mother at that age would have ruined her life, so once she had the baby, a little girl, she gave her up for adoption, then got on with her studies again.'

Jen could barely breathe. Michelle was looking frozen, aghast.

'It worked out quite well, on the surface of it. The little girl was adopted by very rich parents. But in truth she was just another toy they got bored of. So they sent her off to boarding school, abandoned again. She struggled with her studies, despite the expensive tuition. She was bright enough, but messed up in a lot of other ways. On the plus side, it turned out she was pretty good at tennis.'

Michelle

A few weeks ago, Michelle had visited Brendan, her tech-geek financial guy. There was a monstrous PC beneath his desk, the glowing fan inside it spinning like a jet engine as it mined cryptocurrency. That was what her head felt like in that moment as she processed what Kennedy had just said. As she understood the implications, the terrifying implications.

Decades of guilt, lies and misdeeds were coming home to roost. Jen had forgiven her, but that had felt too easy somehow. Michelle had calculated the real price, and she knew that mere forgiveness was not going to save her. It wasn't going to save any of them, especially not Kennedy.

They all thought the danger would be over now that money was changing hands, the 'restitution' being made. In truth, the danger had not even arrived yet, and the restitution would not be made in bitcoin.

Kennedy was looking directly at Jen. 'I'm sorry for what I had to do to you. I was crying in that café because I wasn't sure I could go through with this. I got too close. I like you, Jen. You were kind to me, and you don't deserve this. But as for what I'm taking from her? My birth mother? I am owed every penny.'

There was a growing silence in the room, everyone looking

to Michelle for a response. It would not be the one anybody was expecting.

Kennedy was wrong about almost everything. And the worst thing she was wrong about was who she had trusted.

'We're in danger,' Michelle said, endeavouring to keep her voice steady. 'Worse than any of us thought. You included, Kennedy. You especially.'

'What the hell are you saying? You're finally faced with the daughter you gave up and you're babbling nonsense.'

There was no time to break this gently.

'You're not my daughter,' Michelle told her. 'It's true I got pregnant when I was fifteen, after Jason *raped* me. That's why we moved away. But I never had it. I had a termination.'

'You're lying.'

'I'm not. You didn't find my DNA on any database, because my DNA isn't *on* any database. But I know who *is* lying, and he's on that boat holding Samira hostage. Apart from my parents, there was only one other person who knew I was pregnant. One person who could have spun a yarn you so desperately wanted to believe was true, and who must have used it to manipulate you ever since.'

'I don't get it,' said Nicolette. 'Why are we in danger?'

'Because Jason isn't dead. Jason is the Reaper.'

Kennedy

Just a few moments ago, Kennedy had been planning her escape. With the brace off, she knew how quickly she could cover the distance to the door and was planning how she would use Michelle's grip on the golf club against her, how she would shift her weight to haul her out of the way. She had little concern that Michelle would actually take a swing at her with it. Few people truly had that in them, especially when they had just been told you were their daughter. But then Michelle had hit her with something far harder than any nine-iron.

Broken people could waste their entire lives trying to make themselves whole. Kennedy had instead begun looking for how she might embrace being fractured. She took on ever-changing personae, inhabiting and discarding constructed identities without the weakness of entanglements. This was supposed to be her moment of triumph. She would score a lucrative victory over the mother who had rejected her and the woman who had tried to murder her real father. But in a mouse click she went from fractured to smashed, then Michelle's revelation ground the shards to powder.

What a fool she had been. But as she well knew, the tastiest lies were laced with just enough truth to make you swallow them. Jason *had* been Michelle's high-school sweetheart. And among lies laced with truth, the most tempting still were the ones you desperately wanted to believe. As a teenager she had loved first Cassidy and then Mica, feeling a special connection to the woman on the album covers and the posters on her bedroom walls. What adopted and abandoned stray didn't want to believe her real mother was a superstar?

Kennedy had laced her own lies with truth tonight. She *was* a scam artist specialising in identity fraud. Staying on the move, working health clubs around Europe. It was a good way to find targets. She *had* hacked a DNA database, a subtle breach that allowed her to keep going back for more. Just like she said, she had made money through the resultant extortion scams. She had indeed blackmailed philanderers who would not want certain people finding out who had been screwing their wives.

Then out of an adopted child's curiosity, she got her own DNA tested, just in case she had any blood relatives on the system. To her surprise and not a little trepidation, there was a very close match. She tracked him down, observing him discreetly before she announced herself.

Throwing a curveball into the question of nature versus nurture, it turned out he was a thief and a scam artist too: staying on the move, working beach resorts around southern Europe because he liked a certain lifestyle.

His DNA was registered under the name Sonny Rico because he had been using that name one time when he was arrested and forced to give a sample to exclude him from an inquiry. He was calling himself Don Thomas when she confronted him, but she was soon to learn that wasn't true either.

He sold her a very big lie and then sold her on a long con. It was worth the investment partly because of the potential return, but mostly because it was the only way she was going to get something back from the mother who rejected her. The mother who, Jason assured her, denied her very existence.

It took a lot of planning, months of prep before she took up that conveniently vacated coaching post. Then once she got to Hamilton, it was all about the things she did best: earning trust, garnering the fine details and improvising where necessary.

Nicolette was the easiest to hack. She was very careless with how much she shared online, like she was trying to convince everyone she was living an enviable lifestyle. However, she had all these covert social media accounts too, where she unleashed the dark flip side of all that aspirational stuff. That was how Kennedy discovered Lauren Combe and her amazing house on Clachan Geal. It was the perfect place to pull this off.

The initial plan was to subtly manipulate Jen into having a girls' weekend there, but when Kennedy learned she had got engaged, it provided an ideal pretext.

She was proud of little flourishes, like the playlist, intended to unsettle everybody and let their subconscious tap into feelings of guilt and paranoia. She had asked Jason for some suggestions too, as he had more of a handle on their frames of reference. Some of it was based on specific knowledge, some on playing the percentages, and the rest general malice. She knew Beattie had been in a fatal accident, hence 'Drive' and 'Crash'. She threw in 'Celebrity Skin' to taunt Michelle over the sex tape. She had no idea it would be fucking with Helena's head too.

She felt bad about 'Tsunami' but, given some of the shit Nicolette had been spamming out, she more than had it coming.

Kennedy knew that Jen had sold her company for millions, and she knew Michelle was worth considerably more. That didn't mean it was all liquid, but some of it would be. At the very least she knew from a recent interview that Michelle had a couple of million in bitcoin. The plan was to say they wanted seven, and if it sounded like Michelle and Jen could move more, the Reaper would up the price. Tonight's take was at the lower end of what they agreed they would settle for, but it was still a great score, even split three ways.

A great score that felt utterly worthless even before she learned that Michelle wasn't her mother.

She had believed Jason. He was her biological father, after all, and had taken her under his wing. But that didn't mean she trusted him. There was no honour among thieves, only mutual self-interest and suspicion disguised as respect. And the more she got to know Jen, the more she began to believe Jen's account of Jason rather than Jason's account of Jen.

In an age when we leave digital traces everywhere, Kennedy had become adept at leaving nothing of herself behind once she moved on. What she had not anticipated was the danger of adding something to herself and not wanting to lose it. The version of Jen that Jason sold Kennedy didn't match the woman she had got to know, but it was the version of herself she had become around Jen that made it even harder.

Jen trusted nobody, but Kennedy trusted Jen, and two things she said tonight had troubled her deeply.

The first was that Kennedy had been the public face of all this, while others had been hiding in the background. Getting on the inside had been Kennedy's end. Getting away with it was Jason's. When he introduced her to his proposed third man, Carlos, she had been concerned that he was too eye-catching and therefore memorable, easy to describe. 'Don't fret,' Jason told her. 'We'll be giving them a strong incentive never to mention him. And besides, they would be describing a guy they believed was murdered and his body disappeared, not a suspect.'

That was the theory. But now, not only had the marks sussed Kennedy, they had sussed Carlos's part too. And thanks to her relay app, Jason knew this. That meant she was now his greatest liability, which brought her to the second troubling thing Jen said: that Jason had once threatened to kill his own children.

Jen had believed him. Now Kennedy did too.

Michelle broke the silence that had followed her revelation.

'I'm sorry, Jen,' she said. 'You weren't to know, but I think you fucked up when you told him we had rumbled Kennedy. Now there's only one way Jason and his undead comrade can be sure of walking away from this without being pursued: leave no witnesses. And in your case, Kennedy, they wouldn't only be removing a liability, they would also be increasing their slice of the take.'

This was something that had just occurred to Kennedy. She thought she had a contingency in place against getting ripped off for her share, but Michelle had presented a scenario she was not prepared for. With the exception of her slipping a sedative into Samira's drink, the whole thing was supposed to be non-violent. But as everything else Jason used to sell it to her had been a lie, why not that part?

'Seriously?' asked Nicolette. 'I mean, I never knew the guy and I get from the court case and everything that he was bad news, but what you're saying here . . .'

Nicolette looked to Beattie for support, but she was keeping her head down. She was yet to say a word in response to the news that her brother was not dead. She just stared at nothing, wearing that permanently neutral, slightly disapproving expression of hers, though there seemed something grimmer behind it than Kennedy had witnessed so far. It looked like she was calculating, evaluating. Maybe she wouldn't let herself believe it until Jason was standing before her. But that would be too late for all of them.

'Do you know what the Planck length is?' Jen asked Nicolette.

'No,' she responded, confused.

'It's the smallest measurable distance in the universe. It also accurately describes the extent of Jason's remorse should he have to kill us all. He murdered Ronnie Bryceland just to create cover for the fact that he had stolen Sammy Finnegan's watches. Jason is a narcissistic sociopath. And this isn't just about money, it's about revenge.'

As Jen spoke, Kennedy noticed a glow through the windows. Michelle noticed it too, the pair of them the only ones facing the right way.

'Oh, fuck,' said Michelle.

Every head turned to see lights on the water. A boat heading for the jetty.

'We've got to fortify ourselves in here,' Jen said. 'Lauren, how do we lock this place down?'

The answer was they couldn't. But before Lauren could answer, Michelle was sent sprawling as the door flew open. A heartbeat later, Carlos – aka Joaquin – walked in holding a gun.

Beattie

Were it not for the movies, Beattie would have found it impossible to believe such a small object could keep a room full of people motionless, in thrall to the devastation it might unleash. Though the masked man was tall and muscular, it was the tiny device in his right hand that held seven people under his command, and that command was simply to sit and wait.

Time had moved slowly on many occasions over the course of this traumatic night, but never as pronounced as right now. This was not because of fear, but because of her impatience to see if the impossible was true. Beattie had said nothing, nor allowed herself to feel anything when Michelle said Jason wasn't dead. She knew it was merely a deduction, a supposition.

With no body to bury, she had spent years in this agonising limbo. As the old expression goes, it's the hope that kills. And it killed over and over. She would counsel herself not to, but she couldn't help it: every so often something would happen that caused her to let hope in, such as a reported sighting from someone on holiday, and then she would lose him all over again.

Even when Kennedy confirmed it, while something in Beattie soared, another part of her launched a defence mechanism of caution and restraint. This had been a night of shocks and revelations, but it had also been a night of illusions and deceptions. Above all it had been a night that demonstrated the perils of believing things simply because you wished them to be true.

As she sat and listened to them talking about what Jason was capable of, describing him as a sociopath, she realised that to accept this would mean losing him one more time. One final time.

When she spied him through the window, the only reason she didn't literally jump for joy was that she didn't want to risk startling the man with the gun.

Jason was walking purposefully but unhurriedly towards the house, lit by the lamps along the pathway. He looked different but unmistakably himself. He had always been blond, but his hair was now dyed silver-grey: a concession to ageing, or perhaps it was to make him less instantly recognisable. He was a walking miracle. The beloved back from the dead.

A voice told her that according to the superstitions, the returned were never the same, and you should beware. She didn't want to hear it.

A few seconds later, he strode into the room.

'Surprise!' he said, doing half-hearted jazz hands.

Closer up and in better light, she could see that his nose was different. He had had surgery. Nothing radical, but enough so that if anyone who had once known him caught a glimpse in passing, they would think he was merely someone who reminded them of a man long dead.

Though almost a decade had passed, he appeared even younger than she remembered: the work of Botox, filler, tightenings and tucks. Nonetheless, it did her heart good to see that he had been taking care of himself. Looks had always meant a lot to Jason. Some called him vain, but that was what the envious said when someone more blessed than themselves wore their pride without apology.

He was wearing a tactical vest. Zips, pouches, a sheath holding a knife. A holstered gun. A man on a mission.

Beattie remembered the ski mask worn by the chef so that he would not be recognised, and belatedly understood the significance of Jason *not* wearing one.

The relay app on Kennedy's phone had been muted. Jason didn't know they had worked out who he was before he brought the boat in. He was already on his way, intending to reveal himself. She realised that this had always been the plan. That his plan had always included her.

Jason glanced first at Michelle, then at Jen, a look of calm satisfaction on his face.

'Miss me?' he asked.

Jen did not reply.

'You did, though, in the way that matters. As in, if you come at the king, you better not miss. Rohypnol is strong stuff, but let me tell you: being chucked in the Clyde in November can wake you up pronto.'

He wore a different expression when finally he looked at Beattie, not least because she was the only one smiling at him. It was like they had last seen each other only a few days ago. He was giving her that cheeky grin she recognised from childhood, the one he wore when he was expecting to get away with something because his big sisters would never say no.

She had listened to a lot of talk tonight about who people really were, but in that moment she realised that she alone knew who Jason really was.

She ran over and embraced him, a gesture from Jason reassuring the chef. He hugged her tightly for a few seconds then they stared at each other.

'I never believed any of the lies she told about you,' Beattie said. 'And I know what she tried to do to you. What she did to our whole family. Taking her money is only fair.'

'You angling for a slice, Beattie?' he asked with a twinkle in his eye.

'You've already given me something priceless tonight. I don't need anything more.'

'Do you trust me?' he asked.

'I always did.'

He unzipped a pouch and pulled out a bunch of plastic zip-ties: wrist restraints. Jason handed three to her and three to the chef, then unholstered his weapon, training it around the room.

'All of you on your knees, hands behind your back. Secure their wrists.'

'Jason, this was never the plan,' said Kennedy.

'Her too,' he commanded.

Jason pointed his pistol at Kennedy by way of emphasis. She complied, dropping to her knees. The chef holstered his own gun, needing both hands to fasten the restraints.

'You fucked up, Kennedy,' Jason told her. 'So I'm going to have to defer payment because of that. I need you to hang around in case somebody has to take the fall. You'll get your share if you prove you can keep your mouth shut. But of course, if you do decide to spill your guts, I'm sure the cops will totally believe your story about how your mother's a pop star and the guy they should be looking for is someone who died ten years ago.'

'Who *is* her mother?' Michelle asked.

Jason squatted down so that his head was level with Michelle's while the chef fastened her wrists. 'No idea,' he said quietly. 'To be honest, it could have been one of several. I did pretty well for a guy my age back then.'

'Did you force yourself on them too?'

'Don't pretend you didn't want it. And going by that video, you haven't changed.'

'Fuck you. You're nothing.'

'Quiet,' he warned, pointing the gun in her face. Jason stood up straight again and addressed the room. 'We're all going on a wee boat trip. Like Jen here suggested, I'm going to take you all somewhere to make sure I've got a head start. But I know you won't go telling my former employers about tonight, because if they ever catch up with me, I'll have to tell them all about how Jen attempted to murder me. Would our children like knowing that, do you think?'

Still Jen did not reply.

'Beattie, you'll keep quiet about that to keep the peace, won't you?' he asked.

'If it helps you,' she answered. It wasn't like it mattered now.

'See, there you go. Everybody wins. Now get her tied.'

Beattie knelt behind Jen and slipped the loops of the restraints over her hands.

'He's going to kill us,' Jen told her. 'Don't you get it? He's going to kill all of us.'

Beattie sighed as she tightened the cuffs. 'I never believed any of your nonsense about Jason when I thought he was dead and I'm certainly not going to start believing it now.' She gave Jen's hand a little pat. 'We don't all have as cynical a view as you. Like Zaki told you, not everybody is playing an angle.'

She then tied up Helena, whose hands were trembling as Beattie gripped her wrists. Beattie thought of the first time she had seen her, five or six years old, walking towards Michelle's house. Happier times.

The chef had worked faster. He was tying the last of them, Lauren, as Beattie got to her feet.

Jason looked thoughtfully at Beattie for a moment. 'You still know how to drive a boat?' he asked.

'Better than ever.'

'In that case I have a job for you.'

'Isn't that my job?' asked the chef, a hint of aggression in his tone.

'I've a new task for you.'

'What?'

'Misleading the cops,' Jason replied, then shot him through the heart.

Jen

The air filled with shrieks while the gunshot was still reverberating, the impossibly loud noise shaking everyone even before they took in its bloody impact. The chef was sent sprawling backwards, his head cracking viciously off the edge of the sideboard, but he made no sound nor any physical reaction. He was dead in an instant.

Jason swept the gun around all of them to restore order. Jen couldn't describe it as a calming gesture, but it had the desired effect. They silenced themselves, conscious of what he might do next.

Jason rolled the body over and removed the pistol from the chef's holster. He then pulled a cloth from a pocket and used it to rub down his own gun, the one that had fired the shot. Holding it by the barrel, he walked behind Lauren and placed the pistol in the palm of her right hand, briefly closing her fingers around the grip. He then slipped the pistol into a clear plastic bag before securing it inside another of the pouches in his vest.

Jen hadn't seen him in almost a decade, but she recognised the coolness, the detachment. That was what had always chilled her. Jason didn't need to be angry to do something horrifying. He was at his scariest when he was perfectly calm.

'No need to panic,' he said. 'Just a wee revision to my company's profit-sharing scheme, as well as another insurance policy. See, if everybody stays quiet about what happened here, there's no need for this murder weapon to turn up.'

Jen knew it was bullshit, every word that fell from his lips. He was doing what he always did: giving them a lie they wanted to believe, most of all Beattie. She had been as shaken as the rest of them when he shot the chef, but she had recovered quickest, assimilating this development into whatever narrative she had created to excuse him. She had been doing this all her life, so why would she stop now, when he had been restored to her?

Jason handed his sister a slender flashlight pulled from his belt. 'Okay, let's ship out.'

They walked down the slope in silence, Beattie at the front, Jen and Michelle closest to Jason at the rear. The clouds had dissipated and there was a bright three-quarter moon, its light doubled as it reflected off the water.

As the jetty came into view, Jen could see that Jason had secured the RIB to the stern of Lauren's Sealine. Hope tantalised her. She told herself this meant he was serious about a head start. He could stop the engine, take the keys and leave them to drift while he went ashore on the RIB.

But why would that be any different from just leaving them on the island?

'I want you to know, you're pathetic,' Michelle told him. She was scared but defiant, and Jen guessed she knew she had nothing to lose. 'It must have really burned to see Jen and me succeed in our lives as soon as you weren't a part of them.'

'I'm honestly happy for both of you,' he replied. 'Especially as

323

I'm sharing in your success.' Then his voice became quieter, soft enough so that only Jen and Michelle would hear.

'I want *you* to know, as soon as trading starts tomorrow, I'll be using this money to take short positions on your concert promoter and buying shares in your record company. The latter is about to go right up and the former right down. See if you can work out why.'

Since Jason had shown up, Jen had been asking herself why he had gone to all this bother. If he planned to kill them anyway, why didn't he simply take them hostage from the start and demand they transfer money at gunpoint? Listening to the glee in his voice, she had her answer. It was because Jason had always been this way. He enjoyed making people afraid. He had wanted Jen and Michelle's last hours to be spent in fear, tortured by regret over the things they had done wrong throughout their lives.

As he approached the Sealine, Jason instructed them to sit on the benches either side of the rear deck while Beattie ascended to the fly-bridge.

Stepping off the jetty, Jen noticed a box of diving weights sitting next to the stairs to the bridge. That was when she understood how specifically Jason had planned his revenge. He was going to do to her what she did to him, but without the mercy of being drugged. He was going to do it to all of them. Cuffs so that they couldn't swim, weights looped around the zip-ties to keep the bodies down. He was going to create a *Mary Celeste* scenario, leaving the chef's body on the island and the gun that killed him on the abandoned boat. People would be speculating for years.

Jen found herself seated between Nicolette and Michelle; Lauren, Helena and Kennedy were opposite. Kennedy couldn't look at her, nor the others at Kennedy. Despite what Kennedy had done, Jen still wanted to comfort her. She always had, and now she finally understood why: Kennedy was her own children's half-sister. She must have subconsciously recognised traits that reminded her of Calum and Ailsa. Maybe this was why Kennedy had slipped through her defences, been the one person in this world that Jen was not instinctively suspicious of.

As the engine started up, Jason took position on the fly-bridge, where he could look down on the six of them while also keeping an eye on Beattie at the helm.

Nobody spoke. They all seemed numb. Jen wondered if anyone else had noticed the weights.

'We need to do something,' she urged.

Jason fired the gun over their heads, sending a shudder through all of them. 'Quiet!' he called. 'Not another fucking word from any of you.'

Beattie pulled the boat away from the jetty. She turned in a wide arc around the bay before heading into deeper water. Jen wondered how far out he would decide was enough. How many minutes she had left to live.

Then Kennedy raised her head and called out to Jason. 'I know you said not to talk, but there's something you need to know, about the money.'

'What about it?' he asked.

'It's not where you think. Never trust a hacker, *Dad*.'

'Bollocks. My Toughbook was mirroring your screen and I watched it go into my account in real time.'

'And my screen was showing an animation of a fake transfer. It gets worse, though. It's on a time lock. It can only be retrieved after forty-eight hours, and needs to be unlocked with biometrics. So if you hurt any of us, especially me, you'll never see that money.'

Looks were traded back and forth, tantalised by hope.

'Gosh, sounds like I'm really snookered,' Jason replied flatly. 'Hell of an elaborate fail-safe strategy that you just pulled out your arse this second.'

'I'm serious,' Kennedy insisted. 'Check your laptop.'

'Maybe later,' he replied.

She gave Jen a desperate look. He had called her bluff and she had nothing else.

Kennedy's gaze went to the box by the stairs. Yes, she knew too.

They were quarter of an hour out from shore, in the deepest water, when Jason made his command.

'Beattie, I need you to stop for a moment.'

'What's wrong?'

'Nothing. I just need to sort something.'

Jen felt the boat begin to slow, heard the shift in the engine's tone. This was it. She wanted to scream at Beattie, though she knew it was pointless. She might be the only one of them not cuffed, but she was under an even stronger restraint.

Beattie was the straightest person Jen had ever known: conscientious, caring and dutiful to a fault, especially where it came to family. But that was why she had always suffered a total blind spot regarding Jason. She was standing rigidly by her provenly crooked brother, even after he shot someone right in front of her. Still telling Jen that she was wrong about his intentions. How could she believe that?

Jen recalled Beattie patting her hand after tightening her zip-tie.

We don't all have as cynical a view as you. Like Zaki told you, not everybody is playing an angle.

Then it hit her: Beattie had been telling her *she* was playing an angle. She was presenting herself as someone Jason could trust; or at least as the one person he might believe trusted him. That was why she had recovered fastest after Jason murdered the chef: she was staying in character.

Unfortunately she was taking her sweet time making her move, but perhaps the opportunity hadn't presented itself. Jason had been keeping one eye on Beattie the whole time. He might believe she trusted him, but that didn't mean he trusted her.

'We need a distraction,' Jen said beneath the sound of the engine, her head down so that Jason didn't see her lips move.

'What are you going to do?' Nicolette asked.

'Just trust me,' she told her. The one thing Jennifer Dunne would never do for anybody. And not even 'trust my intentions'. It was 'trust my desperate hunch'.

Helena didn't ask questions, though, didn't need details. She raised her head and spoke loudly, addressing Nicolette opposite.

'I've got one last confession tonight. I want to clear my conscience.'

'About what?'

'I'm the one who's having an affair with your husband.'

'You?' Nicolette asked.

'Me,' Helena replied, defiant.

'And you're telling me now, because I'm tied up and you think I can't do anything? You think I won't fight to keep him?'

Nicolette got to her feet and charged towards Helena, who was already rising to do likewise. They met in the centre of the deck, faces inches apart, hands tied behind their backs, screaming barely coherent abuse.

Jen glanced up. Jason observed with wry amusement for a moment, then fired another shot.

'Quiet,' he called. 'The pair of you sound like seagulls on a tip. Back in your seats.'

327

They both retreated, Nicolette giving Jen a WTF look. It hadn't worked. Nothing had happened.

Then she heard Beattie cry out in alarm. 'Jason, watch out!'

As he turned in response, Jen caught a glimpse of Beattie holding a tube from which something shot out and hit him in the face. It was a rocket flare, orange smoke spewing out of the tail as Jason flailed backwards and tumbled from the fly-bridge.

He landed with a crash, hitting the transom deck right at their feet as the flare continued zigzagging erratically into the night sky. His face was burned, his hands empty. He had lost the gun.

Kennedy reacted first, launching herself on top of him. Jen followed, then suddenly all of them were trying to hold him down with their body weight. He was stunned for a moment then fought like a maniac, lashing out with feet, fists, elbows. Jen felt her head strike someone else's, felt another blow explode in her ribs, saw the world spin as she was thrown off. She righted herself in time to see that Jason had freed both of his hands.

He wasn't punching or grappling with either of them, though. Instead he was urgently unzipping one of the pockets on his vest. That was when Jen remembered he had the other pistol in there.

He tugged the zip across with his left hand and reached into the pouch with his right. Jen threw herself upon him again, but he landed a punch, blinding her with a flash of light and pain. She regained her vision in time to see him produce the gun. It was still wrapped in the plastic bag, his fingers pulling the film apart.

His right hand latched around the stock, his arm swinging to level it towards Jen.

That was when Beattie shot him in the head.

Jen

Jason flew backwards over the transom, then Jen heard the gun report twice more. She glanced up to see Beattie standing at the edge of the fly-bridge pointing the pistol down at where Jason's body lay lifeless in the RIB.

Beattie descended the stairs, a numb expression on her face and a small black object gripped in her left hand. In the dim light Jen thought it was the gun, then saw it was a pair of pliers.

She moved behind Jen's back and took hold of her hand, squeezing it gently for a moment, an echo of her signal in the drawing room. Then she snipped through the zip-tie she had secured there not half an hour ago.

As soon as her hands were free, Jen descended into the galley while Beattie worked her way around the others. Jen found Samira seated in front of a green cloth, still unconscious. The noose was tied to a plastic bracket that had been fixed to the ceiling out of shot. As Kennedy had said, there was no slab of ice.

Jen carefully removed the noose and was joined by Michelle as she began untying the ropes securing Samira to the chair. Michelle had a split lip, which was already starting to swell. Together they carried Samira to the dining area, where there was a bench they could lie her on.

Kennedy appeared next, going straight for the laptop that was sitting on the galley table. Its webcam was pointed at the chair and the green cloth. Jason had referred to it as a Toughbook, and it looked like military hardware. The kind of thing that wouldn't be relying on wi-fi or a dodgy mobile signal.

'Can you access his accounts?' Michelle asked.

'I don't need to. I never sent him the money. I always worried he would screw me, so I had a contingency.'

'I thought that was just a bluff.'

'I was lying about the time lock and the biometrics. Not about the fake transfer. I thought he might rip me off – I didn't think he was planning to kill me.'

'Can we get it back?' Jen asked.

Kennedy turned the laptop around so that they could see the screen. She was setting up a bitcoin transfer from her own account back into Michelle's.

'Doing it now. Do you want to watch?'

'I trust you.'

Kennedy turned the laptop back around and continued working the keyboard.

'What are we going to do with her?' Michelle asked, making no attempt to keep her voice down.

Kennedy looked up, at once anxious and penitent, someone who knew that putting the money back didn't begin to undo this.

'I really don't know,' Jen admitted. Those protective feelings were rising to the surface again. There was a case that Kennedy had been the one most damaged by all of this. The idea of her going to prison made Jen shudder, a thought that reminded her of her own jeopardy in that regard.

'We've got two bodies and a whole lot of awkward explaining to do,' she said.

'Two bodies travelling under fake identities,' Kennedy told her. 'One of whom was already legally dead.'

'A missing person that nobody will miss at all,' said Michelle. 'I think it might be best for everyone if this whole thing just went away.'

But someone had missed him.

'I think that's Beattie's call,' said Jen.

Jen went back onto the deck, but Beattie wasn't to be seen. Lauren, Nicolette and Helena were sitting on the benches, all of them looking dazed and beaten up. Lauren had her head back, holding a hanky to her nose to stop the bleeding. It must have been her head Jen's had clashed with in the struggle. Helena had the beginnings of a black eye.

Behind them she could see the RIB, Jason's body slumped sideways between two benches, his face mercifully turned away.

'You guys okay?' she asked.

'Thanks to Beattie,' said Helena.

'Yeah,' agreed Nicolette. 'Though she cut it pretty fine.'

'It was all about opportunity. That's why I asked for a distraction. With regard to which, thank you. That was inspired work.'

'Nicolette was the one who brought all the energy,' Helena said, a little more insistently than seemed appropriate.

'Yes, but it was a method performance,' Nicolette replied. 'How did you know Paul was cheating on me?'

There was a pause, just a moment too long.

'Erm, I didn't. I just plucked an idea from the air and hoped you would run with it. You're saying it's true?'

'I don't want to go into it right now.'

'How did you know Beattie was on our side?' Lauren asked.

It was not an easy question.

'I knew she was playing an angle,' Jen replied.

Zaki was partly right. Not everybody was playing an angle *all* the time. But sometimes when they were, it was to do the right thing.

Jen ascended the stairs to the fly-bridge. Beattie was facing forward, gripping the helm as though holding on, even though the engine remained idling. Perhaps she had chosen the spot because she couldn't see the RIB from there.

She turned as Jen approached.

Jen didn't say anything. Primarily she wanted Beattie to know she was there for her.

They stayed in silence for a few moments, then Beattie spoke. It sounded like it came from somewhere deep within, strangely calm despite what she had just been through. What she had just done.

'There are superstitions about loved ones who come back from the dead,' she said. 'Revenants, they're called. They say you should beware because although the revenants look like the people you've lost, they're not the same. But the thing is, Jason *was* the same. It took him coming back for me to see what he had always been.'

Beattie glanced towards the edge of the fly-bridge, acknowledging what lay beyond it, though from the helm she could not see what was below.

'I owe you my life,' Jen told her. 'We all do.'

'I wouldn't go that far. We all played a part, and you'll understand if I don't want to dwell on mine. You do owe me a phone, though.'

'What do you mean?'

Beattie produced her mobile from her pocket and woke it. She tapped at the screen, then her voice sounded from the speakers.

'But you did kill him, didn't you? That's what happened to him? You're admitting that?'

'Yes, I killed him.'

Beattie stopped the playback. Then she tossed the phone over the side into the sea. 'It was when he walked in with no mask,' she said. 'That was when I understood. He didn't know you had worked it out at that point: he was already on his way to reveal himself. He wanted you to know it was him. He *needed* you to know it was him. And that meant he was always planning to kill everybody. Including me.'

Beattie glanced at the bench where the gun was sitting. 'I know now that you did what you had to. You had no choice. I'm sorry for how I treated you.'

'And I'm sorry for what I put you through,' Jen replied. 'But ultimately, this wasn't your fault or mine. It was his.'

Beattie's gaze strayed again towards the edge of the fly-bridge. 'I wasn't the only one who continued to believe something because it was preferable,' she said. 'We both have people who would be hurt by knowing the truth, and hurt more by knowing what happened tonight.'

Jen took her hand and squeezed it. She looked Beattie in the eye. 'Nobody has to know. Nobody ever has to know.'

'I don't want to see him,' Beattie replied, wiping a tear. 'Do you understand?'

Jen nodded. She went back down to the lower deck and told everyone the plan. There were no dissenters.

Michelle volunteered to help. They climbed carefully down into the RIB, where Helena passed them several of the diving weights.

'Not all of them,' Jen said. 'We're going to need some for the other one too.'

Jen put the weights into pouches on Jason's vest, then together she and Michelle hauled him over the side. There was a loud splash, sounding an echo in Jen's mind from ten years before.

This time he wasn't coming back.

Helena and Nicolette were waiting to haul them back onto the deck. Michelle went first while Jen trailed her hand over the side of the RIB, immersing it in the cold water. There had been something sticky on it and she wanted it gone.

Helena was reaching down to assist Jen when they were both startled by the sound of a thump.

They turned urgently in time to see a tiny figure stumble groggily through the doors from the galley.

Samira looked around, frowning in confusion and incredulity at her surroundings. She took in the women staring back: cut lips, black eyes, torn and bloody clothes.

'Fuck me. What did I miss?'

Kennedy

Kennedy hung back on the staircase, having glimpsed Helena following Michelle towards the kitchen carrying a mop and bucket. She was moving through the house like a ghost, staying out of sight. She didn't think she could bring herself to meet anybody's eye, but that was moot because nobody seemed particularly keen to meet hers. The effect was to make her feel invisible and yet conspicuous at the same time.

She had no right to expect anything else. These people could not, should not forgive her, and she knew she would have been shown less mercy had their interests not been so intertwined. That they were agreeing to look the other way was all for the sake of Jen and Beattie, though they were not the only ones who had secrets that they would prefer didn't leave this island. It was a mutual conspiracy of silence, of which Kennedy was an undeserving beneficiary.

The plan to cover everything up was agreed on the trip back to shore, its success hinging briefly on the cooperation of Samira. Jen had given her a highly selective breakdown of what had happened, the details deliberately sparse and fuzzy in certain places. Jen told Samira that Beattie had shot the bad guy, but was a lot more vague about the events leading up to her getting hold of his gun. Significantly, there was no mention of the fact that he was Beattie's brother, Kennedy's father and Jen's not-so-deceased ex-husband.

It quickly became clear that Samira wanted to know as little as possible. She had a true lawyer's instinct for the value of plausible deniability.

'We can't ask you to go along with anything you don't want to,' Jen had said. 'Many crimes were committed here tonight, several of them against you.'

'I'm prepared to take a "no harm, no foul" position in pursuit of the greater good,' Samira had replied. 'And right now I'd sign an NDA on anything if someone traded it for two paracetamol and a can of Irn-Bru.'

'But you were drugged and taken hostage,' Jen told her. 'It wasn't "no harm".'

'Maybe from your perspective. To be honest, that's the most consecutive hours of uninterrupted sleep I've had in about six months.'

Kennedy heard Lauren's voice from the drawing room as she reached the foot of the stairs.

'I'm grateful I resisted the temptation to carpet this room,' she was saying.

'The polished wood is lovely, though.'

That was Nicolette.

'I know, but when I chose the design I never considered "ease of cleaning up bloodstains" in the pro column.'

'Who's on disposal duty for this one?'

'I don't mind volunteering. It would be karma regarding the body I *didn't* take responsibility for.'

'I think it's only fair if Kennedy has to help out. I mean, it's the least she can do.'

'I take your point,' Lauren said, 'but I'd rather it was literally anyone else. I don't think I could trust myself not to push her into the sea. Plus, I think she's busy unblocking the internet.'

'Fair enough. I'll come, then. How are we going to get him to the boat?'

'Helena said they found my quad bike at the back of the house.'

Kennedy slipped quietly out of the front door, pulling it softly to but not fully closed. The first rays of sunlight were starting to come through as she stepped onto the grass that would cushion her footfalls while she descended to the jetty.

It had only been dark for a few hours. She hadn't slept but she had another long day ahead of her. It was time to do that thing she did so well. Walk away, shed her skin. Leave everybody behind. If she was a superhero, she would be called Tabula Rasa.

She wasn't sure yet where she would go, but she had options. It would hurt, this time far more than ever before. That was okay, though. She deserved it to hurt.

She unhitched the RIB. She could still see some blood smears where Jen had missed it with the hose as she washed it out on the trip back. The light hadn't been good, but she was determined to ensure Beattie didn't have to see any trace of what she had done. That was Jen all over.

Kennedy winced at the growl of the outboard starting up. She glanced back, but the house was not visible from down here. She wouldn't see anyone coming until they were on the path down to the jetty.

She kept the engine low, not planning to open the throttle until she was a distance from shore. In the meantime, she hoped they were all too busy to look out the window.

She hadn't restored the internet. They didn't need it now that they could get back to the mainland on Lauren's boat, and Kennedy wanted to give herself as long a start as possible before they discovered that she hadn't put the money back either.

When she had shown them the Toughbook, it was running an amended version of the fake screen she had duped Jason with. She doubted she had even needed to. They still trusted her to do right by them even once they knew everything.

They wouldn't come after her either, because going to the police would have implications for all of them. She had pulled it off, got away free and clear. She could start afresh once again. And five million euros would buy her a whole new life.

Tabula rasa.

Kennedy glanced back towards the island, the house getting smaller as the RIB made its cautious initial progress. She reached for the throttle, but an unexpected thought stayed her hand.

If you run when nobody's chasing, then the person you're running from is you.

Five million would buy her a very comfortable life. But could it buy a better one than she had been living for the past seven months? She had a job she enjoyed and was good at. She had people who invited her to their social events, even their wedding. People who cared about her. People *she* cared about, despite herself.

Friends.

She had burned all that, though. Betrayed them, put them in mortal danger and shown she only ever saw them as a payday. She needed a new life because she could not go back to that one. It wasn't there any more.

Then her own words echoed.

They still trusted her to do right by them even once they knew everything.

It was still in her hands if she wanted it. And all it would cost her was five million euros.

Kennedy pulled on the tiller, turned the boat around.

It was time to stop running.

Helena

Helena made a final tuning check at the side of the stage, just a pointless exercise to keep herself occupied in these last few moments before they went on. She had felt less nervous going through that forest with Michelle, being stalked by Joaquin or Carlos or whatever his name was. Less vulnerable too.

She thought she might throw up. How had she allowed herself to be put in this position? How could she have been so reckless, so self-deluding?

Michelle had sold it to her as a special treat for Jen's reception. That was how she ended up spending the entire day before the wedding in a rehearsal studio off the Broomielaw, down by the Clyde. Before the hen weekend, she'd have sooner thrown herself in the river than pick up a guitar and play alongside Michelle, but suddenly there she was, taking part in an impromptu Cassidy reunion.

Jen parent-trapped them, Helena had joked. It wasn't true, though, and not merely because playing at the wedding was Michelle's idea, not Jen's. Helena told herself she was doing it because she didn't want to say no to Michelle, who was not only trying to do something nice for Jen, but probably thought she was doing something nice for Helena too. But that wasn't entirely true either. Because if Helena was being honest, she was doing it for herself.

She had been apprehensive about getting in a studio with Daisy and the terrifying Madeleine. Though Helena had been playing and teaching music her whole life, they were seasoned touring professionals, and she was worried about how she would stack up. In the event, the only note she got was that her style was a bit more metal than they were aiming for, but that was easy enough to correct. She wasn't trying to make a statement or chafe against Michelle's preferred sound. It was just what she had been playing of late.

By the end of the day, they were sounding pretty tight. Tight enough for a wedding band anyway.

The ceremony had been beautiful, really touching. Helena teared up at the sight of it. Jen and Zaki were so right for each other, so very much in love. From the vibes she had given off on the morning they flew to Clachan Geal, Helena feared Jen might have been getting cold feet, but there was clearly not a doubt in her mind now.

She wondered how much, if anything, Jen had told Zaki about the trip. Everyone had stayed the whole weekend to clean up the evidence and because it would allay suspicion if they were all picked up by helicopter and boat as scheduled. Only Lauren went back to the mainland early, to report the death of a neighbour and to collect supplies.

They'd had a decent couple of days, considering. It was quite the bonding session, throughout which the phrase 'what happens on Clachan Geal stays on Clachan Geal' took on a far greater significance than for any previous visitors.

The only person Helena had any concerns about on that score was Samira, who struck her as a bit of a flake. Despite Samira insisting she didn't want to involve the police, Helena had wondered how good she would be at keeping her mouth shut. The answer became obvious when she refused to divulge any details regarding the email they had found on her phone. The only thing she was prepared to disclose was that 'Grimpox' had been the nickname Zaki used for her since she got a particularly gruesome case of chicken pox as a seven-year-old.

They finally discovered the big secret early on during the reception, when Zaki surprised Jen with the announcement that they weren't going to Skye after all. He had been bullshitting about being needed at work, and had quietly arranged cover for Jen's duties too. They were flying out first class to the Caribbean for a fortnight, where a colleague of Samira's was lending them her villa – hence the emails.

The two of them had cooked it up between them, as it was a big deal for Zaki to be paying for the honeymoon. It turned out he was a bit hung up on the idea that anyone would think he was marrying Jen for her money: in particular, Jen herself.

After that bombshell, they had all sat down to a lovely meal, catered by Zaki's firm. The food looked and smelled beautiful, but Helena had barely been able to touch it because of nervous anticipation.

Then suddenly the time was upon her: taking the stage in some cheesy function suite after all. Jen was delighted, though: not because it was a Cassidy reunion in her honour, but because they were Hel and Shell again.

That had been six weeks ago.

It was when they came off that Michelle told Helena the previous day's session was not so much a rehearsal as an audition. 'My tour guitarist broke three of his fingers playing cricket. I need a replacement. Someone who can get up to speed fast and can handle the commitment. Someone I can trust.'

'You don't owe me this,' Helena told her.

'I think we owe this to each other.'

Which was Michelle's way of saying she wasn't asking.

Now here she was, the opening show of the tour, at the SSE Hydro. Her daughters were in the VIP section along with Jen, Zaki and everyone else. Kennedy, Lauren and Darcy, Beattie and Richard.

Nicolette and Paul.

That had been a close call, but not *every* secret had come out over that fateful weekend. Nicolette had opened up to them about her marriage. She didn't know who Paul had been cheating with and claimed she didn't care. But she would care a lot if she found out it was Helena. Helena knew what it was to lose a friend, and now that she had just got Michelle back, she didn't want to lose another.

Helena had intended to tell Paul she was breaking it off. Apart from anything else, her calendar was looking very full for the foreseeable future. Paul had beaten her to it, though. He said Nicolette had come back from the hen weekend a changed woman.

'What the hell were you girls doing over there?' he asked. 'Peyote?'

Nicolette had what she called her 'big new beginning' in a few weeks. She was starting a marketing degree at Strathclyde Uni, where she would no doubt be the most glamorous mature student the place had ever seen.

Helena's big new beginning was upon her right now.

The lights went down, and a roar of anticipation shook the place. They walked on stage, Helena's guts churning.

Michelle stepped nonchalantly up to the mike and spoke. 'Ladies and gentlemen, we have been hired to play for your entertainment, which begins in one, two, three, four . . .'

As they kicked into the opener and she strummed the first chord, Helena felt terrified that she would just stumble over everything. But as she remembered from back in the day, there was a weird kind of autopilot that kicked in when you were on stage. Not merely muscle memory, but a heightened level of performance that only happened when there was an audience, whether it be at a friend's wedding or headlining an arena.

They rattled through three of Mica's hits back to back, each segueing into the next without Michelle speaking. Then she took a moment, waiting for the applause to die down.

'Glasgow, I've a wee bit of an announcement.'

Michelle gave Helena an odd look, a 'got you where I want you' look.

Helena glanced at Daisy the bass player, Madeleine on the drum riser. They were both smiling knowingly. Co-conspirators who had been close to Michelle for longer than Helena ever was.

Helena felt something inside her turn to ice as she suddenly appreciated the extent to which she had placed her trust, her fate in the hands of someone who still had every reason to avenge the dreadful thing she had done. It was now in Michelle's gift to tell sixteen thousand people, including her daughters, that Helena was the bitch who betrayed her childhood trust and leaked her adult sex tape.

But that wasn't what she said.

'I've got a new guitarist. Well, a new old guitarist. Some of you might remember her. Helena, maybe you could give their memories a wee jog by playing something I haven't sung in a while.'

That was her cue. Helena's fingers formed a D and played the opening arpeggio, the intro to 'She Knows'.

The place went mental.

Acknowledgements

I would like to offer my warmest thanks to:

My editor Ed Wood for his invaluable judgement and infectious enthusiasm, as well as Grace Vincent, Richard Beswick and all the team at Little, Brown who have supported my work now for more than a quarter of a century, in particular the late Thalia Proctor, who is deeply missed. Caroline Dawnay, Sophie Scard, Charles Walker and everyone at United Agents for their unfailing support and advice. Marisa and Jack for making our household a welcoming retreat throughout two years of pandemic.

Big hugs and sustained harmonies to Mark Billingham, Doug Johnstone, Val McDermid, Stuart Neville and Luca Veste, my bandmates in the Fun Lovin' Crime Writers. When writing a novel about the nature of friendship, it helps to have such solid examples of the real deal.

Finally, I would like to offer special thanks to Jim Morris and Balaam and the Angel, and to Miles Hunt and the Wonder Stuff, not only for permission to reproduce their lyrics, but for more than thirty years of pleasure and inspiration derived from listening to their music.

You can find the songs mentioned in this novel by searching for 'The Clachan Geal Haunted Playlist' on Spotify.